LEFT

TO

DIE

(An Adele Sharp Mystery—Book One)

BLAKE PIERCE

Blake Pierce

Blake Pierce is the USA Today bestselling author of the RILEY PAGE mystery series, which includes sixteen books (and counting). Blake Pierce is also the author of the MACKENZIE WHITE mystery series, comprising thirteen books (and counting); of the AVERY BLACK mystery series, comprising six books; of the KERI LOCKE mystery series, comprising five books; of the MAKING OF RILEY PAIGE mystery series, comprising five books (and counting); of the KATE WISE mystery series, comprising six books (and counting); of the CHLOE FINE psychological suspense mystery, comprising five books (and counting); of the JESSE HUNT psychological suspense thriller series, comprising five books (and counting); of the AU PAIR psychological suspense thriller series, comprising two books (and counting); of the ZOE PRIME mystery series, comprising two books (and counting); and of the new ADELE SHARP mystery series.

An avid reader and lifelong fan of the mystery and thriller genres, Blake loves to hear from you, so please feel free to visit www.blakepierceauthor.com to learn more and stay in touch.

ISBN: 9781094350202

BOOKS BY BLAKE PIERCE

ADELE SHARP MYSTERY SERIES
LEFT TO DIE (Book #1)
LEFT TO RUN (Book #2)
LEFT TO HIDE (Book #3)
LEFT TO KILL (Book #4)
LEFT TO MURDER (Book #5)

THE AU PAIR SERIES
ALMOST GONE (Book#1)
ALMOST LOST (Book #2)
ALMOST DEAD (Book #3)

ZOE PRIME MYSTERY SERIES
FACE OF DEATH (Book#1)
FACE OF MURDER (Book #2)
FACE OF FEAR (Book #3)
FACE OF MADNESS (Book #4)
FACE OF FURY (Book #5)
FACE OF DARKNESS (Book #6)

A JESSIE HUNT PSYCHOLOGICAL SUSPENSE SERIES
THE PERFECT WIFE (Book #1)
THE PERFECT BLOCK (Book #2)
THE PERFECT HOUSE (Book #3)
THE PERFECT SMILE (Book #4)
THE PERFECT LIE (Book #5)
THE PERFECT LOOK (Book #6)

CHLOE FINE PSYCHOLOGICAL SUSPENSE SERIES
NEXT DOOR (Book #1)
A NEIGHBOR'S LIE (Book #2)
CUL DE SAC (Book #3)
SILENT NEIGHBOR (Book #4)
HOMECOMING (Book #5)
TINTED WINDOWS (Book #6)

KATE WISE MYSTERY SERIES
IF SHE KNEW (Book #1)

IF SHE SAW (Book #2)
IF SHE RAN (Book #3)
IF SHE HID (Book #4)
IF SHE FLED (Book #5)
IF SHE FEARED (Book #6)
IF SHE HEARD (Book #7)

THE MAKING OF RILEY PAIGE SERIES
WATCHING (Book #1)
WAITING (Book #2)
LURING (Book #3)
TAKING (Book #4)
STALKING (Book #5)

RILEY PAIGE MYSTERY SERIES
ONCE GONE (Book #1)
ONCE TAKEN (Book #2)
ONCE CRAVED (Book #3)
ONCE LURED (Book #4)
ONCE HUNTED (Book #5)
ONCE PINED (Book #6)
ONCE FORSAKEN (Book #7)
ONCE COLD (Book #8)
ONCE STALKED (Book #9)
ONCE LOST (Book #10)
ONCE BURIED (Book #11)
ONCE BOUND (Book #12)
ONCE TRAPPED (Book #13)
ONCE DORMANT (Book #14)
ONCE SHUNNED (Book #15)
ONCE MISSED (Book #16)
ONCE CHOSEN (Book #17)

MACKENZIE WHITE MYSTERY SERIES
BEFORE HE KILLS (Book #1)
BEFORE HE SEES (Book #2)
BEFORE HE COVETS (Book #3)
BEFORE HE TAKES (Book #4)
BEFORE HE NEEDS (Book #5)
BEFORE HE FEELS (Book #6)
BEFORE HE SINS (Book #7)

BEFORE HE HUNTS (Book #8)
BEFORE HE PREYS (Book #9)
BEFORE HE LONGS (Book #10)
BEFORE HE LAPSES (Book #11)
BEFORE HE ENVIES (Book #12)
BEFORE HE STALKS (Book #13)
BEFORE HE HARMS (Book #14)

AVERY BLACK MYSTERY SERIES
CAUSE TO KILL (Book #1)
CAUSE TO RUN (Book #2)
CAUSE TO HIDE (Book #3)
CAUSE TO FEAR (Book #4)
CAUSE TO SAVE (Book #5)
CAUSE TO DREAD (Book #6)

KERI LOCKE MYSTERY SERIES
A TRACE OF DEATH (Book #1)
A TRACE OF MUDER (Book #2)
A TRACE OF VICE (Book #3)
A TRACE OF CRIME (Book #4)
A TRACE OF HOPE (Book #5)

CHAPTER ONE

Twenty-nine, twenty-eight, twenty-seven…

The numbers played through Adele's mind like grains of hot sand slipping through an hourglass. She shifted uncomfortably, adjusting the neck pillow she'd purchased at the Central Wisconsin Airport. She pressed her forehead against the cold glass of the Boeing 737, her gaze tracing the jutting wing stabilizers and then flicking across the patches of clouds scattered across the otherwise blue horizon. How many times had she stared out of a plane window like this? Too many to count.

Twenty-six, twenty-five…

Why had he stopped at twenty-five?

Adele closed her eyes again, trying to push the thoughts from her like pus from a wound. She needed her sleep. Angus would be waiting for her back home; it wouldn't do to show up baggy-eyed and frazzled, especially not with what she guessed he had planned for tonight.

The thought of her boyfriend drove some of the worries from her and a small smile teased its way from her lips, hovering in a lopsided fashion. She half glanced through hooded eyes down at her left hand. Adele wasn't much one for jewelry, but her fingers seemed particularly bare. At thirty-two, she had half hoped, in a small, concealed part of her, that at least her ring finger would have been occupied by now.

Soon. If Jessica's texts were to be believed, and the cryptic nature of Angus's last call—soon her hand wouldn't be so bare.

She smiled again.

Why had he stopped at twenty-five?

Her smile became fixed as the thought interjected itself once more. She almost reached for the briefcase she had stowed under her seat, but then exhaled deeply through her nose, her nostrils flaring as she attempted to calm herself. She needed sleep now. The case could wait.

But could it really? He'd stopped at twenty-five. The Benjamin Killer was what they were calling him, after the story of Benjamin Button—a crass, gauche moniker for a vicious murderer. He killed them based on age. Gender, looks, ethnicity didn't matter to him. He had started with that twenty-nine-year-old man—a middle-school coach

1

only a few years younger than Adele. The next was a woman with blonde hair and green eyes, just like Adele. It had stuck with Adele when she'd first seen the woman's photographs.

She'd worked with the FBI for nearly six years now, and she had *thought* she was good at her job. Until now. The Benjamin Killer was taunting them. For the last three weeks, Adele had visited the residences of the victims, looking for a lead, for anything that might point her to the bastard. Every two weeks, another body dropped, yet she wasn't any closer to identifying a likely suspect.

Then, last month, the pattern ceased. The killings had stopped. Adele's weeks of work traveling from Wisconsin to Ohio to Indiana, trying to put together a pattern, had turned up squat. They were at the deadest of ends.

Three weeks wasted, dwelling on the sick thoughts of a psychopath. Sometimes Adele wondered why she had joined the Bureau at all.

The FBI had contacted her directly out of college, but she had wanted to consider her options. Of course, given her three citizenships—German, French, and US—it had been a near inevitability, she supposed. Her sense of duty, her loyalty to the law, had only been further fanned into flame by her father. He'd never managed to rise higher than the rank of staff sergeant over the course of his long and dignified career, but he exemplified everything Adele admired of those in the service. Her father was a bit of a romantic. He'd been stationed in Bamberg, Germany, and married her French mother, who had given birth to Adele on a trip to the US. Thus the triple citizenship, and a daughter for whom the thought of staying put in anything smaller than a country brought on a serious case of cabin fever.

Some people called it wanderlust. But "wander" implied no direction. Adele always had a direction; it just wasn't always obvious to those looking in from the outside.

She reached up and brushed her blonde hair out of her eyes. In the reflection of the glass window, she spotted someone staring at her over her shoulder.

The lawyer sitting in 33F. He'd been ogling her since she'd gotten on the plane.

She turned lazily, like a cat stretching in a beam of sunlight, and peered across the ample belly of the middle-aged man sleeping next to her and contributing a light dusting of snores to the ambience of the cabin.

She gave a small, sarcastic wave to the lawyer. He wasn't bad-looking, but he had a good twenty years on her and the eyes of a predator. Not all psychopaths engaged in bloody deeds in the dead of night. Some of them lived cushy lives protected by their profession and prestige.

And yet, Adele had a nose for them, like a bloodhound with a scent.

The lawyer winked at her, but didn't look away, his gaze lingering on her face for a moment, then sliding down her suit and traveling across her long legs. Adele's French-American heritage had its perks when it came to the sort of attractiveness that men often described as "exotic," but it came with downsides too.

In this case, a fifty-year-old downside in a cheap suit and even cheaper cologne. She would have guessed, based on his briefcase alone, that he was a lawyer, even if he hadn't dropped his business card "accidentally" when he'd spotted her sliding past him into her seat.

"Want my nuts?" he said, smiling at her with crocodile teeth. He waved a small blue bag of almonds in her direction.

She stared him coolly in the eyes. "We've been in the air for an hour, and that's what you came up with?"

The man smirked. "Is that a yes?"

"I'm flattered," Adele said, though her tone suggested otherwise. "But I'm about to be engaged, thank you very much."

The lawyer shrugged with his lips, turning the corners down in as noncommittal a gesture as likely to have ever graced a courtroom. "I don't see a ring."

"Tonight," she said. "Not that it's any of your business."

"You've still got time. You want them?" He offered his almonds again.

Adele shook her head. "I don't like that type. Too salty, small, and old—I'd check the expiration date if I were you."

The man's smirk became rather forced. "No need to be rude," he muttered, beneath his breath. "Bitch," he added as an afterthought.

"Maybe." Adele turned away from the man, rolling her shoulders in just such a way that her suit jacket slid open, presenting the man with a perfect view of the 9mm Glock 17 strapped to her hip.

Immediately, the man turned pale, his eyes bugging in his head. He began to choke, trying to cough up an almond which had lodged in his throat.

3

Joining the FBI did come with its perks. Adele turned back, pressing her forehead against the window once more, trying, again, to drift off to sleep.

***

Her Uber driver pulled up outside the small apartment complex, coming to a squealing halt on the curb across from a large hub of mailboxes. Streetlights glowed on the gray sidewalk, illuminating the concrete and asphalt in the dark. Adele retrieved her suitcase and briefcase from the back seat, her arms heavy from the day of travel.

Three weeks since she'd seen Angus. Three weeks was a long time. She exhaled softly, tilting her head back so her chin practically pointed toward the night sky. She rolled her shoulders, stretching. She had managed to get a little sleep on the flight, but it had been at an odd angle and she could still feel the crick in her neck.

The Uber peeled away from the curb with another squeal and a screech as the driver rushed off in search of his next passenger. Adele watched it leave and then turned, marching beneath the tastefully placed palm trees that the landlord had planted the previous year. She peered up at the orange glow in the second window facing east.

Angus was still waiting up for her. It was only nine p.m., but Angus was a coder for a couple of start-ups in the city and he often kept strange hours. San Francisco: the hub of the gold rush of tech—or silicon rush as some were calling it.

Adele had never expected to be wealthy, but with the equity pay-offs Angus had received from his last company, things were about to change. And, judging by the words after his last phone call, Adele felt they might be changing very soon.

"I need to talk to you about something," he'd said. *"It's important."*

And then her friend Jennifer, an old college roommate, had spotted Angus outside Preeve & Co. on Post Street. If anyone knew the jewelers in this city, it was Jennifer.

Adele approached the apartment and pressed the buzzer. Would he pop the question tonight? Of course, she'd say yes. As much as she loved travel—exploration and adventure were in her blood—she'd always wanted to find someone to travel *with*. Angus was perfect. He was kind, funny, rich, handsome. He checked every box Adele could think of. She had a rule about dating men at the Bureau—it had never worked out well in the past.

No, dating a civilian was much more her style.

As Adele took the elevator to the second floor, she couldn't control the smile spreading across her face. This time, it wasn't the lopsided, wry look of resigned amusement she'd had on the plane while trying to fall asleep. Rather, she could feel her cheeks stretching from the effort of trying to control her grin.

It was good to be back home. She passed apartments twenty-three and twenty-five on the way to hers. For a moment, her smiled faltered. She glanced back at the golden numbers etched into the metal doors of the residences. Her gaze flicked from one digit to the next, her brow furrowing over her weary eyes.

She shook her head, dislodging her troubled thoughts once more, and turned her back firmly, facing apartment twenty-seven. Home.

Lightly, she knocked on the door and waited. She had her own key, but she was too tired to fish it out of her suitcase.

Would he pop the question in the doorway? Would he give her some time to settle?

She half reached for her phone, wondering if she should call the Sergeant before he went to bed. Her father would stay up long enough to catch the rerun of *8 out of 10 Cats*, his favorite British game show, so there was still time to call him and tell him the good news.

Then again, perhaps she was getting a bit ahead of herself.

Just because Angus was spotted outside a jewelry store, didn't mean that he'd already *purchased* the ring. Perhaps he was still looking.

Adele tried to control her excitement, calming herself with a small breathing exercise.

Then the door swung open.

Angus stared out at her, blinking owlishly from behind his thin-framed glasses. He had a thick jaw, like a football player, but the curling hair of a cupid ornament. Angus was taller than her by a few inches, which was impressive given Adele's own height of five foot ten.

She stepped over the threshold, nearly tripping on something in the door, but then flung out her arms, wrapping Angus in an embrace. She leaned in, kissing him gently, closing her eyes for a moment and inhaling the familiar odor of citrus and herbal musk.

He pulled back, ever so slightly. Adele frowned, stiffening. She opened her eyes, peering up at Angus.

5

"Er, hey, Addie," he said, calling her by the nickname he'd used when they'd first started dating. "Welcome back." He scratched nervously at his chin, and Adele realized he had something strapped over his shoulder.

A duffel bag.

She took a hesitant, awkward step back, and again nearly tripped over the item in the door. She glanced down. A suitcase—not hers. Her suitcase and briefcase were still in the hall where she'd left them.

She glanced from the suitcase to Angus's duffel bag, then back at her boyfriend.

"Hello," she said, hesitantly. "Is everything all right?"

Now that she looked, she realized Angus's glasses had distracted her from his eyes, which were rimmed red. He'd been crying.

"Angus, are you all right?"

She reached out for him again, but this time he ducked the gesture. Her arms fell like lead to her sides and she stared, all sense of euphoria that had been swirling in her chest in the elevator deflating from her like air from a balloon.

"I'm sorry, Addie," he said, quietly. "I wanted to wait—to tell you in person."

"Tell—tell me what exactly?"

Angus's voice quavered as he looked her in the eyes. "Christ, I wish it didn't have to be like this," he said. "I really, really do."

Adele could feel her own tears coming on, but she suppressed them. She'd always been good at managing her emotions. She completed another small breathing exercise; small habits, compounded over time. She looked Angus in the eye and held his gaze.

He looked away, rubbing his hands across the strap to his duffel bag in short, nervous gestures.

"It's everything," he said, quietly. "I won't bother you. The place is yours. I'll pay my side of the lease for the next year. That should give you time."

"Time for what?"

"To find a new place, if you need. Or another roommate." He half-choked on this last word and coughed, clearing his throat.

"I don't understand... I thought... I thought..." Again, she suppressed the wave of emotions swelling in her. The way a sergeant's daughter knew how. The way a trained agent knew how. She scanned him up and down and spotted the glinting silver Rolex displayed on his

6

wrist.

Jennifer had been right. He *had* visited a jewelry store. The watch had been something he'd wanted for a while now.

"God, Addie, come on. Don't make this tough. You knew this was coming. You had to have known this was coming..."

She simply stared at him, his words passing over her like a gusting breeze. She shook her head against the sound, trying to make sense of it. But while she could hear him, it sounded like his voice was echoing up from a deep well.

"I didn't see it," she said, simply.

"Typical," Angus said with a sigh. He shook his head and pointed toward the kitchen table. "My key is there. All the bills are paid and the stubs are beneath the coffee tray. You'll need to water and feed Gregory, but I stocked up enough for the month."

Adele hadn't thought about the turtle they'd gotten together. She hadn't had much time to take care of the thing. At least Angus had.

"What do you mean?" she said.

"About Gregory? I figured you might want him. I'll take him if you don't, but I didn't want to steal him if you cared or—"

"You can have the damn turtle. I mean why did you say 'typical.' What's typical?"

Angus sighed again. "We really don't have to do this. I—I don't know what else to say."

"Something. You haven't said *anything*. I come home from three weeks on a work trip to find my boyfriend of two years packed up ready to leave. I feel like I deserve *some* explanation."

"I gave you one! Over the phone. I said we needed to talk when you got back. Well, here's the talk. I've got to go; I have an Uber coming."

Vaguely, Adele wondered with a dull humor if the same Uber driver would come pick Angus up.

"Over the phone? You talked about a movie night, right? Said something about going out with your friends."

"Yes, Addie, and I said that I was tired of not having you with me. Remember that part? Christ, for an investigator you sure suck at figuring out what's beneath your nose. You've been gone for twenty days, Addie! This is the third time this year. Sometimes it feels like I'm dating a phone app, and that's *when* you have time for a quick ten-minute call."

Adele shook her head. She stepped back and retrieved her own luggage from the hall and dragged it over the suitcase in the door. She shook her head as she moved, frowning. "That's not fair."

"Isn't it?"

"I thought..." She trailed off again, still shaking her head. She glanced down at her left hand and felt a sudden surge of embarrassment. Humiliation was the one emotion she had never quite learned how to suppress. She felt it swirl through her, bubbling in her stomach like hot tar. She felt her temper rising and set her teeth. Growing up with three passports, three nationalities, three *loyalties* as some saw it, Adele had been forced to weather all sorts of comments and jibes at her appearance, at her heritage. She had thick skin, with some things. Pervs on board jet planes were easy enough to handle.

But vulnerability? Intimacy? Failing in those areas always left her with a deep pit of self-loathing formed by humiliation and fear. She could feel it clawing its way through her now, ripping apart her calm, tearing down her facade.

"Fine," she said, her face stony. "Fine then. If you want to leave, then leave."

"Look, it doesn't have to be like that," Angus said, and she could hear the hurt in his voice. "I just can't do it, Addie. I miss you too much."

"You have a hell of a way of showing it. You wanna know what's funny? Christ—I can't even believe it." She snorted in disgust at her own stupidity. "I thought you were going to marry me. I thought you were going to propose. Ha!"

Angus shook his head in small, jagged little motions that caused his curly hair to shift. "You're already married, Adele. And you're loyal—I know you won't cheat."

"What are you talking about?"

"I should have known when we first started dating. The signs were there. But you're just so damn pretty, sexy, smart. You're the most driven person I know. I guess—I guess I didn't want to see it. But you're married to your job. I'm second place. Every time."

"That's not—"

"True? Really? Say it if you believe it. Tell me that next time you get a call to go out of state for three weeks that you'll turn it down. You'll request to stay at the office here. Tell me you'll do that, and I'll stay. Hell, I'll march right back in our room and unpack this damn minute. Tell me you'll say no if they call."

Adele stared at him, the hurt in his voice and in his eyes pricking her pride and deflating her once more. She studied his eyes behind the glasses. She hadn't realized just how long his eyelashes were over his dark stare. It hurt to look at him, so she averted her gaze.

"See," he said after a moment of silence. "You can't. You can't promise that you'll choose me first. I hope it's worth it, Addie. It's just a job."

He began to step past her, into the hall.

Adele didn't turn, preferring to stare sightless across the small space of their cramped apartment.

"It isn't," she said, listening to the sound of Angus's retreating footsteps. "It's not just a job..." She clenched her fists at her sides. "It isn't."

She heard him heave a massive sigh. She could feel him watching her, paused in the middle of the hallway. For a moment, she half hoped he would turn back, tell her it was all some big mistake. But after a moment, he said, "There's food in the microwave, Addie. I saved you some leftovers in the fridge as well. You should be good for a couple of days."

Then the elevator doors dinged, there was the sound of shuffling feet and rolling wheels, and when Adele turned back around, Angus was gone.

CHAPTER TWO

Stars winked down at Marion, coy twinkles of light witnessing the twenty-four-year-old woman's progress from the small coffee shop out into the heart of the city's night. The many odors of the Seine wafted on the air, confronting her with the scent of river musk and the residue of the bakeries which had closed until morning. The blare from the horns of impatient drivers replaced the usual sounds of bells which normally tolled across the city. She heard a low, buzzing noise. Listened for only a moment, then placed the sound as that of a tourist boat zipping by beneath the arching structure of the Pont d'Arcole.

Marion exhaled softly as she stepped from the coffee shop onto the sidewalk, taking it all in. This was her city. She'd lived here her whole life and had no intention of ever leaving. One could grow old and still not find all the adventures hidden within the historic place. She nodded in greeting at an elderly couple walking past, recognizing them from the intersection of their nighttime routines.

"Off into the night, I see?" said the old man in rasping, clipped French, speaking with the undertones of a fellow from the countryside. He winked as he passed and then winced as the accompanying madame tweaked his ear.

"As always, monsieur," Marion called back, meeting his smile. "Out to meet some friends."

She bid the couple farewell with a nod and a skip in her step. Then she strolled up the sidewalk, heading toward the river and turning on the corner. She often walked alone late at night—it had never bothered her. This part of the city was well lit, after all, wreathed in security lights and traffic beams which reflected off the glass of the many windows spotting the apartments and shops.

She moved along the sidewalk, turning down another street in the direction of the club where her friends would be waiting. She hotfooted along the illuminated walkways as she checked her phone, spotting an unopened message.

Before she could read the text, however, Marion heard a noise behind her, which distracted her from her phone for the moment. She glanced down the illuminated street, scanning the stone steps and stairwells of the many looming buildings. A stone's throw away, a man limped along, holding a small bundle in one arm. A moment passed. Then the bundle emitted a crying sound, and the man ducked his head in embarrassment, making shushing noises and trying to calm the infant.

Marion smiled at the man and his baby, then returned her attention to her phone. She tapped the screen to read the message. But before she could...

"Hello, little woman, is all things good and well?"

She turned, startled by the broken French as much as the sudden proximity of the man and his child. He was now walking alongside her, making cooing noises toward the bundle in his arms every couple of steps. She frowned at him for a moment, gathering her nerve. Then she stowed her phone. The text would have to wait. She never wanted it said that Paris was as inhospitable as some of those in the tourist districts wished it were.

The man wore his smile like makeup and his eyes twinkled genially, reminding her of the sparse stars above which had managed to push their way through the city lights.

"All things are well," she said, nodding. "How is your evening?"

The man shrugged, causing the wool cap on his head to shift a little. He reached up and tugged it off with his free hand, stowing it on top of the bundle in his arm.

This struck her as rather odd, and she said as much. It was as her mother always said: the women of Paris ought never fear their opinions.

"You will smother the child," she said, pointing toward the hat.

The man nodded as if he agreed, but made no move to adjust the garment. He seemed, almost, to be waiting for something. He scratched at his red hair, which tumbled past his face in loose, sweaty strands.

After a moment, he caught her eye. "The child likes shade," he said. His French still came on with a thick accent. "Say, do you know the course to—to—how do you say it—the water structure? No—hmm, the bridge!"

Marion shook her head in momentary confusion, but then smiled back at the man, meeting his pleasant expression with one of her own. "There are a few bridges. The nearest one is along this street, across the walk and down the stairs near the wharf."

The man winced in confusion, shaking his head and tapping his ear. "What is this?"

She repeated the instructions, carefully. Obviously, this man was a lost tourist, though she couldn't quite place his accent.

Again, the man winced, holding up his free hand apologetically and shaking his head once more.

Marion sighed. She glanced over her shoulder, back up the street in the direction of the club. Her friends would be waiting. Then she returned her attention to the man and his child, her eyes darting to his pleading expression, and she felt a surge of pity.

"I will show you, all right? It isn't far. Follow me, sir." She turned, heading back the way she had come. She suppressed all the bitter thoughts about tourists that half the city circulated in casual conversation. She quite liked tourists, even if they were a bit dense.

The man seemed to understand her well enough this time and fell into step, cradling his child with the cap on top.

"You is a demon," said the man, his tone filled with gratitude.

Marion frowned at this.

The man hesitated, then urgently amended, "No—I mean *angel.* So sorry. Not demon—you is angel!"

Marion laughed, shaking her head. With a wink of her own, she said, "Perhaps I am a bit demon, too, hmm?"

This time it was the man's turn to laugh. The baby cried again beneath the hat and the man turned, whispering sweetly to his child.

They crossed the street and Marion led the man down the stairs by the wharf. Already, the bridge was in sight, but the man seemed so distracted with his child that Marion felt bad about abandoning him without taking him direct.

As they descended the stairs, dipping beneath a dank, stone overpass, the area became less illuminated. There were far fewer people around now.

"We are here," said the man, his French markedly improved all of a sudden.

Marion glanced at him, then noticed something odd. The man noticed her gaze and then gave an apologetic shrug. He dropped the blanket. A small, toy baby—the type that would cry with their bellies pushed—was strapped to the man's forearm. The baby's plastic eyes peered out at Marion.

The man winked. "I told you he likes the shade."

Marion wrinkled her brow in pleasant confusion.

A moment too late, she saw the surgeon's scalpel in the man's left hand. Then he shoved her, hard, the plastic doll crying quietly in the night.

CHAPTER THREE

Adele stood before the stone steps of the school, eyeing the crowd of children with the greatest of suspicion. She shook her head once, then glanced up at her mother. Her gaze didn't have to travel far; already, Adele was taller than most of her classmates. She had hit a growth spurt when she still lived in Germany, with the Sergeant, and it hadn't seemed to stop until this year.

Now fifteen, Adele found the boys in Paris paid more attention to her than the ones in Germany had. Still, as she stood studying the flow of students into the bilingual secondary school, she couldn't help but feel a jolt of anxiety.

"What is it, my Cara?" her mother asked, smiling sweetly at her daughter.

Adele wrinkled her nose at the nickname, wiping her hands over the front of her school sweater and twisting the buttons on the cotton sleeves. Her mother had grown up in France, and had particular fondness for the Carambar caramels which were still popular in candy shops and gas stations. She often said the jokes written on the outside of the caramel's wrappers were a lot like Adele: clever on the outside with a soft and sweet middle. The description made Adele gag.

Adele Sharp had her mother's hair and good looks, but she often thought she had her father's eyes and outlook.

"They are so noisy," Adele replied in French, the words slow and clumsy on her tongue. The first twelve years of her life had been spent in Germany; re-acclimating to French was taking some time.

"They are children, my Cara. They are supposed to be noisy; you should try it."

Adele frowned, shaking her head. The Sergeant had never approved of noisy children. Noise provided only distraction. It was the tool of fools and sluggish thinkers.

"It is the best school in Paris," said her mother, reaching out a cool hand to cup her daughter's cheek. "Give it a try, hmm?"

"Why can't I homeschool like last year?"

"Because it is not good for you to stay trapped in that apartment

14

with me—no, no." Her mother clicked her tongue, making a tsking sound. "This is not good for you. You enjoyed swimming at your old school, didn't you? Well, there is an excellent team here. I spoke with my friend Anna, and she says her daughter made tryouts the first year."

Adele shrugged with a shoulder, smiling with one side of her mouth. She sighed and then dipped her head, trying not to stand out over the other children so much.

Her mother gave her a kiss on the cheek, which Adele returned halfheartedly. She turned to leave, hefting her school bag over one shoulder. As she trudged toward the school, the sound of the bell and milling children faded. The secondary school flashed and the walls turned gray.

Adele shook her head, confused. She turned back toward the curb. "Mother?" she said, her voice shaky. She was now in the park at night.

"Cara," voices whispered around her from the looming, dark trees.

She stared. Twenty-two years old. It had all ended at twenty-two.

Her mother lay on the side of the bike trail, in the grass, bleeding, bleeding, bleeding…

Always bleeding.

Her dead eyes peered up at her daughter. Adele was no longer twenty-two. Now she was twenty-three, joining the DGSI, working her first case—the death of her mother. Then she was twenty-six, working for the FBI. Then thirty-two.

Tick-tock. Bleeding.

Elise Romei was missing three fingers on each hand; her eyes had been pierced. Cuts laced up and down her cheeks in curious, beautiful patterns as if gouged into felt, glistening red.

Tick-tock. Adele screamed as the blood pooled around her mother, filling the bike trail, flooding the grass and the dirt, threatening to consume her, to overwhelm her…

Adele jerked awake, gasping, her teeth clenched around the edge of her blanket, biting hard to stop the scream bubbling in her throat.

She sat there in her bed, in her and Angus's small apartment, staring across the darkened room, breathing rapidly. It was all right; it was over. She was fine.

She reached out, groping for the comforting warmth of Angus, but her fingertips brushed only cool sheets. Then she remembered the previous night.

Adele clenched her teeth, closing her eyes for a moment. The air

15

felt chilly all of a sudden. She reached up and brushed back her hair. Every bone in her wanted to lie back down, to return to the warmth and safety of her covers. Sleep frightened her sometimes, but her bed was always a welcome shelter.

She forced her eyes open, clenching one fist and bunching it around her pajamas beneath the covers.

Safety and warmth bred weakness. The Sergeant had often said, when she was growing up, that the difference between sluggards and winners was their first decision in the morning. Those who put their heads back to the pillow would never amount to much in life.

And while she was no longer a six-year-old little girl, Adele still swung her legs over the side of the bed, kicking off her covers. slapping her feet against the vinyl floor. With practiced and deft motions she made her bed, arranging her sheets and tucking the corners of the blankets beneath the mattress.

She moved across the room toward where the turtle sat in her glass display case. She and Angus had argued about the gender of the creature—they still weren't sure. Angus thought of him as a boy, yet to Adele, the turtle was clearly a girl. The thought of Angus sent a jolt of discomfort through her, and she swallowed, pushing back the surge of emotion.

Using the provided spoon, she measured the turtle's food into its aquarium, watching the creature meander slowly around the habitat of small stones and faux leaves. Gregory had woken up before her—how embarrassing.

She glanced at the red numbers on the digital clock by her bedside. 4:25 a.m. Perfect. She'd woken before the alarm had gone off. The start to any good routine required an attuned body.

Adele quickly dressed into her jogging clothes and left her apartment. There was no sense in waking early unless she put her time to good use, so 4:30 to 6:00 every morning was the slot for her morning run. Some people listened to music while they exercised, but Adele found that it distracted her. Effort and discomfort required attention.

When she returned from her jog, Adele went directly to the cupboard over the stove, dragging out a box of Chocapic. She wiped sweat from her forehead and focused on her breathing as she poured herself a bowl of the chocolate cereal. She ordered it from France—a small luxury, but a childhood favorite. They didn't make cereal the same way in the US.

Adele grabbed her cereal and a spoon, then hurried to the shower. Small habits compounded through time. Minutes wasted in the morning led to minutes wasted in the day. Angus had often teased her about eating cereal in the shower, especially that time when she'd accidentally swallowed soap, but it was another habit of hers she refused to give up. The secret to success lay in routine.

It was as she stepped out of the shower, toweling her hair with one hand and carrying an empty bowl in the other, that Adele heard her phone chirp from the other room.

She glanced at the digital clock beneath the steamed mirror, frowning. She kept a clock in every room. 6:12 a.m.

Strange. Who would be calling her this early?

Adele quickly dried off and got dressed, pulling her shirt on as she hurried out the bathroom door and stumbled into the kitchen.

"Hello?" she said, lifting the phone to her ear.

"Agent Sharp?" said the voice on the other end.

"Yes?"

"It's Sam. We need you to come in."

Adele frowned, lowering her faded, plastic Mickey Mouse bowl into the sink. "As in now?"

"As in an hour ago. You better hurry."

"You sure? I was told I had three days."

There was a sigh on the other end and the sound of voices in the background.

"Vacation is going to have to wait, Sharp."

"Can I ask why?"

"The Benjamin Killer dropped another body last night. How soon can you—"

"I'm on my way."

Adele didn't even clean her bowl—normally a sacrilege in her house—before rushing to don her work clothes, shoes, and jacket and racing out the door.

Twenty-six. Twenty-five. Twenty-four.

CHAPTER FOUR

Speed limits often felt like suggestions when new leads developed in a case. Still, Adele did her best not to rankle San Francisco's finest—especially not this early in the day. The closer she got to the heart of the city, the more the traffic slowed.

She tapped her fingers against the wheel in frustration, berating the drivers around her silently in her head. As she glared out of the tinted window of her Ford sedan, Adele couldn't help but wonder if perhaps Angus was right. Maybe she was married to the job.

A three-day vacation—that's what they'd promised her. Yet, here she was, rushing into work the moment they snapped their fingers and whistled. Just like a good little girl.

Adele clenched her teeth, pushing the thought from her mind. It wouldn't do to dwell on such things. Especially not with what was at stake.

Who had he killed? Would they be able to find new evidence?

"I'm coming for you, you bastard," she murmured. "I'll get you this time." Adele had spent years trying to shed the accent developed over a life lived overseas. But when she got upset or angry, traces of her heritage would peek through, making themselves known in the lilt of her words. "Damn it," she muttered, slowing her speech, flattening the vowels. "Damn it," she repeated, more precise, more careful. No emotion. No accent. "Damn it," a final time. Hours like this, in front of a mirror, had all but chased the reminders of her past from her speech.

She nodded in satisfaction, then glanced over and realized the woman in the lane next to her had her window down and was staring at Adele, her plucked eyebrows high on her fat-injected forehead.

Sheepishly, Adele rolled up her own window. She flashed a smile and a wave, then stared resolutely ahead for the rest of the slow, snail's pace of a drive. She made one more stop just before reaching the office—pulling through a Starbucks drive-through and grabbing a large black, no sugar.

She reached the private lot for the San Francisco field office a half hour later. The two layers of security hadn't caused trouble once she

18

flashed her ID. She adjusted her jacket and doubled-checked the buttons as she hurried into the east branch through the elevator from the car park.

Another row of metal detectors and men in suits with bored expressions, who smelled like stale coffee and cigarettes, eventually gave way to a long, beige hallway.

"Agent Sharp," said one of the older men, tipping an imaginary cap in her direction from where he squatted on a three-legged stool between the metal detectors.

"Hey, Doug," she greeted him with a wave. She smiled at the man, admiring the neat press of his collar and the shine of his shoes. "Looking sharp as always."

He chuckled, a low, rasping sound. Doug had been a field worker about twenty years ago, but had taken some shrapnel on his last assignment which had confined him to the office. His inability to make rank, however, had nothing to do with shrapnel and everything to do with a complete disdain for office politics. Some in the office thought the elevators needed a "Beware of Doug!" sign. He rarely played nice with others, yet had taken a fondness to Adele that had nothing to do with her gender or her looks. She extended the black, sugarless coffee on top of the X-ray machine, leaving the steaming liquid next to the security officer's scarred hand—two fingers were missing, also courtesy of the car bomb that had claimed his career.

"Just how I like it?"

"Thick and bitter with a little bit of caffeine," Adele said, stepping through the security checkpoint and retrieving her briefcase on the other side.

"Just like you, Doug," said one of the other men with a snorting laugh.

"Shut your mouth, slick," retorted the guard. His expression soured, but he turned so the other man couldn't see and winked at Adele, a twinkle in his gaze.

She rolled her eyes. "Sometimes I wonder if I'm enabling you. Caffeine is a killer—mark my words. Give it fifteen years and the FDA is bound to—"

"Yada, yada," Doug said, and then he tipped the coffee, downing half the cup in two gulps. "Feel free to enable me all you want. Anyway, don't let us old fogeys keep you, sport. You got the shimmer."

She turned to leave with a farewell wave, but then paused, heel half

19

raised. "The shimmer?"

"In the eyes. Something's brewing, right? No—don't tell me. Might bump my head."

"Not enough clearance. I get you. But you're right. Something is up. I'll see you fellas around—Doug, Steve." She nodded to both men in turn and then hastened up the beige hallway, her shoes tapping against the marble floor and squeaking every few steps.

She took a turn past an old-fashioned water cooler and some potted plants, then hurried along a row of tight cubicles. The familiar sound of polite murmuring as folks went about their business, answering calls, printing, faxing, clicking away at their keyboards—all of it filled her with a nauseating sense of dread. There were those in the Bureau who wanted her behind a desk. The thought alone terrified her more than any bullet or case.

She reached an opaque glass door set behind a large, rectangular pillar, which nearly completely obscured the door from view. She swallowed, her hand reaching for the handle. For a moment, she paused, listening, gathering her thoughts. Who was this latest victim? Why had he taken a month-long break from his killing? She'd done good work, but he'd slipped through her fingers before. The bosses had to realize that, right?

From the room, she could hear a quiet murmur of voices—one of them soft, even-toned, the other fuzzy and diluted through the glass.

She turned the handle, tapped a courtesy knock with the hand carrying her briefcase, and then pushed into the room.

Three figures waited for her. One sat by the window, a balding man with a long nose, down which he peered into the street below. Another man, taller than average with a strong jaw and a pen behind one ear, sat by a desk, eyeing a large fifty-two-inch TV screen over a conference table.

The other woman in the room was also sitting, but on the edge of the table, her suit pants stained just over the pocket. All three of them, including the face on the TV, reacted to Adele's entrance.

"Sharp," said the tall man with a nod. "Glad you could make it."

"Sam," she said, returning the gesture of greeting. "What did I miss? And who's the pixels?"

"Sharp," said the woman seated at the table, turning slightly so she faced the door. Lee Grant was one of Adele's few friends in the department, and though she kept her tone professional, there was a weight of concern behind her glance. "How was your flight?"

Adele shrugged. "Long, boring. Sleazy lawyer in business."

Grant rolled her eyes. "The usual then?"

Adele chuckled softly. "About the sum of it."

"Well," said Agent Lee, "we were waiting for you to get started. The pixels, as you put it, belong to DGSI exec Thierry Foucault. I believe you two have a history."

Adele's eyebrows invaded the personal space of her hairline, and she circled the table, setting her briefcase down and turning for a better look at the screen. A hawk-faced man with thick eyebrows and even thicker cheekbones glared out from the screen, his eyes flicking around the room. "I don't believe we've had the pleasure," she said, slowly, racking her brain for any memory of the man's face.

"The young lady—this is Sharp?" said the face on the screen, still giving the appearance of scowling, though Adele was starting to suspect this had more to do with the arrangement of his features than of his current mood.

Adele tilted her head in a nod.

"I was still at the embassy when you worked for DGSI." The speakers crackled for a moment, and Adele leaned in, straining to hear. The sound cleared a moment later as Foucault continued. "Four years? Five? A pity you left. France can always use talent like yours."

Adele had no doubt her file sat in front of the executive, but she kept her smile polite. "It was four. I learned a lot in my position in Paris. I doubt the FBI would have recruited me without the experience."

"This is the way of it, no?" said Foucault, smirking through the screen. "France creates the things most valued by America, hmm. It is no matter... I—I did wonder," he said, slowly, his eyes flicking down for a moment, confirming Adele's suspicion about the file. "Why was it you left, eh? Not the weather, I hope."

Lee glanced toward Adele, then quickly interjected, "Perhaps now isn't the best time to discuss it," she said. "We ought to focus on the task at hand."

But the man on the screen was already wagging his finger. "No, no. It is important DGSI knows who it is we work with. France is no jilted lover—it is important we know who we take back, hmm?"

Adele tried to conceal her frown. What did he mean *take back*? Agent Lee tried to interject again, but Adele cut her boss off.

21

"It's really quite simple," said Adele, hiding her frown behind pressed lips and an impassive stare. "I tracked a killer in France, and he didn't turn out to be who I thought he was. I felt like it was time for a change." *Bleeding. Bleeding. Always bleeding.* Adele shivered as her dream flashed through her mind, but she stowed the thought with a swallow and a proud tilt of her chin. She shrugged toward the screen, feeling her suit jacket slide across her shoulders.

Of course, she wasn't mentioning the months of PTSD after tracking the killer and discovering he wasn't the culprit behind her mother's torturous murder. Nor did she feel it appropriate to mention the American forensic psychologist whom she'd traveled to the States with, hoping to set down roots. Chances were, Foucault had all of it in his little file, but as far as she was concerned, it was nobody's business but hers.

"Does that settle it then?" said Agent Lee, glaring at the screen. She pushed off of the conference table and strode past the man with the hooked nose still standing quietly by the window.

"There is nothing to be settled," said the screen.

"Not yet, no," Grant replied, still frowning. "But it might be in everyone's best interests to let the bygones pass and discuss the events of last night."

Adele felt a flash of gratitude for her superior. Lee Grant wasn't just named after two generals on opposing sides in the American Civil War, but she commanded an authority that any agent would willingly follow into battle. Lee's eyes often narrowed in such a way that they became little more than stormy slits in her naturally tan complexion. The child of an American and a Cuban immigrant, Lee was one of the few people in the office who understood Adele's roots, especially given the less-than-six-year age gap between them.

"Well," said Foucault, his voice echoing slightly through the TV speakers. "Do we wait for more, or may we begin?"

Grant glanced at the fellow by the window, who had yet to breach his silence. "I don't see any point in prolonging any further."

"Very sorry, very sorry, Executive Foucault," said the man with the hooked nose at last. He turned away from the glass and leaned his hands against the conference table, staring at the large screen. "Special Agent Sharp has been working this case stateside as Agent Lee mentioned before—we thought it best she was here."

Adele didn't recognize this man, but he had the suit and the attitude of a diplomat, or some sort of low-level supervisor who only came out of the woodwork when agencies needed to play nice.

"As for formal introductions: this is SAC Lee Grant," said the suit, indicating Adele's boss. "She's overseeing the investigation. You obviously know Agent Sharp. And Sam Green works for tech." The tall man with the pen tucked behind his ear who was seated behind everyone gave a polite little wave, but remained silent.

Foucault nodded politely at each in turn. Then he said, "A pity we could not meet in better circumstances. I have more information since last we spoke. The missing girl is named Marion Lucas. Twenty-four years of age. We are still waiting on some tests, but it is with relative certainty that I can inform you the body we found yesterday matches the pictures provided by Marion's mother."

"You mentioned on the call something about shallow cuts," said Agent Lee, trailing off and allowing the silence to fill the space between her and the TV.

For the first time, Foucault's lips formed a thin, grim line. "I'll have someone in the office send the report along." He gave the smallest shake of his head, causing a strand of slicked hair to fall over his eyes, which he brushed back with one hand, sighing with the motion. "I've got to warn you. It isn't pretty."

Adele cleared her throat. "You're sure she was twenty-four?"

Everyone turned toward Adele as if surprised she would interject. An unspoken rhythm governed conversations like these, where a sort of hierarchy dictated the pace of the conversation and permission to speak. But the last thing on Adele's mind right now was office etiquette.

"Yes," Foucault replied. "Verified only hours ago."

Adele shook her head, adjusting her sleeves as she often did when upset or angry. "The killer—did anyone see him?"

"Like I said, we'll send the report over. It's important we all—"

"Did you find the body?"

Foucault frowned at Adele. "Yes. He left it where he killed her. Beneath an underpass near the Pont d'Arcole."

Agent Lee raised a well-manicured eyebrow, her hand absentmindedly passing over the stain on her pocket. Often, Lee would spend full days at the office. She was a notorious insomniac who spent most of her time either working or thinking about work. She cleared her throat now, shooting a questioning glance toward her subordinate.

"A bridge," Adele explained. "In Paris. Cause of death?" This

23

question she lobbed back toward the screen.

"Exsanguination." The same grim line creased Foucault's mouth. "Small cuts, up and down the body. Missing her shoes and shirt. We believe he took those with him. Cuts between the webbing of her toes, along her arms, her cheeks, her breasts. It will all be included in the report."

Adele could hear her own breathing. The air in the office felt very cold all of a sudden and bumps stood up along her skin. "He let her bleed out." She turned sharply toward Agent Lee. "The same MO as the Benjamin Killer."

"The body was found by a couple of tourists," Foucault added.

Adele gritted her teeth, shaking her head wildly. "I don't get it. Why's he in France all of a sudden?"

"It's been a month," Agent Lee replied. "Maybe you were getting close."

"But I wasn't!" Adele looked at the screen and shook her head. "We don't have a clue who it is."

Grant stood framed against the window, standing next to the hook-nosed suit, glancing between Adele and Foucault. Grant said, "Maybe you got closer than you think. Maybe he got spooked some other way. Whatever the case, he could have fled the States for Paris."

"But to kill in another country? So soon after leaving? Most murderers need time to acclimate. He wouldn't be comfortable in his surroundings yet. Why strike so soon?"

Lee Grant tapped her teeth with her fingers. The still unnamed suit by the window glanced between the women, keeping quiet like a spectator at a tennis match.

"It isn't always hard to acclimate," said Grant. "Vacationers can be ruthless. Remember the incident at the resort down in Tijuana?"

Adele wrinkled her nose. "We don't know it's a vacationer, though. What if… What if he's from Paris?" she said, slowly, savoring the thought. "What if he was in the US on vacation?"

Grant pursed her lips, pressing her back against the tall window. "Interesting thought. Maybe. Either way, traveling to Paris gave him the impetus he needed to strike again."

"If that's his mindset, then he'll only get worse," said Adele.

Foucault had been sitting quietly, listening for the last couple of minutes. But at this last comment, he broke his peace. "Exactly. And this is the topic of the day, Agent Sharp."

24

This time, it was Adele's turn to tilt an eyebrow in the direction of her supervisor. Agent Lee sighed. "I wanted to tell you in person. I know you had three days off—I know what the last month must have been like. I'm sure it's been hard on you and Angus." Her lips curved in a sympathetic way. "But you know everything about this bastard, Adele. He's going to kill again. You know it, and so do I."

"What are you asking?"

"They need you in Paris," said Grant. "I've already discussed it with the department supervisors."

Adele was already shaking her head though, and turned her back on the screen, pacing the room before rounding on Foucault once more. Except now, she was watching Lee, framing her friend against the backdrop of the glowing screen.

"No one knows this guy better than you, Adele," said Grant. "The DGSI wants you on the ground. You have ties to both agencies, and with your dual citizenship—"

"Triple," Adele said, softly.

"Come again?"

"Triple citizenship. I'm German, too."

Grant nodded quickly. "Yes, of course. Triple citizenship. You're uniquely positioned, Adele."

"Are you telling me?"

Agent Lee immediately shook her head, causing her chestnut hair, which she always wore in a simple ponytail, to swish back and forth. "No. It's your call. But if you agree, you'll have to go now. There's no time to wait. You'll have to take your vacation some other time."

As static crackled the room, coming from the direction of the TV, Foucault's lips were moving, but she couldn't hear what he was saying.

"Christ, Sam," snapped Adele. "We're the goddamn FBI. Think we could have a clean call?"

The tall tech—who'd remained seated throughout all of this, quiet and watching—was already hurrying over, fiddling with buttons on the TV.

After a moment, the static faded. Foucault tested the mic and then, peering across the room, his eyes slightly off-center—though Adele suspected on his screen, he was staring straight at her—he said, "Well, Agent Sharp? France will have you back. Will you come to Paris?"

"No," said Adele. Immediately, she felt a jolt of worry. The words had come unbidden to her lips, summoned from deep within her, the residue of past decisions bubbling to the surface.

She couldn't go to France. Not now. Not so soon after...

She glanced around the room, realizing all eyes were on her. The lights above felt bright all of a sudden, her own breathing sounded loud to her ears. She reached up one hand, rubbing at an elbow but refusing to stare at the ground, though everything in her wanted to avert her gaze.

Christ, Sharp, you'd really throw away a career just to avoid... Avoid what, exactly? Lee Grant said nothing, studying her subordinate with a compassionate expression. Foucault and the diplomat were frowning, but Adele glanced away, locking eyes with Lee.

Of everyone in the room, Agent Lee had her back. But still, refusing a request like this from the higher-ups didn't come without consequences.

Adele set her jaw and straightened her posture. "I—I can't go back. Not yet..." *Why not, Cara? Come home.*

Adele shivered and shook her head even more adamantly. "No. I just can't...I..." She trailed off, images from her dreams flashing through her mind. Memories of a childhood, of a life once lived, played like shadow puppets across her mind. She thought of Doug in security. Perhaps that was to be her fate: relegated to a metal detector with her own sign, *Beware of Sharp: refuses to play nice.*

Career was one thing... But this... This was too close to home. She inhaled slowly, trying to clear her mind. It didn't *have* to be like last time, did it? Her mother's case was cold. She wouldn't absorb herself in it. Not again. This was about the Benjamin Killer. This was about this girl, Marion, and whoever the next victim would be.

Could she really say no? What was she staying for anyway? It wasn't like Angus had stayed. Why should she?

"Think about it," said Foucault, studying her. "I'll send the case file and the doctor's report. Perhaps you'll have insight we missed, hmm?"

Adele nodded. She could read a report. Where was the harm in that? Just one lousy report.

"Fine," said Adele. "Sam, can you forward it to me?"

One small, measly little case file. Perhaps there'd be a clue, after all. Adele puffed her cheeks, then blew softly, exhaling in an effort to steady her nerves.

Why was he killing based on age alone? What did it all mean? *Bleeding, bleeding, ever bleeding...*

Another crime scene, another killer, another murder. All of it flashed through Adele's mind, leaving cold prickles across her skin as she stared resolutely out the tall glass windows. When would the Benjamin Killer stop? It was like a countdown—a challenge.

He wouldn't stop on his own. It was the wrong question. The real question echoed, unvoiced in Adele's brain: when would someone catch him?

She could feel the eyes in the room staring at her, watching, accusing, waiting…

CHAPTER FIVE

The airplane's cabin echoed with the sound of the churning engines. Adele leaned back in her seat, savoring the comfort of first class. She stretched, arching her back as she clasped the armrests with her hands. She reached up and adjusted the small knob that turned on the air conditioning, and then brushed her hair aside as airflow wafted through the cabin. No sleazy lawyers this time.

It had taken Lee all of five minutes to convince Adele to go to Paris.

Her supervisor always knew what to say. And, in this particular case, she hadn't said anything. At least, for the most part.

Adele could still feel her supervisor's gaze boring holes into the side of her skull. Her own mind had done the persuading. Far too many people were given a pass for the sake of someone else's comfort. Killers escaped because of lazy law enforcement. These murderers, these monsters, didn't deserve Adele's complacency. She wouldn't permit them her exhaustion. Nor would she allow them, ever, her fear of her past.

It had been a while since she'd been in France. And, if she was perfectly honest, she missed it.

She blended in well enough, and could speak the language to a degree few people suspected her of being a tourist.

Adele shifted, readjusting her position against the headrest. She steadied herself, breathing softly, inhaling for seven seconds, then exhaling for eight. A small breathing exercise her psychologist boyfriend had once taught her. The same boyfriend she'd come back stateside with.

That relationship had plummeted in a fiery crash. Adele had never been great at dealing with other people's character flaws. Some thought of her as self-righteous, but she considered herself determined.

And when the psych had cheated on her with a mutual friend, she'd decided the relationship had run its course.

Adele reached beneath her seat, pulling out her briefcase and fumbling for the laptop.

Sam had downloaded the report and the files from DGSI before she left. She hadn't wanted to look at them in the car, on the way to the airport. She'd been permitted to pack a small suitcase, which had taken her all of twenty minutes. She didn't travel with much luxury; besides the few changes of clothes and toiletries, Adele had only packed her plastic cereal bowl and a spoon.

She felt her fingers trembling a bit as she clicked the latch to her laptop and opened the computer. She shifted, turning the screen toward the window and away from the aisle. Her eyes flicked up and spotted a couple of children sitting in business class six rows back. It wouldn't do for them to see the screen, and so she shielded it with her body and turned the lid even further.

Of course, she hadn't wasted the drive to the airport. Going over the files of the previous victims had been no enjoyable task, but it had been a necessary one. The killer seemed to have no particular taste Adele could spot. He chose his victims at random, except for their ages.

Her head pounded, and Adele closed her eyes, loath to witness what she knew she'd find. Images played on repeat across the insides of her eyelids. Angus had accused her of being married to the job.

He was only half right.

She was married to the ghosts of victims past. Wed in sheer will to those whose voiceless lips cried for justice.

Jeremy Benthen. Twenty-nine. Father of two. The Benjamin Killer had rushed this time—his first kill. At least, the first that Adele could trace to him. She could see, in her mind, as clear as if a video were playing before her: Jeremy's body on the ground, shoved between the middle-school gym and the dumpster. He was the head coach of the junior basketball team. Two gloves discarded near a fire hydrant. The lab had failed to pull prints.

Jeremy had been cut along his chest and groin, and one of his eyes had been slashed. Shaky cuts—adrenaline from the killer's first. None of the wounds were enough to kill the middle-school coach. Rather, the killer would incapacitate his victims. He was using a substance, but the toxicology reports still weren't clear. It wasn't chloroform, and it wasn't Rohypnol. Whatever he was administering was a combination of sorts, a home brew.

Then, when he had his victims incapacitated, he would go to work.

The second victim. Tasha Hunt. That's when Adele had determined the killer was using a scalpel. His cuts had become steadier, more confident. Rehearsed. Though, with the single mother from Indiana, he had also used a machete.

Adele gritted her teeth as the memories cycled through her mind. Local enforcement had initially thought the killer was overpowering his victims through other means. But he'd taken off his gloves.

Those gloves by the fire hydrant. A mistake. An oversight—the unforced error of a rookie in his first big game. Except they *hadn't* been the killer's gloves. She'd determined they'd belonged to the victim, to Jeremy. So *why* had the killer removed Jeremy's gloves? Such a strange choice. He hadn't cut Jeremy's fingers…

Between the fingers, nearly imperceptible—that's where she'd found the injection mark. She'd once dated a guy who hid his drug habit by injecting between the toes and fingers. She'd missed it with her boyfriend, all those years ago.

But she hadn't missed it this time. The Benjamin Killer was careful, calculated… But not perfect. No killers were.

Adele knew she hadn't missed anything in the files. But, at Lee's insistence, she had done her due diligence on the drive to the airport.

In the past, she thought perhaps the killer was involved in the medical field, and the drug he used was some sort of dentist's nitrous or some type of anesthetic. But those theories were quickly debunked by the lab. The scalpel was perhaps too obvious a weapon for a surgeon or anesthesiologist.

Still, the most horrifying part: despite whatever substance the killer was using, though it incapacitated their bodies, the victims retained complete use of their minds. They could feel and sense everything done to them.

The killer would cut them in a private setting, then watch. He would witness, for his own viewing pleasure, the slow exsanguination of the chosen target, and then he would leave, long before they were dead.

He never struck a killing blow. He never struck any vital organs or veins or arteries that would allow the victims to bleed out quickly. A weak man? Adele wasn't sure. A clever man? Certainly.

He liked to take it slow. By the third victim, he'd perfected his craft: he'd bled Agatha Mencia for nearly four hours before she finally died.

"Sick twist," said Adele, muttering beneath her breath, her mild accent twisting the "i" sound into "ee." Adele often tried to maintain professionalism. It was the only way to stay sane in a job like this. But every so often, she would come across killers, psychopaths, that beggared one's ability to maintain sanity.

Steadying her breathing once more, Adele flicked through the files on her download folder. Finally, wedged up against the window, blocking anyone behind her from seeing the pictures or content of the report, she clicked the newest file uploaded by Sam.

She studied the pictures with cold, clinical calculations, refusing to miss anything. She cataloged as much of the information as she could, her eyes flicking from frame to frame, reading the doctor's notes beneath each image.

A young woman—shirtless, shoeless. The killer thought he was being clever. But the missing shoes weren't a fetish. He'd injected her between the toes; Adele would have put money on it.

She skimmed to an image of the scene—beneath a dark, dank bridge. Lonely, out of sight. Adele's gaze flitted back to the image of the girl. Not a streetwalker, nor a girl from a low-rent part of town. A nice girl—a city girl. How had the killer lured her beneath the bridge?

Did she know him?

Adele shook her head, her hair rubbing against the headrest of the airplane seat. Unlikely. The killer wouldn't have risked traveling halfway around the world to kill someone he knew.

Could the killer speak French? Maybe he'd lured her. Bundy used to pull a trick, pretending to be a cripple, or pretending to look for a lost pet. Preying on the compassion of his victims.

Perhaps the Benjamin Killer was doing the same?

The bridge underpass was dark in the pictures of the crime scene, and two rows of cement dividers shielded Marion's corpse from view. Planned then, rehearsed. The killer knew where he was taking her.

Just like with Jeremy. Like with Agatha. The murderer plotted his kills well in advance, choosing the perfect location, like a lover preparing for a first date.

Adele stared at Marion's crumpled body. She could see how he'd shoved her, and then he would have threatened her with a gun? No—she doubted it. Not in France. Though it was still a possibility.

A knife would be enough. Maybe even the murder weapon. Then he would remove her shoes and prick her with the needle.

The lighting was too poor to tell much beyond that. Perhaps this was a mercy.

The killer's handiwork was visible across the Parisian's half naked corpse.

Adele thought she could see the young woman's eyes strained in their sockets, conveying a cry for help. Her pupils dilated, though she would have been unable to move. Adele gritted her teeth yet again; she could only imagine the fear, the pain, the sheer sense of loneliness and helplessness.

Adele flipped through the notes and pictures a second time, refused to skip any of it. Any scene, any moment, any fragment of an instance could hold a clue.

She shook her head, sighing softly. Then she read the report again. Nothing new, simply detailing what it was she'd already seen. Adele read the report once more, and then another time, and another. Each time her eyes perused the words on the screen, reading the horrific crime described in clinical detail, she scanned it for clues, keeping her eyes open, her mind attentive, cataloging every second, every pixel, every discarded cigarette butt and graffiti tag beneath the bridge.

She refused to let him get away. Marion Lucas's pleading, motionless eyes demanded justice. The blood pooling around the young girl cried out for vengeance. And Adele, more than ever, was determined to provide it.

CHAPTER SIX

The Charles De Gaulle international airport was one of the largest ones in Europe. Her shoes tapped against the tiles, and then paused on the whirring escalator. She passed through customs and reached the gate.

Adele scanned the waiting room, her eyes flicking from happy families embracing some new arrival, or chauffeurs in dark hats and glasses holding up small signs, to other travelers who set off alone, their luggage trundling behind them.

Her own briefcase rested on top of her suitcase handle, which she'd extended and held tight, rolling her suitcase along behind her.

"Adele Sharp," said a soft, polite voice. Surprisingly, a voice she recognized.

For a moment, if only that, the thoughts of the case were chased from her mind. The way the person pronounced her name, the words plucked from the air, like a florist cutting flowers and presenting them to a customer, brought back memories.

She looked in the direction of the voice and a smile stretched her face.

"Robert?" she said, her cheeks bunching. "Of course they would send you. Of course!"

Robert Henry stood straight-backed and stiff. He wore an immaculately pressed suit, and had a curved, perfectly manicured mustache on his upper lip. His hair was thicker than she remembered it back in their days working at the DGSI—hair plugs, perhaps? Robert had been the one who'd taken her under his wing. He'd saved her life on at least two separate occasions.

A flood of memories came with this recognition. He was smiling back at her, his hands loosely at his side, his polished shoes heel to heel.

Robert Henry was about three inches shorter than she was. Adele was tall, but not excessively so. Robert had once played soccer for a semi-professional team in Italy, but had returned to France when he'd been recruited in the 1950s by the French government, long before

DGSI existed. Now, like his hair, his mustache was also dyed black.

"Robert!" she called, hurrying across the floor, her shoes squeaking against the polished ground. "It's good to see you, old friend."

The small man smiled up at her, extending a hand with a sort of gallant flourish. He took her arm and declared, "You are as beautiful as my sore old eyes remember. I feel the youth returning to my bones as we speak."

Robert didn't even have a hint of an accent. Adele had it on good authority he could speak eight different languages with perfect inflection. As far as investigators went, he was one of the best France had to offer.

"Off to your flattering ways already, I see? And me only fresh off the plane."

"And fresh is the perfect word. Refreshing to have someone who appreciates the importance of sparsity."

His eyes darted to her small suitcase.

"I'll just buy anything else I need. FBI's paying."

"Of course, of course. And how are our American friends?"

"I can't complain. You didn't drive yourself, did you?" Adele grimaced and made a big show of shaking her head.

"Ah," said Robert, a slight frown increasing his otherwise impassive expression. "If you're recollecting that time in Bulgaria, the countryside, I'll have you know, automatic cars are a bane, *non,* a curse on the modern world!"

Adele hid a smirk and wheeled her suitcase around so she could rest an elbow on the raised handle. "Yeah, that's why you hit the light post, is it?"

He scowled in mock severity, clicking his tongue. As he drew nearer, he smelled of a bit too much cologne and a light odor of cigar smoke. "Back to where we left it, I see? No respect. And is it just me, or has your beautiful, glorious accent faded, hmm?"

Adele paused at the smell and the comment about her accent. Her mind wandered for a moment, back to her first days at the DGSI, walking into Robert's office. The same smell had confronted her, as had the same small, friendly man, with far more gray hairs at the time. She could still remember the neat, tidy office, displaying pictures of racetracks and old sports cars. Robert had no frames displaying family photos, as he had no family.

And yet, Adele's lips curved slightly as she remembered the way the man had greeted her then. A strange young girl from America, wandering into his office. He'd welcomed her like a niece and immediately had started asking far too personal questions about her health, her love life, her favorite foods.

It had felt like home.

Adele never had a home. She wasn't German enough, French enough, American enough for anyone to claim her as one of theirs unless they wanted something from her. She spoke with the slightest of accent in *every* language, unable to fully call one hers.

Twelve years in Germany, another fifteen years in France, then the rest in the US. Angus had teased her about traveling so much and never settling. But it never felt right settling anywhere, because... though she hated to admit it, Adele didn't *belong* anywhere. A girl without a home, and no real family left to speak of—moving so much had familial consequences too.

At the time, on her first day, Robert had seen right through her loneliness. He'd seen her as a kindred spirit and adopted her on the spot.

The small, well-dressed, even-toned man kept Adele by the arm, holding it in the crook of his, and began to lead her back toward the exit. They approached the sliding glass doors and slipped into the stream of passengers leaving the airport. Adele allowed her old mentor to guide her along the streets across the gate lane, to where a parked car awaited them—a Renault sedan with dark, tinted windows framed by black paneling. Adele gave her suitcase to Robert, who hefted it into the trunk.

She moved toward the passenger's door, but he quickly beat her to it and opened it, ushering her into the front seat with a gallant wave of his hand.

"Thank you," she said, hiding a smile.

There were some who mistook Robert for a bit of a fool. He was quite showy and enjoyed things like wine and cheese tastings and discussing philosophy. There was a pretentiousness to it, but it didn't bother Adele in the least. Because she also knew he had successfully closed more cases for the DGSI than any other investigator in the history of the agency—albeit, it wasn't a very long history.

He rounded the car back to the driver's side with slow, even steps. As he settled into the vehicle, he glanced over at Adele. "You seem in good health," he said. He paused for a moment, rubbing the steering wheel, then, noticing the motion, he fell still. "Since you were last here… have things—"

"I'm fine, Robert," Adele replied quickly, cutting him off before he could finish the sentence. Her tone fell somber on her own ears all of a sudden. She felt a slight flush to her cheeks. "Last time… The strain— it was—"

"You do not owe me an explanation."

"No, perhaps not." Adele glanced out the window back toward the milling passengers heading to parked vehicles. Her gaze turned back to the vehicle and traced the interior. She paused for a moment, glancing up at the visor above Robert's seat. Two small, weathered photographs were tucked in the corner sleeve, in the same way taxi drivers throughout the city displayed photographs of their families.

Except, this photograph was of the DGSI headquarters, and, the second, smaller one was… Adele looked closer and felt a sudden lump in her throat.

The second photograph was of her and Robert standing next to each other—the first day on the job. She recognized her young, smiling face peering out of the dusty picture. She'd never had a home, never belonged anywhere… And yet, there, sitting in the small car smelling of cologne and cigar smoke, she felt more at home than she had in years.

"It is good to have you back, child," said Robert, glancing over at her with a concerned expression. "Are you ready to work?"

Adele nodded, her eyes flicking away from the visor. "I'm not here for any other case besides this one. Understand?"

Robert's eyebrows inched up. "I will not speak of it; I understand. But do *you*?"

Adele thought for a moment, watching as Robert started the engine and checked his mirror, pulling slowly away from the curb.

One case at a time. That's all she had time for. One case.

She stared out the window as they left the airport, pulling toward the heart of the city. In the distance she could hear tolling bells. It was good to be home…

Her expression softened for a moment as she stared out across the city, her eyes tracing the river and darting across the many old structures. As her gaze flitted to the bridges, little more than arches on the horizon, her expression hardened.

This was home, but there was a rat in the basement, and it was up to her to find it and crush it before it could cause any more harm.

The Benjamin Killer had fled the States for a reason and had already killed once since he'd arrived in France. It would only be a matter of time before he killed again.

CHAPTER SEVEN

Six kilometers from the center of Paris, in the northwestern suburbs of the Ile-de-France region of the capital, Adele found herself staring up at the headquarters of the DGSI.

On the outside, it didn't look like much. A small cafe rested next to the sealed structure, with dull pink and orange bricks providing a quaint appearance in comparison to the bleak gray and black building for which it served as a foot stool.

Adele remembered the building well. In her mind, she had rehearsed the number of turns the vehicle made as it circled the closed parking lot behind the headquarters.

Inside, the building was far nicer than she remembered. Fresh coats of paint and up-to-date technology now filled the offices that Robert led her past.

"One thing to say for terrorists," Robert said as he guided her through the building and noticed her curious glance toward a row of high-powered computers behind a glass wall. "They have a singular way of motivating the allocation of taxes. Here, this way."

Robert led her to an open foyer. A receptionist glanced up from behind a desk and cleared his throat with a polite tilt of his head.

"Here to see Foucault," Robert answered the querying glance.

The receptionist nodded and tapped a button on his phone. There was a buzz, then a thick glass door clicked open, adjacent to the desk.

"They're both waiting," said the receptionist.

Adele followed her former mentor into the room.

It was only as she peered out the windows that she realized they were likely on the top floor. These windows didn't face the street, and they were all tinted black.

Still, the view from so high up brought back another tide of memories. She turned from the city toward the room. Immediately, she spotted the man from TV screen back in San Francisco. His eyebrows were even thicker in person and his glower doubly intense. He sat behind an old desk that looked to be made from carved oak. The desk sat surrounded by so much technology, it seemed somewhat out of

38

place in both time and taste, as did the quill and ink pot sitting near an old dial-phone.

"Agent Sharp," Foucault said, speaking with the same light accent as before. "Good of you to come."

She nodded her greeting.

"This is Special Agent John Renee," said Foucault, gesturing to his left. "He will be your partner on the case. He's already been briefed by SOC Grant on the particulars of the previous cases."

Adele glanced to the second man standing by the oak desk. Perhaps a couple years older, with prematurely gray hair on the side which always accompanied the word "distinguished," Agent John Renee was the tallest man in the room. He had a bold roman nose and a burn mark just beneath his chin, stretching down his throat. He had sharp, intelligent eyes and pronounced cheekbones. Overall, he struck Adele as carrying the appearance of a James Bond villain. Handsome enough to stare at, but rough enough to worry about.

She smiled to herself at this characterization, but hid the expression just as quickly, extending a hand toward her new partner.

"Greetings," she said.

"*Français?*" John Renee replied.

Adele shrugged. "*Oui, un peu.*"

John nodded, his close-cut hair just as dark beneath the ceiling light as it had been in shadow. "English, then," he said, carrying the thickest accent of the three men. "I have read the files, *oui.* But I still think I must ask you some questions."

Foucault interrupted. "I'm sure Sharp wishes to settle. Robert, thank you."

John rolled his eyes, but covered by glancing out the window. "The American princess needs her beauty sleep?"

"The American princess is fine," said Adele, keeping her cool. She glanced toward Foucault. "Actually, if it's all the same, I'd like to see the crime scene while it's still fresh."

Foucault's lips turned down in a sort of shrug and he nodded. "I have no objections. John?"

The tall man with the military hair cut gave a curt shake of his head. "Have you seen the pictures?"

Adele adjusted her sleeves. "Yes. I'd like to track the girl's movements, if it's all the same. Is there anything new I should know about?"

John began to move toward the door without so much as an *au revoir* to the other men. "Lab gave us the results. The body we recovered does indeed belong to Marion Lucas. They found something in her blood."

"That would be the paralytic. Do they know what it is?"

John shook his head, opening the door and stepping through it before her. Robert frowned from within the room and gave a small nod in Adele's direction.

"No," said John. "But they're looking. We had hoped the FBI might know."

Adele quickly returned Robert's farewell, then winced at John. "Afraid not. Never enough of a sample to narrow it down, unfortunately. No matter. How far is the crime scene from here?"

"Follow me, American Princess," said John. "I know a shortcut."

Adele hurried after the brash man as he maneuvered quickly through the halls, leading her toward the elevators set at the end of building. She stepped into the first car that opened with John. The crime scene would have answers. It had to.

CHAPTER EIGHT

Adele inhaled the river air, the same air that had now gone stale in the corpse's lungs. Marion's body had long since been taken to the morgue, but her blood still stained the concrete in haphazard patterns, smothering the dust beneath the bridge in tendrils of crimson.

The area remained cordoned off, with sawhorse blockades obstructing the stairs and the walkway on either side. Two gendarmerie stood sentry, but otherwise, Adele and John had the crime scene to themselves.

Adele dropped into a crouch, pointing her finger at the blood. "Why do you think he bleeds them?" she murmured, then flicked her gaze back toward the stairs.

John gave a noncommittal grunt. "Psychos and freaks do psychotic and freakish things," he said.

Adele pushed off her knees and moved over to the stairs, peering up beneath the blockade toward the sound of traffic and pedestrians above. "She lives on Rue Villehardouin?"

Another grunt. "That's what her mother said."

"She must have come down the stairs then. Shops with surveillance cameras?"

John frowned, testing the word in English. "Surveillance?"

"Security," Adele said in English, then repeated the word in French.

"Still checking."

Adele nodded. "Waiting for the warrants?"

John snorted at this, giving her a long look. He scratched at the burn mark beneath his chin as he wagged his head side to side. "How long has it been since you worked here? DGSI does not need warrants."

Adele tucked her tongue inside her mouth and turned back toward the underpass, nodding slowly. He was right, of course. How could she forget? There were those who felt the reach of the DGSI extended far longer than their purpose. She supposed she didn't disagree. But, from the law enforcement side of things, she certainly wouldn't complain. Less red tape meant less time wasted, which meant more criminals behind bars and more citizens kept safe.

41

Adele shook her head in disgust, glancing around the scene once more. "Nothing new," she said. "Any insights?" She turned, but found John staring across the river, watching the boats pass, a distant look in his eyes. "Hello?" she said. "Is our case boring you?"

He snapped out of his reverie. For a moment, his handsome features hardened, his eyes narrowing over his roman nose. "Yes," he said. "A stupid girl allows herself to be lured beneath an ugly bridge. And now her insides are staining my shoes. So, yes, American Princess, I am bored, and I am tired. Does this count as insight enough for you?"

Adele refused to allow her reaction to play across her face. She knew men like John—men who uttered callous, obnoxious opinions to throw others off guard.

John rolled his eyes, turning back toward the crime scene and facing away from the river. Agent Renee was nearly a head taller than her. His height alone had earned sidelong glances as they'd taken the stairs into the underpass. But Adele refused to let this intimidate her. She stepped right up next to John, surveying the bloodstains.

"The killer must know French," said her partner after a moment.

Adele pursed her lips. "I thought the same. To lure her down here, he had to communicate somehow. Did Marion know English?"

"No. I asked her mother."

Adele jerked her head in a short, choppy motion. "Good. So our killer knows English and French." She exhaled deeply, shaking her head. "Why is he here, though? In France, I mean. Is he French? Vacationing and killing in America?"

"Why must he be French?" John snorted, his accent thicker than ever. "Probably a fat American, eh? Fled to my lovely country like a rat leaving a sinking ship."

"Either way, why continue killing? He got away with it. The killer escaped the US. Why strike again? He could have gotten away."

"Eh. He speaks French and English, but he is not so smart, hmm?"

Adele glanced over. "Perhaps it's you?"

John shot her a sidelong glance, then a smile broke his face. He turned back to the stairs, waving at her to follow. "I wonder that myself, sometimes," he said. "Come—we go speak with her friends."

As Adele cast about the bloodstained ground one last time, a voice jarred her from her thoughts. "Hello!" said the voice in French, echoing down the stairs. "Hello, please, may I speak with you, *madame*?"

Adele turned to find the gendarmerie blocking the path of two elderly folk who were leaning against the wooden barricade and peering into the underpass, waving at her. John had paused on the opposite side of the crime scene, facing a different set of stairs. The tall man rubbed absentmindedly at the burn mark along his chin and flicked a questioning eyebrow in Adele's direction.

"Yes?" Adele said, turning her back on John. "Can I help you?" She peered up, squinting in the sunlight that dappled the stairs and guard rails leading to the sidewalk above.

The elderly couple were well-dressed, with long overcoats and thin gloves. Their silver hair was trimmed neatly: the man with a military cut, not unlike John's—minus Renee's overly long bangs—and the woman with shoulder-length locks that reminded Adele of her mother's.

She swallowed at the thought, but pushed it quickly aside as she ascended the bottom steps, pulling within hearing distance.

"Pardon us," said the man in a rumbling, creaking voice. "But is this where it happened? Where the young girl died?"

Adele watched the man and her gaze flicked to the woman. She hated that her immediate thought was one of suspicion—an instinct honed over years of confronting the worst humanity offered. But, just as quickly, she discarded the notion. Nothing in the killer's crimes suggested a duo.

She kept her expression pleasant, quizzical. Her French, the same as her English, and the same as her German, sometimes carried an accent. She did her best to hide it, but hadn't been in practice as much as with English. "You knew the girl?" she said, carefully.

The old couple shared a glance, peering past the uniformed officer who stepped back once Adele approached.

The old man eyed her up and down. "You are not police," he said, cautiously.

Adele glanced at her slacks and self-consciously tugged at her sleeves. "Er, no—not exactly. I'm working with DGSI, though."

The old woman frowned, clicking her tongue quietly in disapproval.

Adele decided that mentioning the FBI would only have made things worse. The DGSI had only become an autonomous office a couple of years before she'd joined, and there were some in the public who didn't approve of the agency's reputation.

The old woman began tugging at her husband's arm as if to lead him back up the few steps. "Sorry," the woman said, still peering disapprovingly at Adele. "We made a mistake."

"I don't work with DGSI anymore," said Adele, thinking quickly in an effort to save the situation. "I'm consulting. Because of Marion—the girl who died." She made a face like sucking lemons. "Oh, apologies, I-I don't think I was supposed to mention her name." She stepped back, peering down the stairs, but also positioning her body in just such a way so that the bloodstains beneath the bridge were visible over the barricade.

She waited an appropriate number of seconds, then turned back, shielding the crime scene again with her body. "A nasty business," Adele said. "The girl's mother is inconsolable, as I'm sure you can imagine. She's from Paris, too. Living all alone now in her apartment. Such a pity—one should never be cursed to see their child leave the world first."

The old man was peering past Adele, his face turning pale as he surveyed the underpass beyond. The woman had stopped tugging at his arm and her expression softened as she mulled over Adele's words. The woman made the same clicking sound with her tongue, but then sighed. She shook her husband's arm in a permissive sort of way.

"Go on," said the old woman. "Tell the lady."

The man continued to stare past Adele, over the barricade, his eyes fixated like he'd seen a ghost. After another tug on his arm, though, he cleared his throat and his dark eyes leveled on Adele.

"The girl—Marion—we saw on the news. Recognized her from the apartment. She lives on Rue Villehardouin as well."

Adele nodded carefully, her eyes flitting back down the stairs in John's direction, but he was out of sight beneath the underpass. "You knew Marion?"

The old man was staring off again and his wife tugged sharply at his arm once more. "Ahem, yes," said the man. "We would cross paths occasionally on our nighttime walks. A friendly, nice, pretty—er, nice young girl." He cleared his throat and retrieved his arm before his wife could pull it off. He leaned over the sawhorse, white knuckles straining where they gripped the barricade.

The gendarmerie reached out to push him back, but Adele gave the quickest shake of her head and leaned in, staring intently into the old man's dark eyes set in his wrinkled face.

"She walked alone," said the old man. "Said she was going to visit friends—she should not have been alone. Paris is not what it once

44

was."

"No. Most places aren't," said Adele. "You saw her leaving her apartment then. What time?"

"Eight? Nine?"

"Half past seven," the woman chimed in from behind her husband.

Adele nodded. "Did she say anything? Besides that she was off to see friends?"

"No," said the old man. "She said goodnight is all. But…" Here, his fingers gripped the sawhorse even tighter. "Perhaps it isn't my place to say… But—but—"

"—just tell her, Bernard," the woman snapped.

"I do not mean to cause anyone trouble," the old man said.

Adele prompted him with a tilt of her eyebrows. "But…"

"But I saw someone following her. Maybe he was just going the same way… I do not know. But—like I said—I do not wish to cause anyone trouble. However, after hearing what happened to her… I mean, at the time I didn't think anything of it. But now, maybe if I had said something." The old man trailed off and leaned back from the sawhorse, pressing up against his wife in a protective sort of posture.

The wizened woman looped her hand back through his arm and rubbed affectionately at his wrist in a calming gesture.

Adele, though, for her part, felt anything but calm. She tried to keep her tone in check, but found it difficult with her pulse pounding in her ears. "You saw someone following her? You're sure?"

"Yes," said the woman at once.

"Well," said the man, "he may have simply been going the same direction. Like I said, I don't wish to cause any—"

"Sir, if I may, you're not causing any trouble," said Adele, quickly. She inhaled slowly through her nose, trying to steady herself. She could hear the accent in her words the more excited she got. Now wasn't the time to announce to these two citizens that she hailed from beyond Paris. With folk like these it would only complicate the situation. So she inhaled again, and then, her words pressing on the silence between them, she said, "Tell me *exactly* what you saw."

For a moment, she thought of reaching for her phone to record the reply, but then decided it might only spook the couple.

The old man shrugged. "Someone following her. Like I said."

"He carried a bundle," the woman said. "And—yes." She snapped her fingers. "He wore a blue shirt."

The old man frowned, though, his brow crinkling. "No," he said. "The shirt was green. His *shoes* were blue."

"Was he wearing shoes?" said the woman in doubt.

Adele felt her heart sink. She licked at her lips, finding them suddenly dry, and began to step back down the stairs, if only to gain some space to breathe.

"Is there anything else?" she said from a step further down.

The old couple glanced at each other, then, nearly at once, they both replied, "He had red hair."

Adele had been half-glancing back toward where John awaited, but at this, her gaze flew back to the old couple. She stared at them, searching their expressions for certainty. "Red hair?" she said. "You're sure?"

They both shared a look, then nodded adamantly.

Adele felt her pulse racing once more. She'd once had a smartwatch when she'd trained for a marathon. Her resting heart rate had always been far too high for how in shape she was—another side effect of the job. And now, she could practically hear her heartbeat in her ears.

"Would you be willing to give an official statement down at the station?" Adele said. "What are your names? Bernard, you said? Last name?"

The old man began to reply, but the old woman tugged sharply on his arm. "You've heard our statement," she said, frowning. "There is nothing more to say."

"I understand," Adele began, "but if—"

"Nothing more!" The woman had already half-dragged her husband up the steps, leading him quickly away from the underpass.

The gendarmerie officer glanced at Adele as if waiting for an order to stop them. But she shook her head.

"Let them go," Adele murmured. "I doubt there's anything more we can learn anyway…"

She nodded in gratitude toward the officer, then gave a small little salute with two fingers toward the retreating backs of the elderly couple. With a slight skip in her step, she turned and took the stairs, hurrying back toward where John waited.

Red hair. A wig? Perhaps. But a clue either way.

The bastard wouldn't get away. Not this time.

A smile stretched her lips as she rejoined John on the other side of the underpass, facing a ramp with a long metal rail.

"What are you so chipper over?" John said, frowning. He had a phone raised, pressed against his cheek, and he seemed more grumpy than usual.

"I—" Adele cut herself off. "Who is that?" she said, nodding toward the phone.

John lowered the device and clicked a button on the side, sliding the phone back into his pocket, still frowning. "Marion's friends. Some boots were able to track them down. They're waiting for us at the bar."

"Why do you look pissed off? That's good news."

"Oh, yes? It is good? Hmm—well Michael and Sophie are going to be there. You remember Agent Paige, yes?" His tone was now high-pitched and would-be innocent, carrying the malicious undercurrent of bad humor. "She refused to work with you. I cannot emphasize this enough, eh. Refused. Called you a *chienne*—do you remember this word, hmm? It is why I am saddled with our American princess—because Paige would not play nice."

Adele felt the smile fade from her face with each subsequent word. She swallowed, slowly, a prickle of anxiety spreading through her, tingling down her spine. "Sophie Paige? She's an agent now?"

"No longer supervising, hmm?" said John, still in his would-be innocent voice. His mood seemed markedly improved all of a sudden. "I wonder why that is? She wouldn't—no, *god forbid*—she wouldn't blame *you* for her demotion, would she?" His eyebrows shot up in mock surprise.

"Christ, you're such an ass," Adele snapped. She began stomping up the ramp, rubbing her hand against the cool metal of the guard rail. "Are you coming? Or do you want me to interview all our witnesses on my own?"

John didn't reply, but she could hear him chuckling behind her as he followed.

Inwardly, Adele was a tangle of emotions. Sophie Paige had been her supervisor back when she'd worked for the DGSI. And what a mess *that* had been. Surely, after all these years, she wouldn't still hold a grudge…

"Who am I kidding," Adele muttered out loud, picking up the pace as she reached the sidewalk and stomped toward the waiting vehicle.

Sophie Paige was *exactly* the sort to hold a grudge. Interviewing a bunch of Marion's friends with that gargoyle leering over her shoulder sounded about as much fun as pulling teeth.

47

Two steps forward, one step back.
But Agent Paige or not...
The killer had red hair.
Twenty-five. Twenty-four. No more.

CHAPTER NINE

Adele could feel the radiating glare singeing a hole in the side of her cheek the moment she stepped into Genna's, the old, hole-in-the-wall bar behind the college. Adele scanned the crowded room, her gaze flicking across the many low stools arranged around circular tables. The furniture was scattered over what looked like a dance floor converted into a seating area for an elevated stage at the back.

Adele could still feel Sophie Paige's glare piercing the cramped space from the other side of the dingy room.

Adele refused to look over at first. She kept her chin high and maneuvered with surefooted motions through the scattering of tables and cheap aluminum chairs.

John lumbered along next to her, his mood sour once more thanks to the three red lights they'd hit on the way to the interview Marion's friends.

"They come here often?" Adele asked out of the side of her mouth, keeping her eyes rigidly ahead.

John grunted.

"You said they were here when Marion died. Is that verified?"

The especially tall agent grunted again, but then sighed through his nose as if realizing this response wouldn't curb the tide of queries. His voice creaked with rust as he said, "They come here after work."

"And how come we're interviewing them here?"

John raised an eyebrow, glancing down at his smaller partner. "Agent Paige said it would keep them at ease. You would prefer we haul them off to interrogation rooms, hmm? How very American of you."

Adele shook her head, glancing back toward where the small group was seated on the far side of the bar.

It reminded her of her old college days, though the thought soured her mood somewhat. Friends required roots. And roots required one to stay in the same spot for more than a passing second. Adele had never been particularly good at putting down roots. She'd never been taught how. Building friendships had been a thing of the past once she'd left university. Agent Lee, back at headquarters, was, perhaps, the one friend she had; it had been easy befriending a fellow workaholic.

Still, as Adele finally allowed herself a glance across the bar—the atmosphere askew in the daytime, with most stools and booths empty and the stage serving only as a seat for a couple of customers—she found herself examining a group of four young, attractive Parisians.

Agent Paige and her partner stood against thick red curtains covering a window and blocking out the sunlight. Sophie's arms were crossed over her chest, creating pressure wrinkles in her otherwise neat gray suit. She had tucked her lip beneath her teeth in a sort of impatient, disapproving gesture.

The four Parisian friends were all glancing nervously at each other, their hands fidgeting against curled knuckles or twitching fingers. Two men and two women. None of them could have been much older than twenty-five. One of the men, a square-jawed, blond-haired fellow with piercing blue eyes, was tapping a tattoo into the aluminum table, his fingers wiggling wildly. Across from him, a girl with dark hair and dark eyes had clasped her hands together as if she were praying, her thumbs pressed against her lips and her eyes staring at the ridges of her knuckles.

All four of the friends held bleak, somber expressions.

Adele switched her gaze to the babysitters standing by the curtains. Sophie Paige was still glaring. She met Adele's look and communicated nothing, still glowering, still crossing her arms. Her eyebrows, though, inched upward, if only slightly. Her mouth pressed just a little bit more tightly, her lips forming an even—if such a thing were possible—thinner line.

Adele nodded stiffly, offering a greeting to the woman. Perhaps things had improved since they'd last left them. It was often said that time could heal all wounds.

Even as the thought crossed Adele's mind, Agent Paige frowned at Adele, her eyebrows narrowing over her watchful gaze. She turned to her partner and muttered something beneath her breath, which sent the short, round man into a fit of giggling, his dark cheeks wobbling with mirth.

Then again, perhaps time's ministrations were overstated.

"What's the history between you two?" John said, quietly.

Adele had paused, one foot on the single step that led to the raised back portion of the room.

The barkeep leaned against the counter, a bored expression on her face. She'd been unlucky enough to draw the short straw to tend bar during early hours. Adele felt for the girl, and nodded sympathetically in greeting. The girl nodded back and then turned to start adjusting some ornately styled bottles on the lowest shelf above the sink, causing auburn liquid to slosh around.

"It's none of your business," said Adele, growling, still hesitating on the step.

"Ah, so there is history," said John. He clicked his tongue. "I thought so."

Adele ducked her head, hiding her mouth. She lowered her voice even further, practically whispering. "Don't give me that. You knew we had history."

John smiled lazily and leaned against a metal railing as if waiting for Adele to continue leading the way. "I had an idea. You just confirmed it. Tell me; did you take credit for a collar? Steal glory on a case that you both worked together?"

Adele's brow furrowed at this, and she quickly shook her head. "Nothing like that."

She wasn't sure why this particular accusation bothered her so much. The idea that John would think she was the type to take credit for someone else's success particularly burned. She had made her way on her own merit. No one else had given her a leg up.

"Then what?" said John, still leaning against the railing. He glanced toward where the other agents were waiting and flicked up a finger as if to say, *one moment*. He'd been speaking quietly at first, but the more attention they seemed to draw from the customers, the louder he seemed to speak.

"Keep it down," Adele snapped. "Nothing. Nothing important."

"Ah, yes. Of course. Unimportant matters often breed grudges over half a decade, hmm? Which, I might add, can be seen written across both your faces."

"Well, at least you can read; I wasn't sure. Now, could we get on with it? We're here to solve the case."

Adele shoved roughly past John, stepping up onto the raised portion of the room which led into a railed off corner where Marion's friends were waiting with their federal babysitters.

"Hello," said Adele, quickly, formally, nodding at each of the four seated men and women in turn.

51

They looked up, questions burdening their eyes.

She cleared her throat, trying not to glance toward Agent Paige. The woman didn't intimidate her, but she did make it uncomfortable. "My name is Adele Sharp. I'm working with the DGSI on Marion's case. I'm very sorry for your loss."

"You are DGSI?" said the blond, square-jawed fellow. "Was this a terrorist?"

The other man in the group, a dark-skinned young man with high cheekbones, shook his head. "I knew it was terrorists. Didn't I say; I told you, no one would want to hurt her. She was too kind. It had to have been some sort of—"

"Quiet, Antoni," snapped the dark-haired girl who was clutching her hands as if she were praying. "She didn't say it was a terrorist. Why do you always think—"

"—it was, though, wasn't it?" said Antoni, glancing up toward Adele. "It's okay. You can tell us."

Adele sighed and placed one hand on the cold metal table, leaning in toward the four friends who were now all watching her.

Instead of answering them, though, Adele resigned herself to the unpleasant task at hand, and glanced over the friends' heads. "Sophie," Adele said, nodding to her old supervisor with a curt jerk of her head.

At the reluctant greeting, Agent Paige's expression only further soured. "We've been waiting for nearly half an hour," she said, frowning. Agent Paige spoke in a quick, clipped way, the sort of voice oft-burdened by impatience.

The unmet greeting hung in the air between them, stretching the atmosphere and breeding an uncomfortable tension which descended on the group in the daytime bar.

Adele kept her back stiff, her shoulders squared, as she nodded a greeting to Sophie's round, balding partner, which he returned with an equally stiff, uncomfortable motion.

She could feel John behind her, watching, but she refused to give him the satisfaction of a glance back.

"Apologies for the delay," said Adele. "We came as quickly as we were called."

"I'm sure you did," said Agent Paige. She pushed off from the wall and Adele noticed a slight limp to her step as she maneuvered closer to the table. "Jet lag takes its toll on even the best of us, I imagine."

Adele shook her head, moving past the comment without unpacking it. "I'm sorry for making you wait." This she addressed the four friends. "As for the case particulars, I'm afraid I'm not at liberty to discuss much, but any information you provide could prove helpful."

The one named Antoni met her gaze and shook his head. Serious eyes peered from a solemn face. "No one would want to hurt Marion," he said. "We've been telling them; we don't know who did this."

Adele glanced back up to Agent Paige. "You've already interviewed them?"

Behind her, John growled. "Our case, our lead. You should've waited."

Paige shook her head. She adjusted her stance, wincing as she did, limping slightly. Her partner reached out quickly, trying to steady her, but she shook him off with a scowl and snapped, "We didn't interview them. We prepped them for questioning. This isn't America anymore," she said, addressing John's question, but staring at Adele. "Things aren't done the same way. Here, we don't allow bureaucracy to prevent us from doing our jobs."

Adele nodded, tugging at her sleeves. "I remember. It's fine." She glanced back toward the four friends. "I'm sorry if you'll repeat yourselves, but for Marion's sake, I want to make sure we go over everything."

"Christ," John muttered behind her, "this is a waste of time. They said they didn't know anything."

Adele inhaled deeply, steadying herself. She felt assailed on all sides. John, her would-be partner, seemed disinterested in the case, and she hadn't even realized Agent Paige would be there. Adele chewed the corner of her lip, her hands still pressed against the cool surface of the aluminum table. For a vague moment, she wondered about the story behind Sophie's demotion from supervisor back to agent. She sincerely hoped it didn't have anything to do with what had transpired between them six years ago. But she wouldn't bet on it.

Still, Adele wasn't the sort to allow her emotions to control. She suppressed the wriggling mass of roiling guilt, worry, and anxiety, pushing it from her chest into her stomach with a quick swallow and a slow, elongated breath. She inhaled softly, keeping her eyes open, attentive, refusing to betray her nerves. She stepped around the side of the table, circling behind the girl with the dark hair. Next to her, the handsome, dark-skinned man with the high cheekbones studied Adele's movements. The fourth person at the table, who looked like the youngest of the group, an impossibly pretty girl, was still staring at her hands. Every so often, the young woman would glance out the window, looking through the small gap in the thick crimson curtains behind Agent Paige.

"Excuse me, miss," said Adele, "do you mind telling me your name?"

The pretty girl rubbed her fingers along the back of her arms in turns, and shot a furtive glance toward Antoni, almost as if seeking permission. He gave the barest of nods, and then the girl said, "I'm Sarah. And it's like they said; no one would've hurt Marion. She was far too nice. Ask Tomas—he knew her best."

She inclined her head toward the blond boy, then returned to rubbing at her arms, a sadness in her eyes that went deeper than Adele had first thought.

Adele kept her tone gentle. "Can you tell me if she came here the night she went missing?"

"You mean the night she was killed?" said Tomas. "They're not telling us what happened exactly. Did she suffer?"

Adele looked at the blond boy and gave the faintest shake of her head. "I'm afraid I'm not at liberty to release those details just yet."

Agent Paige cleared her throat, gaining the attention of the group. "Actually, I think we're cleared to discuss the case." Once more, she was leaning against the crimson curtains, still crossing her arms over her chest, and still, clearly, favoring her left leg.

Adele gritted her teeth, but refused to meet Paige's gaze. "Perhaps it would be best to *avoid* discussing the details just now."

Inwardly, she seethed. It was one thing to hold a personal grudge, but it was another to bring it to a case. Adele had known she was permitted to discuss what had happened to Marion. But how would that help the girl's friends? Adele needed them open, willing to talk. Fear and horror did not compel people to answer personal questions. Then again, perhaps John was right. This did seem to be a giant waste of time. Marion was killed by a stranger. That much, she would've bet money on. But still, any detail, any clue…

"She didn't come here," said the young man with the high cheekbones. "She was on her way. I texted her, asking her where she was." He trailed off, gnawing on his lower lip. The next words came slow, quiet, a serpentine quality in the way they slithered across the aluminum table and reached Adele's ears. "But she never arrived. We

54

didn't know what happened, well, until later."

Adele nodded sympathetically. She rounded the table again, and this time placed herself between Paige and the four friends, blocking the other agent from view in as subtle a posture as possible. The glower on her former supervisor's face was putting the young women and men on guard. Adele needed Marion's friends to think, to focus. Bad blood and unaired tension wouldn't help.

Adele tapped her fingers against the table. "Did she give any sign of having a stalker? Someone who might have caused her trouble?"

All four of the friends shook their heads. The pretty girl, Sarah, hesitated, then said, "Nothing unusual. There are always people hitting on her at bars. She quite liked the attention, though."

"But nothing out of the ordinary? No one following her home or anything like that?"

Again, all four friends shook their heads.

"American Princess," said John, his words causing her to glance back, "we are wasting our time. They don't know anything. How could they?"

Adele examined her tall partner and held up a finger. "One more question," she said. She turned back toward the friends. "Did she tell you anything about someone with red hair?"

At this, everyone, including John, examined her with puzzled expressions.

Tomas broke the silence first. "Is that who killed her? Someone with red hair?"

"I'm not saying that," said Adele. *I'm not* not *saying that either,* she thought. "I just need to ask. Well?"

She waited, hope spinning through her, causing her heart to pound. But, before she could receive an answer, Agent Paige cleared her throat and stepped forward.

"Can I get anything for anyone to drink?" she asked in an innocent tone. She sidestepped in front of Adele, cutting off her view from the table.

The four friends shook their heads quickly, and Agent Paige shouldered past Adele, moving toward the bar, the limp in her gait more apparent than ever.

A surge of guilt at Paige's limp gave way to frustration at the interference. "We're on the job," Adele snapped.

"Welcome to Paris," retorted Paige, without looking back.

Tomas, a clever look in his eyes, glanced between the two women, and a slight frown creased his expression.

"Well," said Adele, muffling her emotions once more. She glanced back at the young friends. "Do you know anyone with red hair?"

"There's Stephan," said Sarah, who didn't seem to have noticed the tension between the two agents. "He's a few years younger than us, but was in school with us."

"No; Stephan's family moved," said the girl with dark hair. "Besides, he's not interested in women."

Adele shook her head. "I think it would be someone older. Perhaps someone my age, or maybe even older than me. Like Agent Renee."

John cleared his throat in indignation, but didn't say anything, waiting for the kids to reply. Again, they all shook their heads.

"We don't know anyone like that." This came from Tomas, after glancing around at his friends and noting the blank expressions on their faces. "But… Marion was friendly to everyone. Even tourists."

A couple of eye rolls from around the table met the word "tourists."

Adele paused at this, feeling a jolt of sympathy for the murdered girl. Though she'd never met Marion, it mattered that she was friendly to foreigners—especially in a city that had an opposite reputation at times. Adele had spent most of her life moving from place to place, required to prove herself again and again to the locals. It had been a rare thing to have someone greet her with a kind word and a smile.

But had that friendliness killed Marion? The killer had fled the US. Perhaps he'd used his status as a tourist to lure Marion into a false sense of security. But if so, how had the man known the girl's age? Had he stalked her?

Adele's thoughts were interrupted by Tomas. "May we go now?" he said in a weary voice.

The other man with the high cheekbones held up a halting hand. "Hang on," he said. "What happened exactly? If it is true you *can* tell us what happened, Agent Sharp, then why aren't you?"

"It's obvious," said Sarah, full lips forming a thin line as she pressed them tight. "Something terrible happened."

Tomas frowned. "Marion is dead. That's terrible enough." He ignored his friends and pressed on, determined. "Did she suffer?" Tomas demanded, glaring at Adele.

Adele resisted the urge to turn toward where Agent Paige was at the bar; she knew her old supervisor was intentionally going out of her way to make this difficult. Now Adele was in an impossible position. If Marion's friends actually knew what had happened, it would haunt them. But Adele refused to lie. "It was bad. But she's not suffering anymore. And I promise you, I promise," she glanced to each of them in turn, locking eyes, "I'll find who did this. And I'll make them pay."

The four friends slumped even lower in their seats. Then, with a great sigh of resignation, Tomas pushed himself up, stepping backward over his stool and retrieving a coat set on the table behind him. He gestured with a small jerk of his head at the others, and they quickly followed his retreat.

It would take Adele a little bit of time to re-acclimate to the way things were done at the DGSI. There were no checkouts for the interview room, no clerk to escort the interviewees out of the station. They were in a bar in the afternoon in Paris. The French agency often afforded more freedom and less red tape. But, as she glanced toward where Sophie Paige hung her head at the bar, holding a drink which she wasn't sipping, it also allowed the worst sorts too much leeway sometimes.

"Farewell," Paige called without looking back. Her words seem to propel the four friends even quicker out the door, and Adele could hear the scattered sound of their rapid footsteps as they hastened along the sidewalk outside, and then the sound faded with the dull thump of the shutting door.

Adele glared at the Paige's back, frowning. Her hands tingled, her fingers tapping incessantly at her upper thigh.

John stepped forward, his elbow brushing against her shoulder. "Do we go now?" he asked, his voice low. "What is this about red hair?"

Adele ignored him, and she hurried forward, shoving past Paige's partner and surging toward the seated woman at the bar.

"Sophie," the round, balding man barked in warning.

Adele stormed forward, and Sophie Paige turned slowly, glancing over her shoulder and swiveling in her stool.

Adele found her fists were bunched at her sides, and she quickly unclenched them. It wouldn't do to get into a fight in a bar the first day on the job.

"Can I ask what you think you're doing?" Adele snapped.

Agent Paige gave a half smile, presenting the sort of leer that belonged on the mouth of a shark. "You may ask whatever you want. Hells, do what you want. You always have." Page spoke in French, rapidly, as if she were trying to shake Adele off the scent of a trail.

But Adele's French was coming back to her, and she replied just as quickly, "Do we need to talk?"

Paige glared. "The time for talking was six years ago, don't you think? Before you knifed me in the back!"

"I didn't—"

"Go deal with your case and get out of my face."

"I never intended for you to get in trouble," said Adele. "I didn't know you had been demoted."

Agent Paige's left hand tightened around the filled glass, and she spun around sharply, tossing the contents at Adele.

John and Paige's partner rushed forward, but Adele stood her ground, allowing the alcohol to seep down her face and stain her clothing. It dripped from her chin against the faux floorboards with rhythmic taps.

She could feel all eyes on her, including a couple of the daytime customers and the barkeep behind the counter. She inhaled shakily through her nostrils, smelling the whiskey on her chest.

"You're a mess," said Agent Paige. "Clean yourself up." She grabbed a dirty towel from behind the counter and flung it at Adele. Then, without paying, she shoved off the stool and strode away from the bar, toward the door. Her partner quickly fell into step.

Adele found that her left hand was bunched up against her pants, holding her trousers tight.

"I didn't realize it was that bad," said John, his shadow falling over her, cast by the glowing lights in the square fixtures above.

Adele shook her head, causing sticky liquid to slip along her face and continue to drip down her chin. "I knew she was going to be trouble."

"You weren't lovers, were you?"

Adele glanced up at John and shook her head, noting his coy smile and the slight wiggle of his eyebrows. "Get your mind out of the gutter."

"That would've been incredible," John said, smiling fondly, looking off into the distance. Then he glanced back at Adele and sighed softly. "Come, you should clean yourself up. There are bathrooms in the back; I saw a sign."

He pressed gently on her shoulder, guiding her toward the back of the bar, but Adele shrugged off the helping hand and stomped away, her legs stiff, her arms straight at her sides.

She couldn't let past grudges affect this case. Sophie Paige still worked for the DGSI. That couldn't be helped, but that didn't mean Adele would let the older woman and their shared history ruin the investigation.

Adele stormed into the bar's bathroom and stared at herself over the mirror, her eyebrows flicking down in a furrow at the sight of her drenched collar and jacket.

She wiped the alcohol from her face, trying to rid herself of the odor of whiskey. She used foam soap on her chin, scraping the smell away.

As she did, she mulled over the next step. She still had a new clue. The killer had red hair. And he had recently come from the US. How many redheaded tourists could have arrived in the last week? Not many. She would've bet it wasn't many at all.

They would have to place an APB. Perhaps get in touch with the airports. The DGSI had access to more files than much of the FBI. Interpol often shared their own intel. If the Patriot Act in the US was an agency, it would look eerily similar to the DGSI.

The amount of freedom it afforded could create the worst sorts of law enforcement out of people like Agent Paige. Though, perhaps that was just Adele's bias showing.

She twisted the metal knob to the faucet and rinsed off her hands. Adele glanced back up into the mirror, meeting her own gaze. Clearly, the killer was smart. There was no rhyme or reason behind the victims he chose. Their nationalities were different, their genders were sometimes different; only their ages seemed to matter. What did it mean? Why was he so obsessed? Adele had gotten close. Back in Indiana, she was nearly certain she had gotten close… But *how* close? They'd had no concrete suspects. He'd escaped that time. Now, though, she wouldn't let him escape again.

She flung droplets of water from her hands back into the sink, shaking her fingers, then turned sharply and stormed back out of the bathroom, drying her hands off on her already stained shirt. No time for those dinky little air dryers.

The red-haired bastard couldn't be far. If she had to bet on it, she would guess he was still in the city.

Adele now moved toward the exit to the bar, gesturing at John to follow.

59

"Are you okay?" he said, a kernel of sympathy in his tone for the first time.

She nodded fiercely and gestured again. "Come. We have work to do. I have an idea."

CHAPTER TEN

Raindrops rattled the windows in staccato, ushering frigid gloom into the temporary office they'd given Adele back at the DGSI headquarters. She leaned in her chair, staring at the ceiling, studying the fresh paint that glazed the concrete. A small black radiator, of the electronic variety, whirred softly behind her. The office was still unfinished and the heating units were a temporary measure. In the back of the room, a few outlets extended naked wires like the tentacles of some tiny ocean creatures. Back at headquarters in San Francisco, Adele hadn't been given her own office. There were too many agents for that to be considered fair. But again, an agency like the DGSI, which was only a decade old, pulled out all the stops to tempt new recruits. And, like Robert had said, the recent wave of terrorist attacks in Europe, despite all the political implications, had increased the budget for most intelligence agencies.

"How do you fair, my sweet?"

Adele turned slowly, glancing toward the door, her gaze tracing from the figure's polished shoes, up his well-maintained, pressed pants, and lingered on his manicured fingernails. Then she smiled softly and met her old mentor's gaze.

"Not well, I'm afraid," said Adele. She leaned back in her chair, pressing her head against the cold wall, still listening to the rain in the background. "Can't say that we've done much."

Robert ran his hands through his ever-thickening hair, and the early wrinkles around his eyes creased as he squinted in her direction, adopting a look of concern. "You put an APB out?"

She nodded. "John did. Red-haired tourists. Can't imagine there's too many of those; at least not in the city."

Robert stood straight in the doorway, his posture perfect. Most folks would've leaned against the doorframe, or come into the room and relaxed in one of the chairs across the desk from Adele. But Robert stayed where he was, upright, dignified, a bit pompous. He peered down at her, and the short man cleared his throat with a rasping sound. "How is it being back home?"

Adele crossed her legs, pressing her heels on top of the desk. She sighed, ushering a breath in his direction, exhaling the stress and frustration clogging her lungs.

"I'm not sure I am," she said, softly. "Not sure I have a home. But there are worse things, I suppose."

At this, Robert frowned, and he stepped into the room, studying her slowly.

Adele met his questioning look. "I'm not the one who chose to move around as much as we did. A child doesn't always have the options they'd like."

He continued to study her in silence, thinking through his words carefully before speaking. "No," he said at last, a curt, clear word. "But perhaps it isn't you don't have a home. But that you have more than one." He dusted at his dustless suit. "Perhaps it isn't a curse, but rather a blessing. There are those who would be lucky to have more than one home." Robert stepped further into the room and made his way slowly over to the window, peering out into the gray skies. "For me, Paris is my home. I would envy the ability to hold fondness for more than one place."

Adele smiled at the man, but she didn't say anything. She knew what he was trying to do. And she appreciated the effort. But words didn't change the truth of the matter. She had never quite belonged anywhere.

That wasn't a claim for pity. Rather, it was a position of strength, especially as an investigator, to be an outsider looking in. The outsider always brought a new perspective that locals might not possess. Her life, her upbringing—Germany to France to the US—gave her insight that others didn't hold. Each place she lived had its own boon, a gift of experience that it bequeathed her. And yet, whenever she contemplated such things, a slow ache often developed in her chest, not quite unlike anxiety. Perhaps it was closer to loneliness.

She thought vaguely of her mother. But then shook her head, dislodging the thought.

"Have we had any hits yet?" she said, quickly, clearing her throat and speaking more firmly. Robert was still staring out the window. He gave the slightest shrug of his suited shoulders. "I have not heard anything."

"What case are you working on?"

"Nothing new. They have me in an advisory role only."

The way he said it gave Adele pause. There was an edge to his voice that she didn't quite understand.

She stared at the back of her mentor's head, watching him, studying his silhouette framed against the window. "Oh?"

He shrugged again and turned toward her; the droplets stippling the window framed him in a sort of liquid halo.

It's good to have you back," said Robert. "I'll leave you to your work. But you know where I am. My number is the same. If ever you need anything—"

"I know. I really do. And I'm grateful. Extremely grateful."

He flashed one of his rare smiles, which revealed two missing teeth in the front left side of his mouth. For a man who cared so much about appearances, the missing teeth were often jarring to people. Adele had never quite learned the story behind them, but she knew better than to ask.

As she watched him go, she wondered vaguely what he'd meant by "advisory role." She knew the agency liked to hire young talent. But the thought that anyone would try to edge Robert, of all people, out of his job was ludicrous.

As he stood in the doorway and hesitated, he turned back, scratched his chin, and, in a thoughtful voice, said, "Forgive me if I'm wrong, but you said this murderer, this killer, didn't choose his victims based on any particular traits. Nothing except for their age."

Adele nodded, listening intently.

Robert wasn't looking at her anymore, and instead seemed to be studying the carpet on the floor with a frown creasing his face. "If someone doesn't kill because of qualities the victims possess, would it be fair to assume he kills because of qualities of his own?"

"I've thought similarly," said Adele.

"This red-haired man; he's young enough to still have red hair."

Adele glanced up at her partner, refusing to glance toward his own dark hair. She chuckled softly. "I do think there are methods nowadays that prevent the bane of gray. Plus, it could be a wig."

Robert stiffened and shook his head slightly, running his hand through his own hair again, but then he relaxed once more and said, "But not red. A killer who is aging wouldn't dye their hair red, would they? It's too conspicuous. And if a wig, why choose *red*?"

Adele looked at him for a moment, then nodded slowly. "It does draw the eye... So you think his hair is naturally red? Red enough for him to be young; that's what you're saying?"

Robert gave another short jerk of his head. "Young enough to retain the color of his hair, self-obsessed enough to kill people based on qualities he possesses."

"He fled to France," Adele continued, speaking softly. Memories, past brainstorming sessions, much like this flitted through her mind. She and Robert often discussed cases, following one's lead with thoughts of their own, building momentum with back and forth.

A slow prickling chill of exhilaration made itself known as goosebumps across the back of her arms.

She said, "The ages have always been interesting to me. Why would someone flee if they were so obsessed with time? He had a routine; he killed on schedule. Every two weeks. For someone so obsessed with time—and, if like you say, still young, then one might think he's obsessed with their ages for a reason."

"Fled," said her old mentor. "You seem certain of that word."

Adele paused, considering it, her mind racing. Robert often had a way of bringing out the best in her. He would phrase things in such a way that made sense, and would help spark her own deductive process. He watched her, a strange look on his face, not unlike the proud smile of a father toward his child. At last, though, Adele nodded, her teeth set. "I was closer than I thought. I almost caught him. That has to be it. I didn't think I was making any headway back in the States. But he's obsessed with time. A young man, at least young enough to have his normal hair color, who is obsessed with the passage of time. He would have loathed the idea of wasting time. It would have eaten at his core to have wasted the time it took to flee the US and come to France. He killed as soon as he could, and that means he had to have left the US because he *needed* to flee. Because he thought that was the only option."

Robert was nodding now, his lips pursed, his serious face even more solemn with plucked eyebrows curved over his dark eyes.

"That's the only explanation," said Adele. "Barring some personal issue, which I doubt would make someone like this flee, the only thing that explains the interruption of this pattern, this trip to France, is that I was getting closer than I thought. Something I did, something I said, someone I talked to, had him spooked."

"He was scared. Perhaps you need to give yourself more credit."

Adele shrugged, tilting her head until she was staring up at the ceiling once more. "Thank you," she said, softly, but her voice trailed off as her thoughts took over, carrying her into a series of considerations that flitted through her mind.

She tried to think back: when would she have spooked this killer? She thought of the interviews she had, the people she spoke to. She thought of the houses they had warrants for, searching. Dead ends, all of them. No one red-haired. No one mentioning anything about a red-haired killer.

Yet, somehow, the knowledge alone that she was getting close was enough to revitalize her, if only a little. She glanced back toward the door and Robert was gone.

He often did this, leaving without so much as a farewell. Robert was the sort who hated goodbyes. Adele, over the years, had grown numb to them. But perhaps she wouldn't have to this time.

She glanced around the room and looked out toward the skies beyond. The rain was slowing somewhat, and the sound of tapping against the windows was starting to fade. The DGSI was quite like she remembered. There was more freedom in operations than back with the FBI; there was often harder sentiment toward agency overreach from the locals. But also, the agency had resources; they were a smaller nation, with less to keep track of, and so they had resources and time like she wasn't always accustomed to.

She shook her head slowly, scratching absentmindedly at the back of her knuckles. Maybe it wouldn't be so bad to come back here. France wasn't far from being her home. She had spent most of her teen years and her time at university in this country.

Still, something else was niggling at her thoughts.

She lowered her feet off the desk and got up, frowning. She wanted to check the status of the APB, to see if any reports of been filed. Red-haired tourists couldn't be that common. Especially those who had arrived sometime within the last month. But, if it was true she was getting close, and if it was true that this was a man obsessed with the passage of time, obsessed with age, and his victims, then he was also the sort of man who would try to make up for lost time. In the past, he had killed once every two weeks.

Now, though, Adele shook her head, clenching her teeth. Now—she could feel it—he wouldn't wait so long this time. He would kill and kill soon.

CHAPTER ELEVEN

Adele strolled along the boulevard that led to Marion's tall apartment building. He had stalked her here. She had died within screaming distance. Adele glanced up at the safety lights—now off during the day—lining the sidewalk.

She sighed softly, her shoes patting with wet little slaps against the sodden concrete. The streets were still mostly empty as it was a workday, mid-afternoon. The rain also served to rapidly usher pedestrians and drivers quickly on their way. Adele preferred the solitude. She needed to think, to clear her mind. There had to be some clue she was missing. Something she'd read, or spotted, something that would just make sense if she could focus. Adele smiled as a couple of sparrows chattered at each other in the safety of a small decorative tree. The trees were stationed every ten feet or so and had been part of an effort by the French government to bring green back to Paris.

Adele stepped under the trees and winced as cold droplets of water fell from the leaves and tapped against her neck.

She paused at the corner of the street, glancing to her right. Marion's apartment rested within sight now—tall, brown, boasting curving black railings every twenty feet beneath windows—and she could trace the path the girl must have taken the very last time she'd come this way.

Adele turned, heading back toward Marion's apartment, preparing to trace the girl's steps once more. But then she hesitated. She recognized the street.

She turned to the left now, scanning the mailboxes, the benches, and the bus stops lining the gray curb.

She chewed on the corner of her lip, a look of discomfort spreading over her features.

"No," she said, quietly. "Not today."

She turned to the right again and began marching purposefully toward Marion's apartment. But again, before she stepped off the sidewalk into the crossing, she pulled up once more.

Her hands balled at her sides. John was still keeping track of reports of redheaded tourists. So far, the APB had turned up nothing, but Adele held hope. The clue was specific. Specific enough to matter.

She sighed again, huffing slightly. And then she turned sharply; she began striding rapidly up the sidewalk, away from Marion's apartment, away from the crime scene, away from the path the poor young girl had taken before she'd been drugged and bled to death. Away from it all.

As she walked, for a moment, she fell in lockstep with the killer.

She felt like she too was descending in age. Memories from a past life—twenty-eight, twenty-seven, twenty-six… Eighteen, seventeen, sixteen… memories from her youth flooded her mind. She could remember walking these streets before. She turned up one sidewalk, then down another street, cutting between large, looming buildings on either side, the bricks stained red, the windows glinting dully, protected by curtains on the inside.

Adele continued to walk. She missed the city.

She missed the bells tolling in the distance, the smell of the river on the air, the sound of the nightlife, even in the tourist districts. Marion's friends had said she was far too kind to tourists. Far more compassionate than anyone else would normally be.

A girl like that didn't deserve to end up like this.

Adele allowed her own thoughts to propel her further and deeper into the city, walking like a mechanical construct, without tiring, without lagging, and without hesitating.

At long last, she pulled up short.

Adele faced a small store, little more than a curio shop. She stepped inside, and the bell jangled overhead. It didn't take her long to spot the candies she knew would be offered in a place like this. She pointed them out and fished a couple of dollars from her pocket. Then she cursed beneath her breath. Not everyone accepted US currency in France; she waved the dollars toward the man behind the counter. He had olive skin and a soft smile. He nodded once, noting her chagrined look, and graciously bowed his head in her direction.

He wore prayer beads around one wrist, and a red vest with gold lace along the trim. He had kind eyes that studied her, before he reached over and took the dollar bills from her hand.

Marion hesitated, wondering if she should wait for change, but then thought better of it. She nodded her thanks, took the candies, and headed out the door.

She could feel the crinkling of the wrapper in her hand, around the toffee of the Carambars.

Cara. That's what her mother had often called her. Cara—sweet on the inside, witty on the outside. A description that had made her blush as a child.

She didn't blush anymore, though.

Adele took two more streets and then came to a stop in the park. Slow, creeping dread tickled her spine, crawling up toward the nape of her neck with pinpricks of motion.

She shivered, trembling, the air cool but not cold. A few couples were making their rounds along the red cobblestone paths, their arms looped together, their umbrellas protruding skyward. Adele waited for one such couple to pass, rounding behind a series of uniform trees and neatly kept brush.

Then she too stepped into the park, moving past the fountains, along the circular trails around twin ponds, one larger than the other. Some called it the figure eight. To Adele, that path had always looked more like a noose.

She went deeper into the park, toward the back. She knew youngsters would often make out on the picnic tables in the distance, beneath the low-hanging yellow and orange leaves of the park trees. She headed along the bicycle path, the candy bars crinkling in her right hand, her left hand balled into a fist. Then, at long last, she pulled up short.

No one was in sight. She could hear birds still chirping around her, calling to each other, indicating the rain had passed.

And yet, an even deeper, more wretched gloom had settled on her shoulders like a weight.

She stood at the trail head, staring at dirt and mud and patches of dust that had been protected by overhanging branches from the rain.

Trees on either side of this trail sheltered it from view and from the elements. It had also sheltered the scene that had occurred nearly ten years ago.

Adele stared at the patch of dirt and the rivet by the trail. She could see the way the brush had overgrown, covering what had once been clean-cut grass. Had this been intentional?

To her, it felt disrespectful.

Adele fidgeted, tugging at her sleeve, then glancing toward the sky as if looking for insight.

"This was never my home," she said quietly. She listened to the wind and found silence, as she knew she would. "I'm sorry," she said, her voice cracking suddenly.

Her legs felt very weak all at once, and her throat felt scratchy. She reached up and adjusted the sleeves of her jacket, scraping one foot against the dusty trail.

"I don't know what happened," she said toward the weeds and brambles. "I should've found out—I should've. If I was better at my job. If I could have just focused…"

Adele shook her head and turned as if to leave, but something held her firm. She glanced back toward the now overgrown patch of grass on the side of the trail.

She remembered when she had first seen her mother's corpse. Blood, lacing the cuts up and down her body. The killer had let her bleed out, much like the Benjamin Killer was doing with his victims.

Adele felt a slow shudder at the memories. Loathing, like she had only known once before, filled her. A familiar loathing coupled with a familiar reason.

"I'm sorry," she repeated.

What else was there to say? She had failed her mother. She had never caught the killer responsible. And now the Benjamin Killer was also bleeding people. Like her mother. And again, like with that case, she was failing. He would get away. They always got away. Adele snarled, emitting a sound like a wounded creature, and then winced. She didn't like it when her mind went to places like these.

He couldn't get away. Not this time. Men like this, people who did things like this, couldn't be allowed to exist. It wasn't right.

"It's not fair," she said, her teeth clenching at the end of the word, biting the sound off in a short spasming surge of emotion. "I'm not your Cara anymore," she said softly.

The breeze seemed to pick up, wrestling at her hair, glossing her skin with the cool touch of the swaying breeze.

Her hand felt sweaty all of a sudden, and she glanced down toward the candies. She hadn't even realized why she bought them.

She unwrapped one of the candies and popped it in her mouth, wincing at the flavor. She had never liked these caramels. As much as her mother had adored the candy, it was the jokes on the inside of the wrapper that she loved most.

Adele raised the wrapper, about to read it, but then she hesitated. The killer couldn't get away. And she wasn't little Cara anymore. This was not her home. She was a girl without a home. And that was okay. She crumpled the wrapper and tossed it toward the opposite side of the trail, away from where her mother had once been.

She knelt and pressed her forearms against her protruding leg, resting her chin against the back of one hand. She took the other Carambar that she'd bought from the small store and placed it on the trail, next to where her mother had died.

The killer had cut her skin in shallow, intricate patterns, almost like carving some piece of art into a canvas. But Adele's mother had been a work of art in and of herself. The killer had been a vandal, drawing cartoons on a masterpiece.

Adele turned away from the trail, standing still, not walking, but with her back toward where her mother had perished. She couldn't let the Benjamin Killer escape as well.

He had come here, obsessed with mortality, with the descending ages of victims. Someone obsessed with death. And then he had killed again. He would kill soon. But Adele was determined to stop him before he could.

Robert had been right. She knew it now, in her bones. She had gotten close. Far closer than had made him comfortable. Last time, he'd been spooked enough to leave the country. This time, if he could feel her closing in, he could feel the noose tightening, what would he do? A desperate man, with no moral code. What sort of measures would he take?

Adele clenched her teeth in grim resolve. Then she stepped back up the trail, her eyes fixed ahead. She'd walked a great distance from where she'd left the borrowed car. But Adele liked the exercise, she liked the exertion, the effort. It helped her think, to focus. The Benjamin Killer would pay for what he did, and she would see to it that he knew *exactly* who had brought him down.

CHAPTER TWELVE

"Pick a card, my friend, any card," he said, his voice purring through teeth stretched in a Cheshire grin. The man reached up, adjusting his wool cap over his red hair. Now was not the time for conspicuous behavior.

He met the smiling face of a fellow with olive skin, and he winked. The young Parisian frowned in confusion and turned back toward his friends, sipping on a beer.

Sometimes, one simply couldn't help themselves. The man kept his grin fixed across his face, studying the group of locals before him. This was a larger bar than the last one, and the opposite side of town. What had that one been called? Genna's. That time, he'd taken it slow— followed the girl home, kept an eye on her routine. Tonight, though... Tonight he couldn't afford the wasted time.

People were laughing and milling around. This bar was packed, partly due to the rain, which had inserted itself over the city intermittently throughout the day. But also partly due to some sports match. The man didn't follow sports, and he couldn't have named any of the local teams if he had been bothered to. The man had more particular interests.

He smiled at the small group of customers he'd enticed around the jutting edge of the counter.

An easy way to meet friends: magic tricks. Especially in the college bars. The man performed the sorts of tricks one could learn watching videos online, coupled with only a little practice. He was an amateur, even in the most generous of descriptions, but he wasn't here in search of money or praise.

The young man in front of the small gathering of a half-drunk audience watched the amateur magician, waiting as he continued to chatter, fanning the cards.

"And what is your name again?" the magician said, still smiling.

"Amir," the Parisian replied, hesitantly pulling at one of the soft cards, then suspiciously glancing up and moving his hand along to a different part of the deck. Of course, it didn't matter which card he

71

chose. The deck was rigged. The decision, the outcome, was already clear.

"And Amir, memorize your card. Show it to your friends."

A combination of tourists and locals had crowded around for the spectacle, as they often did. The man in the wool cap reached up with his free hand, tugging the hat a bit lower past his bangs, the hem of the wool pressing against his forehead. His smile faltered just a little as his fingernail on his thumb brushed against his ear, eliciting a small amount of pain. The man hated pain.

His lips twisted for a moment, forming into the beginning of a frown. Just as quickly, he readdressed the expression and adopted a smile once more. People loved spectacle.

The man waited for Amir to show his friends the card, and then watched, impatiently, as they shielded the card with their hands so he couldn't see it. The bar's customers waited expectantly for the trick to continue. So many of them were so young. Their flesh was smooth, their eyes clear and bright…

He felt a stirring in his stomach.

"I need to think—think very hard," the magician said, interjecting each word with a playful chuckle or another wry grin. The smile was obviously an act. They all knew it, and he knew it. But the point wasn't to dupe them. The smile had nothing to do with it. They were watching his hands as closely as possible, studying his fingers.

The smile had other uses: it displayed something around his mouth, something so obvious that no one looked too closely. Tucked inside his cheek, the second, duplicate card rested against his molars and his gums. He didn't have a particularly large mouth, but had deposited the trick card before even entering the bar. Any good magician had to do their work before the audience was even watching. The card itself was sprayed with trick adhesive which would keep it from growing soggy in his mouth. Optics were a huge part of it.

Pulling forth a soggy card would immediately tell the audience he'd stowed it long before. But pulling a card that looked new, fresh, gave the illusion that it had been placed there only moments before.

It gave him no small amount of satisfaction to know he could dupe so many people at once. All eyes were on him, everyone was staring, and yet, still, they would fall for it. Amir and his friends waited expectantly, watching him. They were younger, much younger than he was. They didn't value their youth; the young never did. That girl from only a few nights ago, she had been a lively one. He'd enjoyed their time together beneath the bridge.

"Is your card… the three of diamonds?" he said.

Amir's eyes widened, and then his lips curled into a smirk. "No," he replied.

The man inhaled in mock surprise. Of course, this too was part of the trick. Every good hero had to fail at least once before they succeeded. Now, the audience would relax. They would think the trick was over. They would think they had duped the magician—this *foolish* tourist who had come into their bar and demanded their attention. Their eyes would wander from his hands…

And it was in that moment, the man stowed the deck of cards, placing it quickly in his black jacket pocket. Then, just as quickly, he withdrew what looked to be the exact same deck. But this deck didn't have the forced cards with the glue adhesive on the back. Once he did the reveal, they always asked to see the deck. Predictable.

People were similar in their predictability. Be it in France or Indiana. The man's expression soured somewhat at the memory of fleeing the United States. The FBI had gotten too close. The female agent—he'd seen her on the news asking for clues. Little did she know that she'd interviewed his host family the night before he'd fled. She hadn't known he'd been renting a room in their basement, and they hadn't volunteered the information, wanting to avoid any hassle about renter's insurance. They hadn't known who he was.

Besides, how could his host family have known that the vehicle traced back to their home had belonged to him? He'd made sure to ditch the jalopy—he'd paid in cash for it anyway.

Agent Sharp. That had been her name. She'd gotten too close—far too close for comfort. But he was still on vacation. First the US, then France. It wasn't yet time to return home… There was still so much more fun to be had.

The magician smiled at his audience and then clicked his tongue. He could feel the card wedged into the back of his mouth. He extended his hand, beckoning toward Amir, then took the card. He waved it a couple times in a big show, and then snapped his fingers. The card erupted in flame, disappearing as quickly as flash paper could—bought for less than a pound in magician stores around the world.

And yet, the reaction of his small audience sent shivers through the man. Magic was almost as fun as his other activities. It wasn't the same, but it was *nearly* the same. The awe, the spectacle, the complete domination of his audience as they didn't know what would come next. All of it intoxicated him and brought him the satisfaction of knowing what he had always known: he was smarter than them. All of them.

Everyone was staring at his hands now, awed by the disappearing card. Then he made a choking sound and looped his tongue beneath the stowed card; he pushed the card into his mouth and made a big show of puffing his cheeks, turning red in the face and placing his hands against his stomach as if he were about to throw up. Finally, with a gagging sound, he opened his mouth, and the card fell into his hand, slowly curling open. He had to pull the final fold to reveal the jack of spades.

"Is this your card?" he said, grinning at the audience.

The two tables at the bar erupted in applause, all of them staring in awe at the strange tourist and his tricks.

The jack of spades had been intentional, of course. A hero of his, who'd been named "The Spade Killer," had been known for creating late-night art in the park districts, adopting the guise of a gardener when hunting his victims. Such interesting monickers the news outlets would come up with, labeling people like the magician as if they were superheroes. The Spade Killer had operated in France only a decade ago. He would carve up his victims with shallow cuts, creating beautiful patterns on human skin.

The man shivered in delight at the memory, recollecting his first time reading about the attacks in the newspaper back home. It had been better than porn. There had been an artistry to the Spade Killer's work. The artist had never been caught, but photos of his work and his masterpieces could still be found online for those with discerning taste.

"How do you do that?" said Amir, snapping the man's attention back to the moment.

The magician paused, gathering himself, then he simply shook his head, and smiled. "Would you like to see another one?" he asked.

Another one. He needed another one. It had taken so long, stalling, when that FBI agent had gotten too close. She'd asked the wrong questions in Indiana. It had been time to leave. He still wasn't sure how much she knew. At least that was behind him. The agents in France would have to start from scratch to catch him. That gave him a good amount of time to enjoy this new playground. Like the Spade Killer, he too wouldn't be caught.

But he couldn't wait another couple of weeks. No, he needed to catch up. Time was of the essence. Always ticking, time. He swallowed, and his smile faltered just a little.

"Would you like to see another trick?" he asked, louder this time, glancing around at those clustered near the counter, trying to regain their attention from their bottles and half-filled glasses.

"Yes!" someone said, "Do me!"

He turned, eyeing an old, silver-haired woman smiling at him, pearl earrings glinting beneath the low light of the bar. She wouldn't do.

He turned away from her and smiled his crocodile grin and said, "I need a little information first. This trick will only work on certain people." They were in a bar behind the college, after all. The clientele was far younger than usual. "What are your birthdays? Year and month—it's important. I have a sense; tell me, is anyone here twenty-three?" He said it innocuously, casually, but with enough flair and gusto to arouse curiosity. He glanced around at the few spectators seated at the bar.

"My friend," someone said at last. The magician glanced over to a young man with a scraggly goatee. He had the look of some sort of starving artist, complete with an artisan's cap and a black shirt which read *"Rock & Roll."* The magician tried not to allow his distaste to show. Music was like wine; when treated with indifference, it could only give someone a stomachache.

"Yes?" said the magician. "Are they here?"

Scraggly-beard nodded quickly, and he hurried over toward another table at the back.

The magician's French wasn't great, but it wasn't as bad as he often pretended. And he could understand the conversation well enough. Even over the din of the bar, he heard the man with the scraggly beard saying, "Come, he has a trick to show us."

The friend seemed reluctant, but at the insistent pulls on his arm, got slowly to his feet and allowed himself to be guided over.

"And you're twenty-three?" the magician asked, glancing at the man with a curious look. He could feel his mouth go dry all of a sudden, but resisted the urge to wet his lips.

The newcomer nodded slowly, his eyes wide beneath dark hair. "Yes, my birthday was in July."

The magician flashed his crocodile grin. "Count out twenty-three cards. Here."

The newcomer hesitated, frowning. "Does this trick take very long?

75

What is it?"

"Patience," said the magician, still smiling. "I'm about to show you."

CHAPTER THIRTEEN

Adele turned up the final street, her arms straight at her side, her brow crumpled over glaring eyes. If the APB didn't get a hit soon, he could leave Paris. He could kill and escape.

She turned the corner, facing the side of the street where she had parked her loaner. There, sitting on the hood of the Nissan sedan, the lanky form of John waited, his arms crossed, a look of impatience on his face.

He reached up and adjusted the collar of his shirt over the burn mark which stretched down his throat and across his neck. He muttered a few choice words, which Adele couldn't hear. John passed a hand through his hair, pushing it back and adjusting stray bangs behind his ears. DGSI had a dress code, but it was considered more suggestion than coercion. And John, with his military cut sides, messy bangs, and unkempt stubble seemed particularly averse to persuasion.

Adele could still feel her frustration swirling inside her, trying to lay claim to her thoughts. The killer couldn't escape.

She muttered to herself and stomped forward, approaching her sedan. A surge of annoyance twisted through her at the sight of John sitting on the car, leaning against the windshield as if he owned the thing. While it wasn't hers, it didn't hurt to treat government property with a bit of respect.

"There you are," John said, noticing her for the first time. If he knew his posture would frustrate her, he made no move to alter it. He shifted a little, causing the hood to protest with a metallic groan, suggesting he could easily put a dent in the thing.

"Could you get off," Adele said in a patient voice, though she didn't feel like it.

John raised his hands in mock surrender, peering with dark eyes down his pronounced Roman nose. "It's all right, American Princess. How come I couldn't reach you?"

She shook her head, then tapped at her pockets and pushed a sigh skyward. "Dammit. Must've left the phone in the car."

She stepped past John and peered through the windshield, noting the phone sitting in the cup holder through the tinted window.

"I just needed to clear my head," she said, glancing at her partner. "I'm serious, get off. You'll put a dent in the thing."

John nodded, adopting a look of sincerity. "Oh, of course. I'm sorry."

He made no move to rise. "Maybe, just a suggestion, in the future you shouldn't leave yourself completely without any mode of communication." He shifted again, the heels of his shoes at the end of his long legs tapping against the metal rim of the front right tire.

"Could you stop," Adele snapped, feeling the annoyance rising in her like bile in the back of her throat. "I'm not in the mood."

He smirked. "Any new leads?"

"I'm serious. Get off the car—Christ, you're like a teenage boy."

"You know what your problem is?" he said, still making no move. "You think the world owes you. You think you're entitled. Well, I'm here to tell you you're not owed anything. This city is my city. American princesses can't just come here and—"

"—Stop calling me that. Get off the damned hood."

The frustration in her chest was now turning to anger, which, aided by John fanning the flames, was quickly turning into rage. She didn't like that he had this effect on her. He was behaving like a child. This attitude never would've been permitted at the FBI. She vaguely wondered about his story. He didn't seem like a very good agent. He was bored half the time, sarcastic the other half, and angry throughout it all. So why had they hired him? And, most importantly, why was he still sitting on her car with that enraging smirk?

She reached forward and grabbed him by the arm, preparing to bodily drag Agent Renee from the hood. He tensed the moment she touched him, his eyes narrowing, his other hand dropping instinctively toward her chest with rapid speed.

He didn't hit her, but it was a close thing, as if he'd been trained to react violently to physical contact.

"Don't touch me," he growled.

"Get off my car."

He slammed a hand against the side of the metal, far too hard. "This car?"

"Jesus, John, maybe we better just go back and ask if they'll set us up with different part—"

Before Adele could finish, she heard the quiet chirping sound of her phone, the ring tone drifting through the tinted windows.

A split second later, a louder ringing sound of some French rock song began playing from John's suit pocket. He glanced at her, frowning, still tensed, the muscles in his neck straining like someone on the verge of action. But as the song played, he fished the phone from his pocket and began to relax. He pressed the speaker to his ear, still frowning at Adele, and snapped, "What?"

Adele waited, also frowning.

John continued to glare, but then something else crept into his expression. "You sure?" he demanded.

Adele couldn't hear the reply on the other end, but she did hear indistinct sounds. In the distance, car horns blared. The rain stopped, but a quiet dripping sound resonated as water fell from gutters and leaves and moved in slow spurts toward the sewer grates.

Adele leaned in closer to John, listening. He smelled like expensive cologne and gunpowder. It was a scent she recognized from her father. The gunpowder anyway. Her father never spent a dime on cologne. He would've thought it wasteful. But he spent enough time at the gun range that he always came home smelling just a little bit like smoke and metal. Adele's least favorite part of the job was target practice— perhaps due to her father's opposite influence.

"What is it?" Adele could feel goose pimples rising across the back of her arms.

John slid off the hood of the car and began hurrying over to a large black SUV parked behind her.

"A hit on the APB," he said quickly. All signs of his bored, annoying personality had vanished, replaced by an excited air that propelled him quickly toward the side door of his car. "Red-haired tourist, the Hyatt Hotel downtown."

Adele stared, stunned. "Is he there now?"

"Right now. He has a girl with him."

Adele cursed and fumbled for her keys, racing around the hood of the car toward the driver's seat. "I'll follow you!" she shouted over her shoulder.

John was too busy gunning his own engine and turning away from the curb, ripping up the street. A second later a siren blared from the SUV, coupled with flashing red and blue lights.

Adele settled, didn't bother to buckle, and tore after him, roaring through the French streets. She would get the bastard this time. This

79

time, he wouldn't escape.

CHAPTER FOURTEEN

The cold metal of her firearm pressed against her cheek. She kept it close, angled upward, out of the line of sight from the eyehole in the large metal door that led to the hotel suite. Red numbers: 57. A single eyehole, trimmed with bronze.

Behind her, she could feel the presence of the concierge who'd given them the key card and escorted them quickly to the room.

John flanked the other side of the door from where Adele pressed against the wall. She could feel the metal frame of some bland hotel art jutting against her shoulder. She breathed slowly, calming herself, waiting. She had never been particularly good with a firearm. It was the one area that she needed more practice in. John, though, seemed in his element. He was crouched low, his extraordinarily tall form somehow compact all of a sudden. The gun he held with as much skin gripping the metal as possible, putting Adele's own teacup grip to shame; the Glock .22 seemed an extension of his hands.

A wildfire glinted in John's eyes, and he nodded toward the door and mouthed the words, *"Ready?"*

She glanced back down the hall, toward the stairs. They hadn't wanted to take the elevator. Grunting and low muttering resounded through the thick door to suite fifty-seven.

As they'd entered the lobby earlier, it had sounded like backup was at least three minutes away. Three minutes was a long time. A lot of pain.

The concierge had confirmed a girl was with the red-haired man. A victim.

For a moment, Adele hesitated. This didn't seem like the killer's MO. He didn't take his prey back to some lair. He preferred to kill them in quiet, secluded places. Places that couldn't be traced back to him. A new country, a new MO, perhaps? Whatever the case, she could hear the sounds growing louder through the door.

A second later, a woman screamed.

No more waiting. Backup would have to get here when it did. Adele jammed the key card into the door slot, and John shoved past as she turned the handle.

"Show me your hands!" he shouted, his booming voice filling the room.

Weapon raised, left arm bent, she followed John into the hotel suite, the sound of their footsteps muffled by thick carpet, but the sounds of their voices blaring forth, attempting to control the room with sheer volume, resonating in the large space.

The suite was at the top floor of the hotel, reserved for affluent clientele. There were ebony counters along a small area that served as an en suite kitchen; a chandelier dangled above the two agents, illuminating marble tiles on either side of the stretch of red carpet leading from the door, down two steps, and into a lounge area.

Adele was mediocre with firearms, but in surveying a crime scene, there were few better. She instantly cataloged three adjacent doorways in the suite. Two of them were shut, but one was propped open. Large, tinted windows circled a bulging, spherical wall, giving a view of the city below. And there, lying over the top of a mauve, cushioned sofa, a redheaded man had a woman pinned beneath him.

The man wore a strange black outfit. Beneath him, Adele could hear the quiet shouts and fearful cries of the woman.

The man's hands jutted skyward, as he spun to face the two agents. "Please!" he shouted. "Please don't shoot!"

John hurried over to the woman, keeping his gun trained on the man.

Adele couldn't see any blood. Adrenaline laced through her body as she took quick stock of the man. He didn't seem to be armed.

She felt a slight jolt of discomfort as she realized he was wearing black latex all up and down his body. Her gaze flicked to the woman and realized she was wearing a similar outfit. There were conspicuously cut holes in the body of the outfits, allowing no room for decency, but ample room for intimate access.

John had pulled up sharply, and clicked his tongue in a disapproving sound. "Christ, put that away, will you?"

The man hesitated, his cheeks turning the same color as his hair. He began to lower his hands to zip up his suit, but just as quickly, Adele barked, "No sudden movements!"

The woman also covered herself, trying to keep some modicum of decency by placing herself between the couch and the agents. No blood. No weapon. No injuries.

"Dammit," Adele said. She lowered her gun, shaking her head in disgust. "Mademoiselle, are you hurt?" This, she directed toward the woman.

The woman shook her head wildly and pointed toward the man. "He's a friend," she said. "Purely a friend. We're not doing anything illegal. I'm here for free!"

John's gun also lowered, and he sighed. "Interesting comment to volunteer," he said, with a wry shake of his head. Some of the burning wildfire in his gaze had faded now.

Adele could feel her frustration mounting, but John seemed to have found the humor in the situation. He winked at the woman and gave her a quick glance up and down. "What's the going rate?" he said. "I might have some spare time tomorrow."

Adele stared in shock at her partner, but then, when the woman didn't react in outrage, she glanced back.

Agent Renee holstered his weapon and winked at the woman. "Pretty sure while this is outside of my jurisdiction, you're not supposed to be paying for it. It's not 2016 anymore, my friend."

The man, who had, with slow, careful motions, managed to zip up his latex suit for some amount of decency, shook his head. Adele noticed a long, leather strap on the ground, as well as a riding crop. She noticed a couple of bruises on the exposed side of the woman's hip. But nothing in the woman's posture suggested she was afraid of the man next to her. If anything, she seemed embarrassed.

"It isn't like that," the man said, taking a shuddering breath. He continued to fidget nervously, his hands still down by his waist. His gaze flicked between Renee and Adele, the red hue of his cheeks now matching his hair. "Perfectly consensual. Tell them—well? Tell them!"

The woman glanced sidelong at him and hesitated for a moment, a shrewd look coming across her eyes. She considered the comment, and Adele could see the wheels turning in her brain as she seemed to mull over her options. At long last, though, she sighed, and said, "He's right. Perfectly willing."

The red-haired man sighed in relief.

Adele tried to suppress her frustration. Clearly, this wasn't the Benjamin Killer. It couldn't be. Could it?

John moved over to the couch and plopped down, leaning back and crossing his legs, tossing his feet onto a footstool. The lack of professionalism sent another jolt of annoyance through Adele. Their argument from earlier had faded to the back of her mind, but the cavalier way in which John conducted himself put her ill at ease.

"Well," said John, addressing the red-haired man, "I'm going to guess that you aren't French. I haven't heard an accent like that since American Princess first spoke back at the office."

This, Adele thought was entirely unfair. It was true that earlier it had taken her a couple of hours to get back into the stream of conversation, but this man spoke with a terribly thick accent. She couldn't quite place it. It wasn't American.

"British?" she said.

The man glanced sharply at her, worry wrinkling his face in rigid lines around his eyes. He began to reply, but then caught himself.

John chuckled, thoroughly enjoying himself. "Does the missus know you're out and about, playing with the French toys, hmm?" John said. "It would be a pity for her to find—"

Before he could finish, the man let out a quiet yelp and bolted for it.

Adele snapped her gun up, and there was a brief window where she could have fired, but, though her finger stayed on the trigger, she didn't squeeze. The man's face was covered in sweat and streaks of red as he barreled into Adele, knocking her roughly to the side. He shouted incoherently and bolted toward the door.

Adele stumbled back, slamming into one of the couches, throwing out a hand to steady herself on a metal railing that led up the two steps.

She aimed at the man's retreating form and shouted, "Stop or I'll shoot!"

But he didn't stop. In his black, skintight latex suit, the man bolted into the hallway and then disappeared from view, the sound of his thudding footsteps reaching them from the open doorway.

Adele hesitated for only a moment to glance back at John, raising an eyebrow in exasperation. "Gonna help?"

John leaned back, crossing his hands behind his head, and smirking in the direction of the prostitute against the wall. "I'll cover her," he said. "You can chase the one with the wood in the rubber suit."

Adele huffed and resisted the urge to roll her eyes as she stowed her weapon, and then broke into a sprint, racing up the stairs along the red carpet and out into the hallway of the hotel.

She spotted the man pushing through the doorway that led to the stairs, his fingers shoving against the metal push bar, and the latex of his suit reflecting the red from the exit sign above.

Adele lowered her head, racing toward the man and covering the distance rapidly. They were at the top of the hotel, and the man hadn't opted to wait for the elevator.

She reached the stairwell and could hear him a flight below her, cursing as he circled the stairs, sprinting down.

"Stop!" she shouted.

The retort of slapping footsteps indicated he had no desire to comply. She saved her breath and continued her pursuit without further comment. Adele took the stairs four at a time, leaping down the steps rapidly.

Just below her, she could hear the ragged gasps of the man as he continued to flee. Her own breathing was steady, calm. She could feel the way her body responded each time she pushed off one foot and rounded the banister, circling down the staircase one flight at a time. She spent most of her life running, training. Every morning, without fail, she would exercise for moments like these. The man had made a mistake in thinking he could outrun her.

Already, even though they'd only covered a few flights, she could tell the man was lagging. She was gaining now and reached the top of a flight of stairs as he reached the bottom. Another flight of stairs, and he was only halfway down. One more, and he was within grabbing distance.

Adele didn't try to shout this time. The man was gasping, heaving, his breath coming in huffing puffs.

For her part, Adele's breathing was elevated, her heart rate higher, but she could still keep this up.

The red-haired man could hear her approaching footsteps, and he turned, his eyes wide with panic. They widened even further as Adele launched through the air, tackling him from behind and bringing both of them slamming to the marble landing.

The man's breath *whooshed* from his body as he thumped to the floor, cushioning her fall.

Adele tried to control her temper as she rolled the man over and pulled his hands sharply behind his back. Just another tourist who liked his French prostitutes and bondage games.

"I suspect you're going to enjoy this," she said, grimly. There was a slight squeak of his rubber outfit against the floor as she shifted him into a better position and then reached for her handcuffs, pulling them out and shackling his wrists.

"How long have you been in France?" she demanded once the man was secure. She kept her knee in the small of his back, crouched over him like some gargoyle above a hapless victim. Frustration and fury cycled through her body, carried by pulsing adrenaline and an elevated heartbeat.

She shook him roughly, pulling at the handcuffs until he loosed a painful grunt.

"How long have you been in France?" she repeated, speaking in English now.

The man sighed softly, deflating like a leaking balloon, and then, with a grunt, he said, "Only a week. You can check my tickets on my phone. Please—don't hurt me."

He had a British accent. London, by the sound of it.

"A week? How come you're just now checking into the hotel?"

It took another shake of the man's cuffed hands, but again he grunted, and, reluctantly, gasped out, "Third hotel. I switch after... After each one."

"Each what?"

The man whimpered, shaking his head, his red hair shifting back and forth and his rubber suit squeaking against the marble floor. "They're better in France. You don't understand. I'm not a bad man. I pay them well, and always follow our safe words, I promise! You're not going to tell my wife, are you?" At this, the British man's voice cracked.

Adele muttered in disgust—not so much at the man's actions but at the outcome of the APB. This wasn't the killer. Of that, she was nearly certain.

She gently guided the man back to his feet, some of the anger deflating from her at his docile posture. With a sigh, trying to steady her breath and allowing the man to do the same, she guided him back up the stairs.

As she did, her vortex of annoyance and anger began to recede, giving way to another thought... She glanced sidelong at the man, pushing him along in front of her. He had a British accent. A Brit in France.

While this man clearly wasn't the killer, she'd been operating under the assumption that the killer was from France or the US. That he either fled the US to escape to a foreign country or that he'd been vacationing in the US and returned home to Paris. But, as she shoved the man along, back up the stairs, she realized there was a third option.

What if the killer wasn't from France or the US? What if he was from a different country entirely? What if he'd been just visiting both the United States and France?

The thought haunted her, niggling at her mind as she returned up the stairs and rejoined John in the suite.

By then, uniformed police officers had arrived for backup. Gendarmerie could also be glimpsed through the windows, far below, waiting outside in their quasi-military vehicles. The police took the prostitute and her client from there. Before leaving with their charges, they conducted a brief interview with John, who seemed to enjoy the whole situation. Adele stood in the doorway, watching her partner answer the final question of the leading police officer. She watched as he sauntered across the room, beaming at her. "That was fun," he said.

"That's one word for it."

John chuckled, and began to slide a piece of paper into his pocket.

Adele glanced at the parchment. "What's that?"

John smirked, but shrugged with one shoulder. "Don't worry about it."

Adele glanced at the paper, noticing a couple of numbers before he finally slid it completely from view.

She lowered her voice to a hoarse whisper. "You didn't." She resisted the urge to reach out and shake the man. "Is that the girl's number?"

John chuckled again and patted Adele on the shoulder in a gesture he had to know would infuriate her. "My American princess, what you don't know can't hurt you."

"I can't believe you. I can't—"

"—you know what I feel like? A drink. You should come. You look tightly wound. I heard Agent Paige was talking about you with Foucault, by the way. She's not very nice in her report."

"I don't—I just—" Adele didn't know what to say. She glanced toward John's pocket, then back up at his smirk, and then down to the hand which he was still pressing against her shoulder. There was something condescending about the gesture, but also familiar.

Strangely, this invitation to get drinks seemed to suggest he had warmed to her somewhat. If not for the burn along his neck and up his throat, John would have been quite handsome, with his bold nose and disheveled bangs. It was little surprise, in his position, with his personality, that he would leverage his authority to coerce the number from the prostitute. Adele sincerely hoped it was just a joke, but decided it wasn't worth pursuing; she had more serious matters to commit her thoughts to.

If Agent Paige was causing trouble back at the office, there was nothing Adele could do about that either. Their history proved that.

She shook her head, mouth slightly agape, and glanced back toward the two black-latex-wearing suite occupants. The tickets on the phone had confirmed the man's claim—he'd only arrived last week, and he hadn't come from the States. She sighed softly, breathing through her nose as she surveyed the arresting officers and then turned back to John. "I don't even—"

"A rough night, I know. You got your hopes up." For a moment, it almost seemed like John's voice was sincere. He reached out and began to guide her, tugging insistently at her arm and pulling her toward the elevator. "Come. I'll show you my favorite spot."

"I don't know…"

"It's back at headquarters. I know how much you like the office; you can pretend you're working."

"A drink at headquarters?"

John nodded and continued to guide her along with a strong but surprisingly gentle grip. "You need to unwind as much as I do."

Adele loosed a sigh, lifted her eyes skyward as if in silent prayer. But at last, she nodded, numbly. What else was there to say? The killer had evaded her once more. The APB had been useless. Perhaps a drink was exactly what she needed.

CHAPTER FIFTEEN

Adele could feel the exhaustion from the last couple of days taking its toll. The thought of her morning run tomorrow filled her with dread, but she hadn't missed one in years and she wasn't about to start in Paris. Still, as John drove his SUV wildly up the nighttime streets, darting beneath the vibrant light posts lining the sidewalks, she couldn't help but feel the last vestiges of her energy being spent on an emotion eerily similar to unease.

"I thought we were going to get drinks," she murmured from the passenger seat. Her cheek was pressed against the cool window, and her hair cushioned the side of her face. She stared out the front windshield, her eyes tracking the buildings ahead of them.

"We are. Back at headquarters."

"You said that. Sounds awful. Why not just go to some bar—"

"Just hang on. I'm about to show you."

"You sure they won't tow my car?"

John kept his long arms out, holding the steering wheel, but still managed to evoke a shrug from a shoulder followed by a slight tilt of his head.

"Even if they did, so what. It's a government car. They'll have to give it back. You're too tired to drive."

Adele sighed again, closing her eyes, if only for a moment, like someone on a diet inhaling the scent of chocolate cake. "If I didn't know better," she said, "I'd think you were worried about me."

John tutted quietly and said, "I thought you were a good detective. I'm worried about my own ass. Follow the clues, American Princess."

They pulled into the parking lot outside the DGSI headquarters, nodding at the night guards as John flashed a badge and Adele handed hers to John so he could poke it out the window.

One of the guards nodded in familiarity to Renee, a gesture which the tall man returned. Adele was reminded of her own relationship with Doug, one of the security guards on the third floor.

John parked beneath the dark overpass, the concrete lot illuminated only by rectangular incandescent lights in the enclosed space's ceiling.

Adele followed after her partner, an uneasy gait to her step. She couldn't sleep, not now. Not after the day's events. Her idea of a good time and relaxing with a drink rarely involved the workspace, but she hadn't wanted to turn John's invitation down. John's personality took some acclimating, and she didn't want to shoot down his one offer of camaraderie. He was a strange one. A rebel, in the most juvenile sense of the word. But there was also something deeper. Something she couldn't quite make out about him. It piqued her curiosity.

She had to walk double pace to keep up with his long, steady strides as he moved down the nearly empty office hallways.

"APB was a bust, but the tox report should be on my desk," he said conversationally, leading her toward the stairwell.

"Not more stairs," Adele groaned.

"It will be worth it. Don't worry."

John's office was on the seventh floor. But instead of heading up, he took the descending flight.

Adele stared uneasily after the tall man. "You're not going to kill me, are you?"

John glanced over his shoulder up at her and flashed a jack-o'-lantern grin. "Haven't decided yet. Just come, American Princess. You see killers everywhere. Makes it hard to recognize comrades."

"Yeah? You're a comrade, not a killer, is that it?"

"Perhaps I'm a bit of both." He gestured at her and, without waiting, continued down the stairs.

With a rising sense of malaise, which made her feel silly, Adele followed after John, taking the stairs much slower than earlier.

He led her down to the basement and pushed open an old rusted door. A dusty, cracked hallway filled with chipped paint and dull lights stretched before her. At the far end, she spotted an evidence locker and a couple of interrogation rooms that seemed little used. John pushed open the door to interrogation room three and glanced inside, looking around. "Coast is clear," he said, conspiratorially.

Adele didn't know what or who he was looking for or expecting to find in the old, abandoned interrogation room, but she didn't care to ask. Out of the entire building, this floor was the worst she'd seen.

Large flakes of paint peeled off the walls, and watermarks scoured the floor, suggesting the basement had flooded more than once. Lettering marked some of the doors as interrogation rooms, displaying words beneath thin layers of dust. The building had been serving the

DGSI for a decade, but the basement had been left, it seemed, to fend mostly for itself.

John moved further down the hall until he reached Interrogation Room Six. Then he fished a key from his pocket. He tried the door handle, which wouldn't turn. He nodded in approval, humming quietly to himself—the same tune that served as his ringtone. Then he inserted a small key, turned the door handle, and pushed it open.

He glanced up and down the hall, only further adding to the burden of unease on Adele's shoulders. As the door opened, she was assailed by a strange, fruity smell. She'd been to vineyards before, and the odor of fermentation in the basement was overpowering.

John inhaled it, though, like a matron coming home to fresh-baked cookies. He stepped into the room, and, reluctantly, Adele followed. She scraped past the rusted metal frame and stepped into a room that was entirely dark. A second later, the door slammed shut, sealing off even the illumination from the hallway.

Adele felt her heart lodge in her throat. "John?" she barked. "This isn't funny."

She heard chuckling from the darkness, but then, a moment later, there was a quiet clicking sound. Lights sputtered into being above her, illuminating the enclosed interrogation room.

Except, instead of a metal table and cold chairs, there was a large, oversized couch pressed up against the back wall. A small distillery leaned against the wall, set on a wooden plank table that looked to have been handcrafted. A couple of pictures hung on the wall opposite the distillery, and miniature wooden barrels were stacked in the far corner, next to a sealed blue plastic tub with a thin layer of duct tape circling the lid. The fermentation smells came from this pile of barrels and the rectangular plastic container.

Adele saw a couple of bags of sugar, some clear tubing, and two hard corks on the ground as well as some other ingredients that she knew went into making wine and moonshine.

"You're joking," she said, staring at the place.

John whistled a cheerful tune and retrieved a couple of glass cups from on top of the window ledge. The window glimpsed the adjacent interrogation room, but it was too high for Adele to see much.

"Glasses are clean, don't worry," he said.

"By the smell of it, this stuff is strong enough that even if they weren't clean it wouldn't matter."

91

John raised an eyebrow at her, then gestured toward the couch. "Has a reclining lever on the side. TV's over there—turn on whatever you want. Actually, second thought. If it's not sports, you won't be able to find it down here."

Adele wasn't sure what to make of all this. Somehow, John had managed to build himself a secret mancave in the basement of the DGSI headquarters. By the looks of things, and the number of glasses, he either used it regularly, or he had guests over on occasion.

"Do you bring all the girls down here on their first day?"

John snorted, but any retort was interrupted by the sound of liquid trickling into a cup.

"You in for some sangria? Or would you prefer something from the distillery?"

Adele hesitated, then said, "The hardest thing you've got."

John nodded in appreciation, and after a moment, he returned with two cups. Both held clear liquid.

Adele accepted her glass from John. She leaned back in the couch and pulled the handle on the side, sighing as the footrest lifted up and the back of the chair reclined.

John sat on the couch, also, but preferred the arm, his boots on the cushion of the couch.

John faced Adele and leaned against the wall. He grabbed a remote lodged between the back of the couch and the wall, and pointed it toward the small screen attached to a swinging arm in the middle of the room. He clicked the remote, and the TV sputtered to life, filling the room with French commentators chattering about some recent soccer game.

"Do you like football?" said John.

Adele shrugged. "I played a lot of sports growing up, but I was never particularly interested in watching them."

John tutted, sniffing in mock offense.

Adele inhaled the contents of her glass and winced as a powerful odor assailed her, clearing her nostrils and raising the hairs on her neck. She could feel John's eyes on her. She pressed the glass to her lips, tilted it back, and swallowed a gulp.

Immediately, she regretted this decision.

The moonshine scorched her throat and filled her mouth with a strange, gingery taste. It wasn't unpleasant, but it was powerful.

She felt the burning sensation turn to a tickling one, threatening to elicit a cough. She clenched her teeth, refusing to give John the satisfaction of seeing her react to the liquor. Her eyes watered, but she managed to keep the drink down. A small victory.

Adele glanced over at John, who had already downed half his glass.

"Good, isn't it?" he said with a smirk.

Adele shrugged and leaned even further back. Above her, she spotted a couple of the pictures she'd initially noticed from the door. Both photographs displayed men with guns and wearing uniforms.

She stared. "Were you part of the Commandos Marine?"

Absentmindedly, his hand reached up and massaged at the burn mark on his neck. The handsome man shrugged and murmured quietly, "Once upon a time."

"My father served in the military."

John nodded to show he'd heard, but offered no comment himself. He took another long swallow from his drink, downing the rest in a giant gulp, and then swung his legs over the couch to retrieve some more.

"I've heard stories about you guys," she said, nodding toward the picture. "Some people say you're the Navy SEALs of France."

John gave a harsh, barking laugh. "We're better than those Americans," he snapped, an undercurrent of anger to his words. "We sacrifice more and take harder jobs."

Adele didn't see the point in arguing.

"Well, I should've figured you for a military guy. You have the manners of a soldier."

John flicked an eyebrow up and downed another glass in two quick swallows. He poured himself a third from the distillery spigot.

"We still have work tomorrow," Adele reminded him.

"Never stopped me before," John said with a shrug. This time, he took the glass back to the couch. He once more sat on the armrest, facing Adele, his dirty shoes pressed on the dusty cushion.

"Thanks for inviting me here," she said.

She couldn't get a good read on John. Was he trying to make a move on her? If so, he was sitting far enough away for them to be siblings. She had no interest in becoming romantically involved with anyone at this point. John wasn't bad looking, but he was ill-mannered and seemed to hate his job. She wasn't sure the career path that led from special forces to DGSI agent. The way he carried himself, his weapon drawn, back at the hotel, had suggested more than basic field

93

training.

The memory of the hotel room came rushing back. Adele visibly winced, shaking her head and taking a long sip from her cup. She swallowed, savoring the burn as the alcohol did its work.

Stupid. So stupid. Redheaded tourists—just a john and a prostitute. Adele refused to see the humor in the situation.

The killer was out there, probably preparing to strike again. She needed another clue, a directional signal. The APB had been a bust. A wig, then? Probably. Red hair was too obvious. Robert had been right. She was back to square one. Nothing to show for it.

She felt her hand squeezing tightly around the cold glass and she resisted the urge to chuck the thing across the room.

A replay of some soccer goal displayed itself on the small color TV. She watched, mesmerized by the lights, looking for some source of distraction. What next?

She stared at the glass in her hand, at the clear, trembling liquid. She was missing something. There had to be a way in; some way to break the killer's defenses. To figure out where he'd made a mistake. He was clever, but he couldn't be that clever.

"You really love the work, don't you?" John said, breaking the silence.

She glanced over and noted no change in his appearance. His voice wasn't slurred either. But, by her count, he was almost finished with his third glass.

"It's what I do," she said.

"You're obsessed. I used to know men like that. Back in, well… where I used to work. Obsession got them killed."

His voice choked for a moment, and Adele look sharply away, hoping to spare his pride. John did not seem like the sort who would appreciate sympathy or pity.

"I don't know what that life is like," she said, softly. "But I do know what it's like to lose someone."

She thought of the overgrown grass next to the bike trail. The sheltered portion of the park, hidden from eyes. She thought of cuts and intricate patterns, like some patchwork art, lacing up and down her mother's body. She thought of the mutilation, the pain, the loneliness, the terror. She thought of how helpless she'd been to do anything. And, afterward, how miserable she'd been in solving the case.

This case taunted her in the same way. There were eerie similarities between the two. Of course, Adele highly doubted they had anything to do with each other. Still, she could feel the killer, the one from ten years ago, and the one now, teasing her, mocking her, leering at her from the dark, waiting for her to fail again.

"Death comes for us all," said John. He tipped his glass in a sort of mock salute toward Adele, and downed the rest. "You think, sometimes, that if you're skilled enough, trained enough, if you put in more hours than everyone around you, that you will be able to protect them. You know? Pitiable thing. Much easier not to care. Either way, the outcome is the same."

Adele kept her gaze on the TV. She hadn't heard John speak like this before. It made him seem a little less annoying. He was now staring off at the wall, his eyes fixated on the two photographs of military men.

"I…" she began to say, not sure where the sentence would lead. She paused, though, staring now at the glass in her hand. She frowned, slightly. "You said the tox report would be on your desk tonight?"

John didn't seem to have heard her and continued to stare blankly at the wall.

"John?"

He grunted.

"The toxicology report. From the lab. You said it would be on your desk?"

"That's what I was told by the technician. He said by tonight." John shrugged. "The lab is good at their job. I don't expect there was a delay."

"Have you read it yet?"

Some of the sarcasm and scorn returned to Agent Renee's gaze. "I said it would be on my desk by tonight. I've been out with you all day. When would I have had time to read it, hmm?"

Adele was getting to her feet, though, ignoring his comment. "We need to see what it says. Now."

John shrugged, rose from his seat, and poured himself a fourth glass, nearly to the brim. Then, ignoring the concerned look on Adele's face, he sidled past her with steady movements and pushed open the door. Adele followed him back up the stairs to the seventh floor—by the fourth he'd already finished his fourth glass and yet, somehow, it didn't seem to affect his surefooted movements.

Either he knew how to hold his liquor very well, or years of training his physical body had a greater effect than that of the alcohol.

John's office was far larger than Adele's, and there were no pictures or photos here. Instead, his walls displayed posters of scantily clad models and actresses that most agencies would've considered grossly inappropriate.

John played his role well—just enough to keep people offended and at arm's length. But Adele was starting to discern more about the man.

Still, right now, the source of her curiosity wasn't the man himself, but what lay on his desk. She spotted the manila envelope the moment she stepped into the room.

John left the door ajar behind them and approached the desk with her. She beat him to the envelope and opened it with quick, deft motions.

She scanned the document a few times, hesitating, trying to place the results. It wasn't formatted the same way the FBI did, so it took her a moment, but at last she found what she was looking for.

"Dammit," she muttered. She lowered the report.

"What?" said John, sounding bored again.

Adele gnawed on the corner of her lip, shaking her head slightly from side to side, her hair swishing against her ears.

"It's the same as the FBI. They know the chemical compound; a powerful paralytic, but they don't know what it is."

John sat on the edge of his desk, massaging his forehead. "What do you mean?"

"I mean they can identify its components, but they don't know where it would be sold. It's not over-the-counter, obviously. But it's not even in medical distributions. They've not seen anything like it."

Adele tapped her fingers against the manila folder, grinding her teeth in frustration. A clear, powerful liquid. Not unlike John's alcohol.

Could the killer be making it himself? She highly doubted it. Whatever substance he used was powerful and immediately effective. To make that sort of stuff from scratch would take a level of clearance and competence the killer couldn't have possessed while simultaneously maintaining anonymity. But then where was he getting it?

John asked, "FBI didn't know?"

Adele shook her head.

"DGSI doesn't know?"

"Great rehashing."

"My point," he said with a sniff, "is that perhaps Interpol might have a clue. America and France aren't the only places with records of tox screens or chemicals."

Adele glanced to John, her eyes widening. "Do you think Interpol will help?"

John smirked. "DGSI has a great relationship with Interpol, unlike the US. Besides, their headquarters are in Lyon—it's not far from here."

Adele tapped her fingers against the folder, her excitement mounting. "Genius. If we can find out where he's getting that drug, we might be able to find out where he's from."

"I thought you said he was from France," said John, frowning.

Adele placed the folder back on the desk and turned, heading toward the door once more. She could feel exhaustion still pressing down on her like a blanket, trying to smother her. Her morning run loomed large in her mind, and she shuddered at how she would feel when the wake-up call came for her in her hotel room. Still, if John was right, and Interpol could identify the substance, it would clear things up.

"I thought he had to be, at first," said Adele. "But what if he's not from the US *or* France? What if he's a vacationer? We didn't consider that. What if he's from somewhere else, and what if that's where he's getting the substance from?"

John tried to hide it, but he looked impressed, if only for a split second.

She patted him firmly on the arm. "Good idea, grab the report, we can fax it over from my office."

John shook his head and waved at her. "No need. I have an old military buddy who works there. I'll give him a call—send a picture of the report. Give me a second."

Adele felt a surge of gratitude toward her partner, which she hadn't felt up to this point. Perhaps he wasn't as disinterested and useless as she'd first thought.

It took a couple of moments, but after a murmured phone call and some legally questionable pictures of the document, John turned back to her, clicking his phone off. "They're on it," he said.

"How good is this friend of yours?"

John shrugged. "I saved his life, twice. He saved mine three times. You could say we're close."

"No—I mean how good is he at his job? He works in the lab?"

John smirked as if sharing a secret joke with someone not in the room. "No, he works at Interpol. He wouldn't know a chemistry set from a distillery. But they'll do what he says."

John turned and exited his office with Adele, locking the door behind him. "I'll drive you back to your hotel," he said.

Adele shook her head. "Not after four drinks you won't."

He groaned and complained, but Adele stood her ground, and, at last, he relented.

"Fine, here are the keys," he said, tossing them to her. His aim was just a bit off, and the keys scraped against the wall, leaving a small gash in the paint. He groaned and began to walk down the hall, back toward the stairs.

"You need me to drop *you* off?" she called after him.

He waved a dismissive hand. "Sleep downstairs."

She pictured the small interrogation room with the couch and the TV.

It was an oasis in a place like this. But it also held a sadness. She wanted to protest, but then thought better of it. Perhaps John didn't have anyone to go to. Back in San Francisco, Agent Grant Lee often slept at the office.

Adele took the keys and hurried toward the elevator. She was sick of stairs.

The toxicology report would be the key. As smart as the killer thought he was, she was getting closer; she could feel it.

CHAPTER SIXTEEN

The cool breeze introduced itself to the night with gentle swirls, brushing against leaves and sidling along buildings down the cramped street. Enes made his way, stumbling a bit on the stone curb. In the distance, he spotted a police car pulling by, lights flashing.

The man puffed his cheeks, breathing in quiet relief. "Stupid Peter," he murmured. He was glad he'd turned down the ride from his dorm mate—five drinks in and still behind the wheel.

Still, prudent decisions did little to stave off a nip in the air, and the young man wished he'd brought a jacket. He'd left his umbrella back in Peter's car, but thankfully the rain seemed to have stopped, at least for the hour. He shivered, rubbing at his arms as he made his way along the street.

Enes glanced back in the direction of the bar and blearily surveyed the glowing orange and yellow lights emanating from the streaked windows. He could hear the raucous cries of people reacting to the football match, and, perhaps, to the magician. It hadn't been a very *good* magician. The trick with those twenty-three cards had been easy enough to spot. An engine, in statistical parlance, where no matter what, a chosen card would be revealed after a series of mathematical estimations.

The university student shook his head and pulled his shirt collar over his ears for a bit of warmth. He rubbed his arms a second time.

Normally, walking through the parks at night, especially in Paris, was an ill-advised option. But it was just so cold. He didn't want to circle the park to reach his dormitory. Besides, it wasn't like he was some defenseless child, worried about being attacked. He could take care of himself.

Enes jutted his chin forward and nearly slipped off the curb as he took another step. Quickly, with a spring, he righted himself, testing his suspect foot. He winced.

Through the tingling pain, Enes paused, teeth still clenched. Behind him, for a moment, he thought he heard footsteps.

Uttering a string of expletives, he glanced back, but spotted no one.

The row of parked cars glinted beneath the moon, winking ominously at him. Still cursing, he jerked his foot back onto the sidewalk, testing it gingerly. Then, with added respect toward the alcohol cycling his system, he began to move toward the park.

There had been a killing in Paris not long ago. It had made the news. But it was on the opposite side of the city, nearly an hour and a half away in bad traffic. He figured he would be fine.

Enes reached the park and scanned the darkness. Safety lights flanked the trails, illuminating the waving trees and the vegetation responding to the influence of the wind.

He wished he'd carried a knife. Still, it was only a short walk to the other side of the park, and then he'd be within sight of his dormitory.

Again, for a moment, he had the uncanny feeling of being watched. The back of his neck prickled, and he turned, peering across the park once more.

Still, he spotted no one. For the faintest of moments, he reconsidered the trip through the park. The place was notorious for muggings and worse, but even muggers didn't like the rain.

Enes lowered his head and began to limp through the park, keeping quiet, his arms at his side, as if presenting as small a target as possible would allow him safe passage beneath the shadowed trees.

At this point, everything seemed quieter. Living in a city like Paris—a beautiful, messy, *loud* city—one could forget what quiet was. Even at night, the sound of passing cars and the noise from the apartments or bars would taint the air. The park, though, while not entirely removed, was still spacious enough and serene enough that Enes thought he could pick up the quiet buzz of the safety lights.

Then he heard footsteps.

A chill crept up his spine, prodding at him like fingers of ice. He turned sharply and spotted someone coming rapidly toward him.

For a moment, he felt a flood of fear. He tried to break into a sprint, but found his twisted ankle wouldn't hold his weight. He stumbled and quickly righted himself, turning once more to face the oncoming person.

As the stranger in the dark drew nearer, Enes's breathing eased.

It was the magician from the bar.

The young man muttered beneath his breath, allowing a sardonic smile to twist his lips. He felt silly all of a sudden, reacting as he had. The tourist with the thick accent had been annoying, but clearly nonthreatening.

Enes shoved his hands in his pockets, refusing to return the small wave flashed in his direction from the magician.

"Excuse me," said the tourist, his accent grating.

"You shouldn't sneak up on people," Enes snapped. Some of his friends liked to slow their speech when speaking to tourists. It allowed the foreigners to understand better. But he had no such aversions to rapid cadence. Tourists, as far as he could tell, were a bane on the city. They robbed Paris of much of its identity.

The magician continued to approach, smiling genially. He had a wool cap pulled tight over his head with stray strands of reddish hair poking out from beneath the hem.

"You forgot something," said the magician.

Enes frowned. Instinctively, he checked his pants pocket, but his wallet was still there. He glanced back at the tourist and shook his head.

"Come with me," said the stranger. "I left it back over on the trail by accident."

Enes scowled now. He didn't like this tourist, and he didn't like that he'd been startled at night in the middle of the park. He glanced around and thought he spotted a couple teenagers on a bench in the distance. But they weren't looking his way.

"Go away," he said.

"Come, you forgot something. Your wallet. It's just back that way."

Enes checked his pocket again, this time pulling his wallet out enough so he could glance at it. He opened it slightly and spotted all his cards and the ten-euro note he'd expected.

He shook his head. "Not mine," he said. "Go away."

The magician had stopped, both his hands out of sight behind his back, a quizzical expression on his face. "You really are twenty-three? What's it like?"

This took Enes off guard. Now, part of the earlier fear had returned, once more circling his system. Perhaps he'd been too quick to dismiss the threat presented by this tourist. He began to turn to walk away, limping along quickly, heading toward the opposite end of the park.

He continued to glance back, refusing to leave the strange, creepy man out of sight.

"It must be nice," the magician said, following in his footsteps, moving quickly, but confidently. Like a predator stalking its prey. "Youth is wasted on the young. I'm only a bit older than you. Look at me; can you guess how old I am?"

Enes shook his head wildly, and began glancing around for a tree branch or some rock he could use as a weapon.

"I'm only forty," said the magician. "But I don't look much older than thirty-two, do I? That's what my friends say. I've had a lot of work done." He laughed in a would-be disarming manner.

The young man felt anything but put at ease. He felt a hand suddenly reach out and grab his wrist, gripping him tight and sending his heart catapulting into his throat.

Enes caught a wicked gleam in the magician's eye, followed by the flash of something metallic as the tourist's other hand came darting forward.

A needle. Enes shouted and swung a wild punch, which missed the magician, but did enough to knock off his aim. The twenty-three-year-old turned and tried to sprint away, but again his ankle failed him.

Now, the tourist snarled and lunged after him.

Enes kicked, bit, and scratched, trying to go for the magician's eyes. But the tourist held on tight; there was a pause, a quick grunt, and Enes felt a sudden sharp jab of pain in his waist. He glanced down, realizing suddenly that he somehow found himself on the ground in the dirt with the magician above him.

A horrible, pale little syringe was stabbed into his hip. The plunger had been pressed.

Enes stared, stunned. Then he tried to rise. A second passed… two… His arms felt funny.

The magician emitted a cooing sound and reached down to caress the young man's hair in tender, affectionate strokes.

Another chill crept across the college student's skin. But, just as quickly, the sensation up and down his spine faded. He tried to regain his feet, but found they wouldn't move either.

Had he broken something in the fall? Terror filled him. A childhood spent playing sports, fearful of injuring his spine, flooded his mind. But, as he tried to speak, he found his lips wouldn't move either. His arms hung limply at his side like wet strands of pasta. He could hear, see, he could feel the dirt trail pressed against his chest and cheek. He could feel the sharp pain now, returning to his side. His senses, if anything, seemed heightened. The magician was twisting his arm, evoking further pain as he tried to roll his prey over.

Enes wanted to resist, but his muscles, his tendons, his limbs didn't

102

respond. He could feel, but he couldn't move.

Now fear pumped through him, swelling his system with adrenaline. But the adrenaline only stirred him to more anxiety. The adrenaline wasn't being used; it had nowhere to go. He was helpless.

He tried to scream, and he could hear the shout, the bloodcurdling screech in his own mind, but there, beneath the moon-laced tree branches, staring up at the dark sky, he heard nothing. His lips remained numb.

He saw a glint of something metal, and then a muttered oath. The magician was shaking his head and murmuring something to himself in a language the young man didn't understand. The tourist grabbed his victim by the wrists and began to drag him roughly along the trail, toward a darker portion of the park.

"Have you ever heard of the Spade Killer?" said the magician in a low voice, grunting in between the words. "He once created artwork in a park too. Not this one, but close enough. I must thank you for leading me here. It's fate."

Enes couldn't respond. He could feel dirt getting into his shirt though, scraping against his back as he was dragged along the path. Somehow, the sensation was double. The pain in his shoulder sockets worsened, the rash along his back rubbed with dirt and gouging rocks.

He felt himself deposited unceremoniously beneath a dark tree.

Above him, he glimpsed another flash of metal. The magician was holding a small knife. He stared down at the young man, a tender expression on his face. He stooped, still smiling, and removed Enes's shirt. The college student couldn't resist; he couldn't fight.

The magician loosed a shuddering gasp, an orgasmic sound. He studied his victim's exposed chest. "Where to start?" he said. "Twenty-nine was too old. This park—it's funny we should be here. Not far from here, in another park, the Spade Killer had his first. She was forty-one, you know? Twenty-three, forty-one. The numbers both add up to five—get it? That's where he started. He stopped at thirty—imagine that? Forty-one to thirty. The authorities don't even know all of his tapestries. I picked up where he left off. You're just a youthful piece to a grand tapestry. I once had a body like yours, you know? I still do. Look."

The magician lifted his shirt, revealing a trim, pale body, and he seemed to flex his abdomen, trying to press his muscles against his skin. The vanity and the terror of the moment mixed, settling on Enes's helpless form like a smothering blanket.

"Rock hard," said the magician, slapping at his abdomen. "And the work," a long, pale finger traced his cheeks. "Most people can't tell it's professional." He reached up, prodding at his nose and beneath his eyes. He smiled down at the shirtless victim. "This is going to be fun. Please, whatever you do, don't scream." He chuckled at this. "Not that you could…"

Then the knife flashed forward, descending toward Enes's chest.

Voices exploded from behind them.

"You! What are you doing with him!"

The magician froze, a horrified look curling his features, his leering grin morphing to a wide-eyed look of fear.

Hope surged in Enes's chest. He wanted to cry out, to plead. But the words wouldn't come.

"It's nothing," said the magician, keeping his face forward, refusing to glance back toward the sound of the voices.

Enes thought of the teenagers he'd spotted on the park bench. Perhaps they had noticed him. He'd never much liked teenagers in recent years. They were notorious for leaving glass bottles around the park or vandalizing the statues.

"What are you doing with him?" came an angry voice.

"We're in love," retorted the tourist. "Leave us to our privacy!"

"Hear that?" said a second voice. "I told you not to bother them. Pervert."

The first voice, though, didn't seem convinced. "He's not moving. Look at him."

"It's fine," said the magician, still stiff, frozen, staring ahead. "Go away. It's been a long day for him. This isn't something your parents would want you to see. It's a private thing. You're being rude."

A couple of voices were snickering now, giggling to each other at the tourist's words.

Enes felt terror coming back. Hope fading. Would the teenagers leave? The magician was convincing, and had even leaned down to tenderly caress the young man's chest. The giggling voices seemed convinced.

The sound of dirt scraping beneath shoes reached Enes's ears. "Sorry, sir!" called one of the teens. "We're going."

But the first voice retorted, "I don't believe you! You have a knife in your hand. Look—it's a knife! We're calling the police!"

At this, the magician gave up all pretenses. He cursed and shoved roughly off the young man, pressing hard against his chest for leverage, and then he bolted in the opposite direction of the voices, fleeing into the trees.

"Sir, help is coming. Are you hurt?"

Two faces, then a third crowded above him. Enes spotted phones pressed against each of the teenagers' cheeks, but though he tried to react, tried to speak, he found he still couldn't move a muscle. Still, tears of sheer gratitude traced the inside of his face and tickled the underside of his chin.

CHAPTER SEVENTEEN

The gated mansion loomed over Adele, its shadows sweeping the well-maintained streets of the cul-de-sac. Her breath plumed into the night, twisting toward the sky in foggy ribbons. Adele paused for a moment, checking her watch. Exactly one hundred. The small symbol of a heart on the smartwatch pulsed next to the steady number.

The skies were still of dark countenance, and sheets of still quiet draped the streets—especially in the upper end of the Parisian suburbs.

Adele pushed a few strands of hair back behind her headband, clearing her vision. Normally, she never broke routine. But sleep had played coy with her, and Adele had needed to clear her head. Running along the empty sidewalks at night had been refreshing. She needed those lab results; but it would take time…

Time she didn't have to waste.

A light switched on in the white-bricked mansion, beaming out through a multifaceted atrium window and swaddling vanity pillars stretching the yard.

Another flood of memories bubbled up. She smiled through the gate, toward the light, sourced by the only other person she knew in France who kept horrible hours. When she'd been younger, many of her nighttime runs had ended up outside this place.

Adele winced against the glare of the light, and then flinched as the gate suddenly opened, splitting in the middle and swinging inward with the quiet, churning sound of an electric motor. Adele glanced up the long driveway toward the house.

Again, she was filled with memories of her time in France when she'd first joined the DGSI. Smiling to herself and attempting to push aside thoughts of the case, of the tox report, of the ticking time, she broke into a jog up the trail and toward the mansion.

The door swung open as she ascended the patio steps.

Robert stood in the doorway, wearing fuzzy pink slippers and a luxurious silk robe.

"Were you up?" she asked, breathing heavily between her words.

Robert lifted his right hand, his thumb pressed between the pages of a book. "Just doing some reading. Come in."

Adele hesitated, glancing over her shoulder. She had lived at Robert's mansion for a year last time she'd been in France. She didn't know why a man who'd inherited so much worked for a government agency, especially as it wasn't the kindest of jobs, nor did it facilitate interactions with the most pleasant of people. If Robert had wanted to, he didn't have to work a day in his life.

Then again, perhaps that's what he feared.

She shut the door behind her as she entered the pristine marble and tile atrium. In her estimation there were far too many statues and paintings adorning the area, not to mention the overly resplendent chandelier dangling from the ceiling. But taste was a matter of preference, and Robert's tastes were more high-minded than most.

The small man stepped quietly across the tile floors in his fuzzy slippers, leading her through a side door and into a study, entirely unperturbed by her unannounced visit. In the study, a slow fire crackled behind a grate, and a couple of red chairs faced the flames. Robert plopped down in the seat on the left.

In one corner of the room, a dusty billiards table lodged between a bookcase and a wall. The pool cues were also covered in dust and stood unused in a rack by the table.

The house was large, and though there were two chairs, Robert lived alone. He'd never been married, and had never had kids of his own. He'd been brought up in a generation where his preferences in a romantic partner had not been smiled upon.

Adele's breathing quieted and her heart rate calmed as she approached the fireplace, feeling the warm pulse of the flames as they crackled in the hearth. Robert propped his feet onto a footstool and leaned back, melting into his red chair with a look of contentment on his features.

"Sit, please," he said, waving a small hand toward the empty chair. "Couldn't sleep?"

Adele collapsed in the chair, as she'd done so many times before. She couldn't count the number of nights she'd fallen asleep like this with Robert reading a book next to her. For some reason, this memory filled her with a flood of guilt.

She ran her hands along the arm rests, twisting at a couple of metal buttons. She knew she should have done better keeping in touch with Robert. He'd seen her as a daughter, and she'd just up and left.

107

But Robert hated goodbyes, so Adele had never offered him one.

She squirmed in her seat and stared at the flames. Perhaps, predictably, Robert had a glass of red wine set on the coffee table next to him. He lifted his book, propping it with one hand, his eyes scanning the pages while his other cupped the wine glass; cradling it with three fingers, he lifted it toward his lips. "Your old room is still available," he said, softly. He glanced at her. "I know you won't be here long, but you're welcome to it. I haven't moved anything, and the cleaners have kept it tidy."

Adele paused and swallowed. She shrugged with one shoulder. Staying in a hotel was easier, but sleeping in one, especially for the first few nights, always interrupted her routine.

"There's Chocapic in the kitchen," said Robert, after a moment. He glanced over the top of his book, inclining one wispy eyebrow beneath his thick hair.

Inadvertently, Adele could feel her stomach grumble. She had packed her bowl and spoon, but she hadn't had time to go to the grocery store.

She knew that chocolate cereal filled with sugar wasn't the most nutritious breakfast for a law enforcement agent. But some habits were hard to shake.

"That's not fair," she said, "you're tempting me."

Robert pursed his lips and lowered his wineglass. His eyes twinkled, but he kept his expression serious. "I'm just offering a guest some cereal."

"Aren't you the one who gave me grief all those years for eating that, what was your word—junk?"

Robert chuckled and got to his feet, closing his book with a snapping sound. His slippers still made no noise as he padded across the room to another adjacent door. Adele followed, and they reached the large, polished kitchen with cherry wood cabinets and ebony-black countertops.

Adele went over to the cupboard where she knew Robert had kept the cereal once upon a time. She opened it, and immediately spotted three boxes of the chocolate cereal. She glanced back at her once mentor. "These look new," she said.

Robert shrugged. "I often keep some there. Throw them out if they expire, and then replace them, just in case." His voice trailed off at this, and he offered no further explanation.

She felt another surge of guilt.

Next to the cereal, a small stack of plastic bowls displayed Mickey Mouse cartoons. Identical to the bowl her mother had given her when she'd been a child, and the bowl she now carried in her suitcase.

She stared. "Where did you find those?"

Robert chuckled. "If I'm honest with you, I just asked someone to find them. Apparently this internet thing is all the rage. Can't say I'm very familiar with it myself."

Adele shook her head. "You didn't have to."

"I know."

Adele could feel Robert's eyes on her as she poured herself a bowl of cereal and then went to the fridge for the milk. A few moments passed in silence, expanding the space between the two of them, and Adele ate her first bowl of cereal in quiet.

After a moment, she lowered her spoon, tapping the metal quietly against the edge of the plastic. "I'm sorry for leaving like I did last time," she said, softly. "I just couldn't stay here. Not after what happened to—"

Robert shook his head, clearing his throat. "No need," he said, hurriedly. "You don't need to apologize. You lost your mother. I remember what that was like for me too. It's painful. Sometimes change is warranted."

Adele leaned against the cold counter, the ridge pressing into the small of her back. This room was colder than the study had been, but not unpleasant. "What was it you'd said back there in the office?" she said, clearing her throat and changing the subject. "Why are you only in an advisory role? They're not trying to bully you out of the agency, are they?"

Robert waved his hand airily. "It's the same with all these places. When I came over from homicide to work for the DGSI, they wanted me in a mentoring capacity. But now that the agency has grown, and they've recruited, they're looking to replace all the old gentlemen of yore. It is what it is. Can't cry about it."

Adele shook her head in disgust. "You've closed more cases than any of them. You're the best they have."

Robert cleared his throat and puffed out his chest, if only a little, beneath his bathrobe. He chuckled. "You flatter me. I am quite good though, aren't I?" He smirked and glanced away, intentionally striking a profile like a portrait of a gentleman detective from fiction.

Adele chuckled and flicked her spoon toward him, causing a couple of droplets of milk to land on his cheek.

The older man immediately clucked like a hen and hurried over to the sink, wiping his face and frantically checking his bathrobe. "This is silk," he said, scandalized.

Adele held up her hands in mock surrender, the spoon clutched between her pointer and middle finger. "Sorry. I got carried away. I promise not to flick milk at you anymore."

Her smile faded somewhat as Robert washed his cheek, and her own thoughts returned to the matters of the day. She could feel her phone in her pocket, pressed against her leg, silent. Far too silent. She had told John to call her the moment the tox reports came in. But it was just too broad. The technicians, even at Interpol, would have to spend days sifting through data and records, trying to locate matches of the substance in Marion's system. They needed a way to narrow down the search. But how?

"I'm serious about staying here," said Robert. "Only if you want to. But—"

"I don't know how long I'll be here for," said Adele, wincing as she did. She knew that living in this giant mansion on his own was a source of loneliness for Robert. She knew he saw her as the daughter he never had. And, unlike the Sergeant, he was one of the more affectionate people she knew—a rare quality in fathers, in her experience. Robert actually seemed to enjoy things.

And yet, it felt a great burden to be the medicine for someone's loneliness. Though, with Robert, if there was anyone deserving of her affection, it was him. He'd done her a good turn on far more than one occasion. Still, she was in France to do a job, not to rekindle old friendships...

"Robert," she said, softly, "remember that case, three years ago, the one you emailed me about?"

Her old mentor frowned, scratching at his jaw. "Which one?"

"The one with that museum, where they tried to spend the night in the bathroom stalls to avoid the security cameras."

"Ah, yes. A bomb attack. I remember. Foiled."

Adele nodded. "You said something interesting about that case. I—I wanted to ask you about it, but it was hard to communicate what I meant over an email."

A lesser man might have said something like, "Phones work too,"

110

or, "My door is always open." But while Robert definitely felt the hurt that could have spurred such words—she could see it in his eyes—he didn't say it. Instead, he just watched her, a kind look on his face. "Ah, yes. I think I remember. It was a strange thing in an art museum."

"It wasn't the museum so much, but what you said about the man planning to kill the curator, and plant that bomb. He was going to kill fifty people if it had worked, maybe more. A monster. But you've never seen those people like that, have you?"

Robert studied her a bit and rubbed his finger across the spine of the book that he still held closed.

"What do you mean?"

Adele sighed, thinking of her time back stateside. Thinking of hunting down this killer, of what had been done to Marion, what had been done to her mother. "You have a compassion for these killers, too. Don't you?"

Robert hesitated, staring at the plastic bowl in Adele's hand. He shifted against the cherry wood cabinet, and then winced and quickly jerked away lest he stain his expensive bathrobe. He stood, straight postured, chin high, but eyes thoughtful. "I remember," he said, his voice fading in thought. "I believe I do. I know how to use email; there is that. Perhaps the internet isn't so bad after all. But I remember because it was a strange thing to happen in a museum. There were some paintings there that sold for hundreds of millions before being donated. Beautiful paintings. Statues and art encapsulating human history." He trailed off, a vacant look in his eyes as he stared through the skylight into the dark skies above.

Adele said, "I've never appreciated art that much, but what little appreciation I have comes from how you talk about it."

Robert didn't seem to hear her, and he continued, leaving where he left off as if he hadn't even stopped. "That museum held so much beauty, but when I hear about plans to kill people, be it the victim or the killer, all I feel is sadness." He shook his head. "It's easy to think of people as monsters. And perhaps some of them are. But they didn't have to be. It's like a vandalized *Mona Lisa*. It's like seeing Notre Dame burning. Human beings are far more valuable than any piece of art. We are walking, breathing, thinking, loving, hoping masterpieces who flit about on the surface of this world. Think about how large the universe is. Each of us could have had our own planet, alone, standing in solitude as the rarest of things. Think about how diamonds are

111

treated, as if they are the most valuable thing in the world. People guard them jealously. We build safes and hire security and carry guns to protect them. Imagine if people thought of others, other humans, with the same sense of value…"

Adele tried to track what he was saying, but whenever he started to philosophize it oftentimes went over her head. It wasn't that she couldn't understand, but more so that she didn't think in such terms. Sometimes he would quote famous authors or wax poetic, and while there was a beauty to it, Adele was far more of a realist. Still, she held her silence and listened, waiting.

"The thing is," Robert said, softly, "these killers could have been so much more. And the people they kill are so valuable. It's like seeing a book burning or a painting destroyed for the sake of destruction. It saddens me." He shrugged. "I don't know if that answers your question." His eyes seemed to refocus, and he noticed her expression. "I'm sorry; I didn't mean to prattle on like that."

But Adele quickly shook her head. "No; that's beautiful. I was just thinking about something myself."

"Well, you're welcome to stay here as long as you want. But I do need to get some sleep. I've managed to whittle it down to only three to four hours a night." He chuckled and shrugged.

"Thank you, but I should probably—"

Before she could finish, the phone in her pocket started to vibrate. Adele frowned and whipped out her device, pressing it to her ear. "Yes?" Adele listened, her eyes widening with each passing moment. "Tonight? In the park? You're sure it was him?"

Another pause.

"I'll be right there."

Adele turned and began hurrying rapidly away from the kitchen and through the study, back toward the atrium. "What is it?" Robert called after her.

"The killer," she shouted over her shoulder, pausing only for a moment. "He attacked someone in the park, and they survived. I need to get back to the hotel. I'll talk to you later; have a good night!"

Adele sprinted out the front of the mansion and ran breakneck down the street, hurrying back in the direction of her hotel where she'd parked the car.

CHAPTER EIGHTEEN

Her wheels jumped the curb, jolting Adele forward in her seat and causing her shoulder to slam into the edge of the steering wheel. She cursed, wishing she'd taken the time to buckle; but without correcting the parking, Adele flung open the borrowed car's door and sprinted between the two gendarmerie vehicles flanking the entry of the park with flashing lights.

In the distance, she could see men milling about beneath the trees, guns saddled against their shoulders. The gendarmerie were technically a military branch, but they would often serve in keeping order among the citizenry.

Elsewhere, she spotted regular police officers searching through the park, flashlights at the ready, leashed hounds with black and brown fur leading the way.

The nighttime park, normally a quiet affair, echoed with barking, shouting, and urgent cries.

Adele frantically scanned the vehicles in front of the park, and she spotted the ambulance.

She sprinted toward the vehicle and managed to glimpse a limp foot on a stretcher just as the back door slammed shut with a metallic *clang!*

"I need to speak with him!" she shouted, hurrying over to the ambulance. She flashed her temporary DGSI credentials and brushed past one of the gendarmerie who reached out a hand to intercept her.

"Who's in charge here?" Adele demanded, avoiding the insistent hand. "I need to speak with the victim!"

Before she could reach the ambulance, though, two police officers inserted themselves between her and the vehicle. One of them glared at her, his eyes stony beneath his blue and black hat. The other one held out both hands in a pleading gesture, and kept repeating, "You can't; he's unconscious. You can't."

Adele thought to push past the two of them, but then reconsidered and hesitated. "Are you in charge?" she asked, directing the question toward the scowling man.

He gave a brief shake of his head. "The captain is over there," he said, curtly.

Adele glanced to where he was pointing, and spotted a group of officers milling around near a park bench upon which sat four kids. They couldn't have much older than fourteen, and a couple of the smaller ones swung their legs over the edge of the bench. All of them shared the same nervous fidgeting gestures and sidelong glances.

"You're sure he's unconscious?" she demanded.

The pleading officer responded before the scowling one could reply. "He hasn't been able to say a word. He responds to light, he's alive, but we have to get to the hospital, now. We think he was drugged."

Adele cursed, running a hand through her hair. With a sudden jolt of embarrassment, she realized she was still wearing her sweaty jogging headband. Great. So much for first impressions.

Reluctantly, she dragged herself away from the ambulance. If the victim couldn't speak, then he wouldn't be much use to her anyway. No doubt the killer had dosed him with the same substance he'd used on the other victims. But how had this one survived?

She spotted John talking to a gendarmerie near a cluster of trees in a particularly dark section of the park. But she ignored her partner for the moment and headed directly toward the kids sitting on the bench.

As she went striding beneath the trees, the park seemed cold all of a sudden, or perhaps stepping on the dirt trail only reminded her of the frigidity of another night in another park. There was a reason she didn't take her morning runs within spitting distance of a park—not even stateside. She shifted past two officers with another flash of her credentials, and then hurried over to the bench.

"You interviewed them yet?" she asked, glancing toward the female officer standing by the kids. She could see now that all were teenagers: three boys and a girl. All of them stared wide-eyed at her. Two of them had the freckles and upturned noses suggesting they were brothers; one of them had darker skin, and the fourth, the girl, looked a little bit like Marion.

"Never mind," Adele said, cutting off the officer's response. "Were you here? Did you see what happened?"

The teens glanced uncomfortably from her to the officer next to them. The police officer gave a small nod and gestured encouragingly for them to answer the questions.

The girl shot a look at the others, then spoke first. "Furkan saw them first," she said, her voice lower and raspier than Adele had expected. "We thought they were lovers."

The freckle-faced boy on the far end of the bench giggled, but then quickly disguised the sound as a cough.

"We went to investigate," said the one who Adele assumed was Furkan. He was taller than the others and had a baby face. "Called out at them. Something was off."

"Looked like he was going to stab the guy on the ground," said the girl. "We thought he was mugging him. Furkan here was mugged last week. They took his watch."

The baby-faced, dark-skinned boy nodded in confirmation.

Now they seemed less nervous all of a sudden. Adele's undivided attention propelled them forward. They still fidgeted and shared glances with each other, as kids only know how, but the information continued, and Adele slowly pieced together what the kids had seen.

"What did he look like?" she said once they'd finished recounting the events.

"He was just stiff," said the girl, "lying on the ground, like a plank of wood."

"I—no, not the victim, the attacker. Did he have red hair?"

Two of the children shrugged simultaneously. "The baby-faced boy said, "He was wearing a hat. A big jacket, too."

Adele almost growled in frustration. "Was he tall? Short?"

Again, the children shrugged.

Adele suppressed the emotions swirling through her. She wasn't an amateur. Frustration was part of the game. She'd been doing this long enough to know how to be a professional even when things didn't turn out how she wanted. She inhaled, counting quietly in her head, then exhaled and counted for a longer portion of time. Then she said, "You were all very brave; you saved someone's life tonight. I hope you know that…"

"Wait," said the girl, "there was one thing."

Adele paused, listening.

"He spoke funny."

Adele frowned.

At this, the other children all nodded, their heads bobbing as one. "It's true," said the baby-faced boy. "My parents speak with an accent. But his accent was even stranger."

The other children nodded again. The one on the end began muttering beneath his breath, and sent his assumed brother sitting next to him into a fit of giggles. Adele listened for a moment, and her eyes narrowed sharply. "What did you say?" she said, turning on the boy at the end.

He immediately stiffened, his hands clutched tightly in his lap, his legs going rigid against the wooden bench.

Adele amended her tone, struggling to stay calm. "No, I'm sorry, you're not in trouble. But what were you just saying?"

The boy hesitatingly glanced at his friends, then up at Adele. "I was just joking; I'm sorry."

"No, I heard. You were mimicking his accent. Please, could you do it again?"

Hesitantly, the boy cleared his throat, then blushed and shook his head.

"He's embarrassed," said the girl, cheerfully.

The other children giggled except for the one under scrutiny, who scowled at his hands.

Adele hurried over and dropped to a knee in front of the boy. "It's all right, I promise you're not in trouble. You were incredibly heroic tonight. All of you. But please, this man has hurt people and I need to stop him. I need you to tell me what he sounded like."

The boy didn't look at his friends this time, mustering the sort of courage that required solitude, but then, responding to the earnest tone in Adele's voice, he, in a very quiet way, repeated the phrase he'd said to his friend.

"You're sure he said it like that?" said Adele. "With the aspirated stop?"

The boy looked at her, his nose wrinkling in confusion.

Adele shook her head. "Never mind. I mean with that *s* instead of the *t*. He mispronounced the word?"

The boy nodded. And, hesitantly, the others also nodded in confirmation.

Adele had the freckled boy repeat the phrase in French a couple more times, just to be sure, and each time he mimicked the voice of the killer, the elation in her chest only grew.

It's a private thing. You're being rude. A simple enough phrase. But a very telling pronunciation.

"Thank you," she said, quickly. "Thank you very much. I owe you."

Then she turned sharply on her heel and jogged over to where John was. Her heart thrummed in her chest, and she could practically hear

116

her blood sluicing through her ears.

"Renee," she snapped, gaining the attention of the tall agent. He glanced over the head of the smaller gendarmerie in front of him and raised an eyebrow. His eyes were bloodshot, and his cheeks puffy, but Adele didn't have time to worry about her partner's drinking habits. "You need to call that friend of yours at the lab."

John frowned, wincing against the loud sounds in the park. "I didn't know you were good with children. Have some of your own?" He raised an eyebrow.

Adele ignored the question. "You friend at the lab—*call him*."

"Call him? It will take some time, like I said. There won't be results."

"No, I know. But I have a way for him to narrow it down. It should speed things up a ton." Adele motor-mouthed her way through the sentence, propelled by her own excitement, her fingers tapping against her thigh in impatient spurts.

"How?" said John.

"The accent," Adele said, trying to keep her calm.

"I don't understand? What accent?"

"I spoke to the kids, and they heard his accent! You know how kids are, like parrots, they can mimic anything back. Well, I was insecure about how I spoke when I was younger, when I first moved to France. My mother was kind enough to hire someone to help me. They did strange tricks, even including chocolate chips placed on the tip of my tongue to help me learn how to stretch my consonants. But, most importantly, I learned about aspirated stops."

John was staring at her now like she was crazy, but she pressed on. "The attacker clipped his aspirated stops. He dropped the 's' instead of a 't.'"

"I really don't—"

"He's German!" Adele cried. "It's dialectical. He's not American. He's not French. He's *German*. Call your lab tech, tell him to narrow down the tox reports based on German companies, both private and public. Understand?"

John frowned, shaking his head. "You can't know for sure based on the mimicking of a child—"

But Adele shook her head again. "I'm sure. I feel it. The pronunciation is like a fingerprint to me; I've heard the differences in language my whole life. I know he's German. Just do it. Please."

Renee sighed, but then shrugged and reached for his pocket, pulling his phone out. He pressed it to his ear and then waited, peering out into the park, toward the dark trees and leaves, along the abandoned trail with scattered dust.

Adele also turned, glancing back toward the children, her eyes settling on the girl. She did look quite a bit like Marion.

"…Yes. German companies," John was saying behind her in a murmur.

Adele continued staring out into the park, allowing herself the faintest of smiles.

They had him now.

CHAPTER NINETEEN

Gasping, hands jammed into his jacket pockets, cap pulled low over his forehead, the man stumbled through the streets. He resisted the urge to curse with every shuffling step. He had to stay calm, stay collected. He could already hear the sirens in the distance, tolling like wedding bells announcing his marriage. But he was a runaway bride. They were here for him, but they wouldn't catch him.

The tourist forced his breathing to calm, willing his pounding chest to still. He rounded a corner, curling past a shuttered newsstand and ducking beneath one of the safety lights, keeping his head low.

He bumped into someone and nearly lashed out with his knife. managed to glance up just in time. He noticed the blue and black uniforms of gendarmerie.

Immediately, he smiled politely, suppressing the tingle of excitement creeping up his spine. Fear was not for him. Fear was for others. No, he was in control.

He tried not to look at their rifles, nor did he glance past them toward the flashing sirens of their parked vehicles.

"Good evening," he said, politely, and then continued on his way, not moving too quickly nor too slowly.

He could feel their eyes boring a hole into his back. Any moment now, they would call out after him. He was sure. But he was smarter than them. So instead, he turned, facing the officers.

As he suspected, one of them had a hand half-raised, his mouth open in preparation to cry out in the nighttime street. But at the sudden about-face, the gendarmerie frowned.

The tourist pretended he hadn't noticed, and he approached the officers once more. A criminal fled the scene of a crime, but an innocent civilian would be curious. Because a citizen who had nothing to do with the crime would want assurance of safety. They would want to know the comings and goings in their city. Why the flashing lights, why the sirens at night?

The man was not a stupid criminal. He wasn't a criminal at all, but the evolution of a species.

He adopted a grin, but then notched it down and kept his expression nervous. "What's going on? Not another terrorist attack, is it?" He knew his accent would come across, but it didn't matter. France was filled with tourists. The gendarmerie glanced at each other and eyed him up and down, likely searching for a weapon.

But he kept his arms at his side, loose, his hands now facing open-palm toward the officers.

Inwardly, his emotions raged, but he couldn't allow them control. The Spade Killer hadn't been caught—it would be a pitiable testament to his hero to fail where the savant had succeeded.

"Where are you going?" one of the officers snapped.

"Back to my hotel. Is everything okay?"

The other glanced at his partner, and they whispered to each other, then addressed him again. "Hurry back to your room, you don't want to be out at night. Go!"

"But is everything okay?" he said, selling it with a final flourish.

"We can't discuss it. You need to leave, now!"

The man held up his hands in mock surrender and then turned, hurrying away again. His neck prickled, but he didn't look back. He could feel the tension in the air; he could taste the fear over the city.

Now was time to go home. His feet thumped into the sidewalk in long, angry strides. He clenched his fists, then paused for a moment beneath a light post, listening vaguely before turning the corner.

The gendarmerie were whispering again, but taking less care to lower their voices.

"Did they find the man?" said one of the officers. There was a click, followed by the buzzing sound of a radio.

The static continued for a second. Then a replying, fuzzy voice said, "Agent Sharp is at the scene. She thinks she has an idea. We don't know; keep an eye out."

The man continued moving. Any moment, they might call after him. He had to get away. He turned down a side street, then another street.

The fuzzy radio words haunted him with each step.

He cut through a couple of alleys between tall, looming red brick buildings. His hotel wasn't far, but he'd have to get back to the bar where he parked his car.

He was sure he'd make it, though. They wouldn't find him. Not now. He had to head home. He wasn't done yet in France, but his vacation had been cut short. He would have to return again some other time.

The name, though...

He knew that name.

The man ground his teeth, scowling into the black as he moved through the city streets back toward the bar. Agent Sharp. The FBI agent had been called Sharp, too. The same agent who'd interviewed his host family back in the US. The one who'd been hounding him for months now. Agent Sharp.

The name fueled him forward, out into the night, and away from the crime scene.

CHAPTER TWENTY

"Christ, American Princess, you were right. I can't believe you were right."

Adele's foot tapped a tattoo into the floor outside Executive Foucault's office. Her thumbs scraped back and forth on the rigid edge of the wooden armrests in the chair facing the DGSI executive's glass door. Through the opaque glass, lined with long seams of partitions, Adele could just barely make out the shape of the executive leaning against his desk.

Beyond that, she couldn't see anything. But she knew he was on the phone. Most of the DGSI had been on the phone for the last two hours, after the expedited lab results had come in.

John reclined next to her, the chair serving far too small a fixture for his lanky frame. His long legs extended across the hall, his toes jutting up against the freshly painted wall, and his back hunched uncomfortably in the chair.

"How did you know?" he said. Despite his uncomfortable position, he was now looking at her, casting a sidelong glance down his long Roman nose. He had worn a turtleneck today, which disguised the burn mark across his neck. Adele hadn't seen him wear anything to disguise the scars before, and vaguely, she wondered what had changed.

"I told you to stop calling me that," she said.

John frowned, confused, and then he turned back to face the glass door. "Would you prefer American Queen?"

"I prefer Adele. Or Agent Sharp. Or, if you'd really like, you could call me ma'am."

John snorted.

"But I suppose I can let this one pass," Adele continued. "You were right about your friend at Interpol. They are quick."

John nodded, shifting uncomfortably again and causing the chair to creak precariously beneath him. "You really do have an ear for accents. A German killer in America and France." John reached across the small coffee table next to him and pulled the manila folder they'd been copied in on, flipping it open to examine the contents once more. Adele had memorized the thing already when it had first arrived two hours ago—they'd gone directly to Executive Foucault with the results.

In the opposite room, Adele could still hear the chatter of urgent voices in the office.

Every train station, bus stop, airport, and border would be watched for red-haired German citizens trying to flee the country.

But it was too late.

She knew it in her bones. He had been one step ahead the entire time. Last time, in the US, when she'd gotten close, he had fled the next day.

After the debacle the previous night, with his victim escaping, surviving, there was no way he would have stayed in the country. He'd had ample time to get out. He wouldn't have waited.

Too late. Always just a moment too late…

Adele shook her head firmly. "What's taking them so long?"

John shrugged, scanning the folder once more. "You know how the BKA is," he said. "Germans are official folk. Not like your FBI. Not like DGSI either. They have more red tape than both our agencies combined. Especially with Interpol presiding."

Adele shook her head. "You'd think with Interpol's help we could get something done."

John shrugged. "It's always been difficult tracking criminals across borders." He sighed, puffing out his chest. "I doubt that'll change now."

Adele clenched her teeth. "But he's killed in the US and France. For all we know he's killed in Germany too. Everyone should want him caught."

John shoved the manila folder beneath her nose, flapping it up and down and causing the sides to wiggle like butterfly wings. "He's not identified. All we know is that the substance in the victim's veins is from Lion Pharmaceutical in Hamburg."

"Yes," said Adele, keeping her tone patient. "But it was an unreleased substance. It didn't meet approval standards." Adele kept her gaze fixed on Foucault's door. "Which means the only people with access to it would be working *for* the pharmaceutical company. That narrows down our suspects by a lot. How many of them do you think travel frequently to the US and France? How many of them do you think have red hair?"

"Could be a wig," said John. "Think of that?"

Adele hesitated. She had thought of that. But Robert had seemed so

123

confident in his deduction that the man wouldn't have displayed red hair if it hadn't naturally been his. A man of vanity, clinging onto his youth. That had been Robert's prescription. And her old mentor was rarely wrong. Still, maybe he had lost a step. Time passed; he had aged. Maybe it was a wig.

Secretly, Adele hoped it wasn't. Not only would red hair make it easier to track the killer down, but it would mean that Robert was right. That he was still one of the best investigators in France.

"One step at a time," said John. "I don't want to go to Germany anyway. What do the Germans have that we don't in France?"

Adele rolled her eyes. This time she did look over at her tall, hunched partner. "We're not going on a vacation. We need to find a killer; is that a good enough reason to take a sabbatical from your beloved Paris?"

John scratched his jaw, and shrugged with one shoulder. "Not really."

Adele would've continued harassing her teammate in part good humor and part exasperation, but the glass door to Foucault's office opened, nearly whacking John's extended legs.

Adele's partner jerked his feet back, and the door scraped across the thin carpet, revealing an older woman with pursed lips and intelligent eyes.

"The Interpol correspondent," John whispered to Adele.

"I know; I was here before you."

This time John rolled his eyes.

Behind the correspondent from Interpol, the executive was on the phone, the receiver pressed to his ear. He yammered away in accented English, but then his eyes flicked toward the open door, and he turned, shielding his mouth and lowering his voice.

The door shut, and the Interpol correspondent stepped over John's extended legs.

John made no move to pull back a second time, allowing the neatly dressed older woman to primly step over him one leg at a time.

Adele jammed her elbow into her partner's shoulder, but received only a grunt for her efforts. Renee kept his legs out, smirking after the lady from Interpol.

This wasn't John's lab friend. Rather, the woman had been sent to help coordinate between the BKA and the DGSI, serving essentially as moderator, a babysitter between the intelligence agencies of France and

Germany.

"Well?" Adele called after the woman as she continued down the hall. The correspondent paused and glanced back.

"Do we have permission to enter Germany?" Adele called again, this time pushing off her chair and standing up. She moved after the agent and kicked John's leg until he pulled it out of the way.

The Interpol agent glanced from Adele to John's slouched form and pursed her lips again. Her silver curls were pressed tight to her head by the stems of thick glasses. She was a larger woman, but with a pleasant face. Her intelligent eyes twinkled behind her glasses, and she said, in a careful, precise tone, "I think it is best if you speak with the executive. He'll fill you in on the details."

Agent Renee harrumphed and slid lower in his seat, like a child outside the principal's office.

Adele, though, took another few steps up the hall, her expression pleading. "We can't wait," she said. "Each moment that passes is another moment where he could escape. He could try to change his identity. He could *leave* Germany. We may not be able to find him if we don't hurry." Adele realized her voice was rising, and so she took a quick breath, steadying herself before finishing, in an even tone, "For now, he doesn't know we found the source of his paralytic."

The Interpol correspondent raised a calming hand. "I'm not in charge of DGSI employees. Like I said, it's best to speak with the executive. He should be off the phone soon. Good day."

The correspondent nodded and then turned, hurrying back up the hall and turning a corner out of sight.

Adele stared after the woman, shaking her head side to side. "Well, that was cryptic as hell. Do you think Germany's going to play nice?" She glanced over at John.

Agent Renee had his eyes closed, his head tilted back against the wall, and he looked like he was trying to sleep.

She growled and resisted the urge to kick him again. Instead, Adele stomped back to her seat and flopped into the chair. It also creaked as John's had under the sudden jolt of her weight. Vaguely, Adele wondered if perhaps she should stop eating so much cereal. She reached out and patted her stomach, but determined if she was still in healthy enough shape to chase men down stairwells and tackle them, then she was allowed the occasional bowl of Chocapic.

"Could you stop that? It's annoying."

John was glaring at her fingers with one open eye and the other one still shut. Adele glanced down and realize she'd been tapping a rhythm against the wooden chair.

She flung up her hands in mock surrender and glared at the opaque glass of Foucault's door once more, and then surged back to her feet. "If he asks, I'm in Robert's office."

John shrugged and closed his eyes again.

Adele hurried down a couple of flights of stairs and then moved along a stretch of hall, brushing past only one other man moving quickly in the opposite direction.

Adele had left Robert's mansion in a rush the previous day. His offers of lodging were still fresh in her mind. It would be nicer than a hotel to stay in the old room she'd occupied for a year back when she first joined the DGSI. But then again, she wasn't going to be in France for long.

She paused at the thought. She thought of Agent Renee, of her trip to the park, of the smell of the river and Robert's kindness. It wasn't as bad as she remembered. The pain of losing her mother had faded somewhat. The double pain of failing to capture her mother's killer was still fresh in a way, but it too had lessened. Adele needed time to think, and space to do it. John was distracting. It was like working with a monkey. A very dangerous, deadly monkey in the right circumstances.

The Commandos Marine were renowned for their operations throughout Europe and the Middle East. But from an investigative perspective, John seemed to have the subtlety of a jackhammer.

Adele reached Robert's door and tapped on the glass. There was a pause, then a voice called, "Come in!"

Adele pushed into her old mentor's office. It was as sparse as when she'd first visited, but he was no longer in a bathrobe and slippers, and wore his neat, pressed suit where he sat behind his large desk, staring with a frown at a computer screen.

It had only been eight hours since she'd left him in his house, but he looked well rested, carrying no bags under his eyes.

For her part, Adele had only managed two hours of sleep in the parking lot, waiting for the expedited tox report to come in. She could feel exhaustion taking its toll and envied Robert's ability to get by on such little rest.

He looked cheerfully up at her and flashed a smile. He pushed back from the desk, folding his hands in his lap and adjusting his posture so he sat straight-backed in his custom leather chair. "I hear there's good news."

She nodded and leaned against the doorjamb, glancing out the window of her mentor's office toward the city beyond. "I think we have a shot of getting him this time. We just have to hurry."

Robert nodded and scratched at his wrist. "I…" he began, but trailed off.

A moment of silence fell over the room as both of them seemed lost in their thoughts. Robert always considered his words carefully before he spoke. This time, it took nearly another minute before he opened his mouth. "It wasn't fair of me to offer you your old room back," he said, softly. "I apologize."

Adele looked up, jolted, for a moment, from her worries about the case, Executive Foucault's phone calls, and Germany's compliance.

"Excuse me?" she said.

"I know it wasn't fair of me. I apologize."

Adele frowned, but then corrected her expression lest her mentor think it was directed at him. "What do you mean? There isn't anything unfair. It was very kind of you."

But Robert held up a quieting hand, and waited for her to dwindle into silence. "That's accommodating of you to say. But I think we both know that your heart isn't in France. And it is true that my house feels empty at times, but that was my choice; a choice I made years ago."

"It's not a choice you still have to make," Adele said quietly with a shrug. It was a conversation she'd tried to have with him before, and one he'd masterfully avoided on many occasions.

"Perhaps not. But either way, it isn't fair of me to put you in that position. I hope you know that I do care for you. Greatly. And I want to see you succeed. There are very few agents that I've worked with who are as talented as you. You're more relentless than any of them. And more determined than even I was at your age."

Adele smiled at this, but then fidgeted. She thought of her father, and how little chance she'd had to become accustomed to kind words, the thought propelling her into a flush of gratitude toward Robert.

"I care about you too," she said, glancing out the window again. "You've been like a father to me; I hope you know that. And my heart may not be in France, but a piece of it is. I don't know quite where I belong. I hope to figure that out. You'd think in my thirties I would have some idea."

Robert chuckled at this, though, and shook his head. "It doesn't get any better toward the end of sixty either. Trust me."

Adele chuckled. She hesitated, then said, "If it's all right with you, I would like to stay in my old room instead of that cold hotel. I don't know how long I'll be in France. And if the phone call with Executive Foucault goes well, Germany will be allowing us temporary jurisdiction as soon as possible. But when I return, I might have to spend a couple of nights in France still. It would be nice to have a home."

Robert watched her for a moment, his face expressionless. For a moment, Adele wasn't sure if she'd offended him somehow. But then she spotted the moistness in his eyes, and his right hand trembling slightly where it was tucked over his left.

"I would very much like that," he said, clearing his throat. "There are a couple of books that I think you might like. I'll have them placed in your room before you get there. Should I have someone retrieve your things?"

Adele shrugged. "If you'd like. It's only really a suitcase. In fact, I haven't even opened it yet, except for a change of clothes."

Robert grinned, revealing his two missing teeth; his gap-toothed smile clashing with the rest of his immaculately maintained appearance. Adele allowed herself a quiet chuckle, remembering the many farfetched stories her mentor told about how he lost his teeth.

"Well," said Robert, "I'll—" But before he could finish his sentence, Adele felt a hand grip her shoulder.

She jolted and whirled sharply around, resisting the urge to strike out with the flat of her palm to distance herself from an attacker. Agent Renee was staring down at her, his eyes holding a mirth that Adele couldn't quite place. But it was similar to the look he'd carried when he'd teased her about inside information pertaining to Agent Paige.

"What?" Adele snapped.

"Foucault's off the phone. He sorted it with the BKA."

Adele's eyes widened. "Sorted it? What do you mean?"

John cleared his throat, and his expression soured. "I mean we're headed to Germany. We don't have time to pack bags. Anything we need we can buy there. But BKA is willing to work with us on this temporarily. They want to catch the guy too."

John turned and began stalking up the hall, not waiting for Adele to fall into step.

128

For a moment she stood in the doorway, staring after a partner, her mouth wide. An FBI agent partnered with a DGSI operative, heading to Germany to work with the BKA, all under the supervision of Interpol. It was unheard of.

Adele shook her head in mild shock. The killer wouldn't escape. Not this time. They were going to catch him. She knew it. They had to.

At the thought, a strange sensation came over her, like shivering after being doused with ice water. She frowned at the ominous feeling, unsure of its origin for the moment. Somehow, though, as the dreadful feeling spread, she knew that what came next wouldn't be easy. The killer was not the sort to go down lightly. He was arrogant and dangerous; a deadly man. She would have to do her best to make sure no one else was hurt in his apprehension.

Adele glanced back over her shoulder toward Robert, raising an eyebrow. "You still think he has red hair?" she said.

Robert paused, thought, then nodded. "I'm confident he does. I don't think it's a wig. But I think you shouldn't underestimate this man. He's confident and has been leading the chase for a while now. He won't go down easy. And if he can, he's going to take bodies with him."

Adele pursed her lips. "I think you're right. See you in a few days, hopefully."

Robert gave a small rolling finger wave, but he was no longer smiling as he watched her exit the door and hurry after John, racing down the hall to catch up with his long strides.

CHAPTER TWENTY ONE

So many flights in so few days. Adele could feel the exhaustion weighing on her like sandbags strapped to her limbs. Still, as she settled in the limousine, with Agent Renee against the other window, she glanced toward the young woman seated across from them.

Their German attaché couldn't have been older than twenty. She had a nervous, excited energy about her as she surveyed the two agents settling in the back seat of the limousine. If the age of their BKA connection didn't suggest the German authorities were sending a message, then the provided vehicle certainly did. Adele had never been picked up by a limousine in her life.

A twenty-year-old tour guide in a gauche limousine—the BKA were having a go and Adele wasn't amused.

Through the window, Adele spotted passengers streaming through sliding glass doors toward waiting vehicles or toward the taxis lining the gates. She heard the sound of jet engines rumbling the sky above and could smell gasoline and stale smoke on the air, settling in the still cabin.

Adele moved her right hand between her leg and the door, so the others couldn't see, and she pinched herself, trying to propel the pain through her system to jolt herself awake. She needed caffeine. They'd served coffee on the plane, though, and it had done little to revive her.

"You're the BKA correspondent?" said John, eyeing the young attaché.

The German shifted uncomfortably and adjusted in her seat. "Yes," she answered in nearly flawless English. "My name is Beatrice Marshall. You may call me Agent Marshall." She inhaled and then, in a rehearsed fashion, declared, "The BKA is happy to work with the FBI and the DGSI, but where you go, I'm required to go—understand?"

Adele smiled at the young woman, remembering her first year working for the DGSI fresh out of college.

Agent Marshall tapped politely on the window divider between them and the driver. "Please take us to Lion Pharmaceutical now," she said.

"That's it?" Adele asked, frowning. "We don't need to shake hands with some supervisors or make nice with your boss?"

Agent Marshall shook her head primly, crossing her legs and then adjusting her position to face Adele with an uncomfortable sort of pivot. John was watching her, a small smile curling his lips, like a lion who'd spotted a gazelle.

Adele glanced at her partner and rolled her eyes. "We're heading directly to the pharmaceutical company?"

"Is that a problem?" replied the young agent.

"No, of course not."

Inwardly, Adele had hoped she would've had time to at least get some sleep. She'd managed to snatch about a half hour of rest on the plane, but scrunched up in business class next to John, with worries and fears cycling through her mind, had made true slumber an impossibility.

Adele settled into the back of the car, listening to the chugging engine and the spinning wheels as the limousine left the airport.

Germany. It wasn't as jarring to travel from France to Germany. It was only a couple hour flight at best. The transition from US to Europe was a far different kettle of fish as most of the travel was over an open ocean. Now, though, Adele felt a strange sense of nostalgia descending on her. Germany had been her home until she'd turned twelve. Her father still lived here... perhaps a visit was in order.

She thought of Robert back in France, of his offer for her to reclaim her old room. It would be nice, at least, to swim in the indoor pool after her run. Her trip to France was taking unexpected turns.

Perhaps none more unexpected than the latest twist. It seemed like the start to a joke. A BKA officer, a DGSI operative, and an FBI agent all walk into a bar...

Then what? Whatever the punchline was, Adele desperately hoped it involved a red-haired killer.

The limousine carried them through the city, slicing through traffic. They exited the city on a gray highway not long after, pulling out into the suburbs, then eventually a series of fields on the outskirts of Hamburg.

Lion Pharmaceutical wasn't too far from the airport, but it would still take some time.

John was going over the manila folder as they traveled, and every so often, making eyes toward their young German babysitter. Though the young agent mostly fixed her gaze ahead, facing the backseat from the middle, every so often, she would look up to meet Renee's gaze and smile. Her legs were still crossed at least.

Adele suppressed the urge to vomit and closed her eyes, trying to focusing on her breathing and steady her nerves. Tired as she was, she couldn't allow it to slow her thoughts. Her target was in her crosshairs… now it was only a matter of time.

Finally, after nearly an hour, the limousine pulled into a side road that led toward a large metal fence topped with barbed wire.

Adele perked up, peering through the tinted windows toward a large structure in the distance. A giant building of glass and curved windows centered the stretch of fence. The building looked like an aquarium from this distance, except for the rows of barbed wire between the road and the compound.

A couple of men armed with rifles stood outside the gate, holding up halting hands toward the car.

Marshall nodded politely through the window and leaned out, extending identification. "I'm here with the BKA," she rattled off in German. "My supervisor should've called ahead."

John wrinkled his nose at the foreign language, but Adele listened intently.

Marshall continued, "These are agents Renee and Sharp from the DGSI and FBI. They're under my supervision; there shouldn't be any problems."

A few exchanges later, following a phone call from the gate, the guards stepped aside, and the gate split, rolling on a metal track and allowing them entrance into the parking lot.

The driver guided the limousine further into the compound and pulled up outside the curb closest to the front doors.

Lion Pharmaceutical was displayed in large golden block letters above the giant glass doors. On each of the front windows, a crisp design of a white lion head stenciled the glass.

John exited the vehicle first, pushing open the back door and swinging his long legs out onto the curb. He extended a hand, gallantly offering his arm toward Agent Marshall. Adele rolled her eyes again as the young German operative accepted the French man's arm and climbed out from the back of the limousine. Adele followed.

She glanced back at the long, black vehicle with the tinted windows. She'd never been one for the German sense of humor. This, though a small one, was a jab in their direction. Sending a young agent in a limousine was the German government's way of putting them in their place.

Adele adjusted her sleeves and stared up at the enormous blue glass building. Somewhere in that structure, somebody knew who the killer was. She was sure of it.

The chemical compound had been a perfect match for a drug created in this very building.

She turned to John. "You have the files?"

Renee continued chatting with Marshall but wiggled the band of a briefcase strapped over his shoulder in Adele's direction.

The limousine pulled away from the curb in search of a proper parking spot while Adele and her two teammates made their way toward the large glass doors with angled metal handles.

Conspicuous red letters were scrawled across the door: "WARNING: Authorized Personnel Only."

Elsewhere, stenciled beneath the lion logos, other warnings ornamented the glass, as well as a yellow triangle with black marks over the word: "TOXIC."

Before they reached the doors, Adele spotted someone through the glass and both doors were pushed open. A man and a woman stood on either side, flanking the entry, both wearing business suits and gesturing politely at the agents to enter.

"Director Mueller is upstairs," said the man on the right side of the door.

He had no distinguishing features whatsoever. He had an average face, was of average height, and had light brown hair. His complexion was hard to place ethnically, and his voice wasn't deep nor was it high-pitched. As if to complete the image, he was also wearing a charcoal gray suit.

The woman on the other side of the door didn't say anything, but kept the door ajar, still smiling politely at them with the sort of feigned excitement a car salesman might have envied.

"Who are you?" John growled in English.

"Personal assistants to Director Mueller," said the young man, with a light, airy accent, flashing a Colgate smile. "Please, if you will... we've been expecting you."

Adele followed the two young assistants into the lobby of a large white-walled atrium. Strange decor, like the type found in hotels or banks, had been arranged tastefully throughout the space, including a small koi pond beneath a fountain in the center of the room. The sound of trickling water created a peaceful atmosphere in the otherwise intimidating building.

"Director Mueller is quite busy today," the male assistant began, turning to face the agents with a smile, his hands on his hips. "If you wouldn't mind waiting—er, excuse me, *miss*!"

Two sets of stairs ascended the back of the room, and an elevator door presented itself at the base of the stairs.

Adele marched toward the stairs without invitation, ignoring the calls of the assistant. She ignored the elevator, while John hesitated, his hand hovering, about to push the button. She started stomping up the stairs, heard John grumble behind her, but, reluctantly, she could hear him follow after her, leaving the elevator.

The hurried footsteps of the assistants followed also, and both of them were now calling after Adele. "Excuse me, please! Wait! Director Mueller was very express in his desire *not* to be disturbed!"

But Adele ignored them and continued her trek up the stairs.

While it was true that Interpol had gone to great lengths to connect her with the BKA and designate temporary jurisdiction in this country, that didn't mean she had to play nice. Someone in this laboratory had killed at least six people, and had attempted to kill a seventh. Most likely there were bodies she didn't know about.

Somehow, Lion Pharmaceutical's drug had ended up in the hands of a serial killer.

They had to act quickly. Before he escaped. She reached the top of the stairs and glanced around. A long hall led toward a circular waiting area with glass windows on all sides. Various doors lined the hallway. A couple of them looked like offices, one a bathroom and another a supply closet.

Adele strode quickly past these doors and reached the waiting area. Two giant brown double doors held the opposite wall.

Adele reached for the handle, and, still ignoring the protests from the assistants behind her, she pulled the door open and stepped into the room beyond

"Director Mueller, I presume?" she asked, projecting her voice across the large office. The floor-to-ceiling windows displayed a breathtaking view of the surrounding countryside and a distant glimpse of the city center.

A handsome man with features a little too fixed to be natural stared across her over a chic, slim desk. It was one of those standing desks Angus had gone on and on about back in San Francisco. In one corner of the office, a treadmill faced the window, flanked by a small rack of dumbbells.

The man standing behind his desk was on the phone, but stopped mid-sentence at Adele's unannounced entry.

He glanced at her, then his dark eyes flicked past her, and he raised an eyebrow toward his assistants. At least, he tried to raise an eyebrow. Surgeon's scalpels and injections had long limited the man's ability to properly express, however, and all he managed was a generic twitch of his forehead.

Adele cleared her throat. "I apologize," she said in English. "But it's a matter of some urgency."

Director Mueller eyed her up and down and slowly lowered the phone into his pocket.

"No English," he said, quietly. Then, in German, he said, "Why did you let this American in without giving me until the end of my phone call?" His voice was clipped but patient.

The bland-featured assistant and his partner hurried past Adele, trying their best not to touch her, but moving with urgency so they brushed against her as they slipped into the room. "Sorry, sir," said the young man in German. "But BKA is with them. You said they'd called ahead."

Director Mueller nodded a couple of times. "They did. But that doesn't mean I don't still have work to do. I can't shut everything down the moment they want, BKA or not. Which of them speaks German?"

He glanced past Adele toward the other two agents. John was scowling again and doing his best to look intimidating. Agent Marshall, though, stepped forward, raising a small hand. Before she could speak, though, Adele raised her voice. "I can speak German."

She felt the eyes in the room dart toward her, settling on her in surprise.

"I actually grew up here."

She glanced back and noticed the look of surprise on John's face. For some reason, this gave her no small amount of pleasure. She smirked in his direction, and then turned back to the man at the desk. "I'm sorry for the intrusion, Director Mueller. I promise to be in and out as quick as possible. I know you have business to conduct and

135

research to complete. It is not my intention to intrude beyond a reasonable capacity."

Director Mueller's already high eyebrows flicked up even further. "You do speak German. And quite well. Well, darling, what can I do to help?"

Adele tried not to show her displeasure at the familiar term. His tone suggested an air of condescension.

She knew men like this. Men in positions of power and authority who didn't take kindly to anyone intruding on their turf. Adele wasn't some activist, and she didn't desire to alter the way people thought; it was simply an observation. As an investigator, it was up to her to notice things. And to use them.

There were some agents, if looked down on, who might take offense. But Adele wasn't in the business of changing hearts and minds. She was here to catch a killer.

She adjusted her posture. Instead of squaring her shoulders, she slouched, instead of standing with her arms at her side, she crossed them, in a defensive, submissive position. She put one leg over the other for a second, fidgeting and scratching at her ankle with her foot in an awkward, ungainly gesture. She shuffled again, trying to find purchase, and muttered quietly to herself as if trying to gather her nerves.

"Sorry," she said, quickly. "I'm so sorry." She even raised her voice a little bit, softening her consonants and extending her vowels in a sort of childish way. "I know how busy you must be. Please, could you tell me about this compound? It's quite difficult to understand."

"I have to finish this phone call," said Director Mueller. At her words, he seemed to calm somewhat. "You could come back in a half hour, say, and I'd be happy to answer whatever questions you have."

Adele fidgeted, gnawing on the corner for lip, playing clueless. She did have boundaries. But if she needed to play the sheep, she would play it. If she needed to flirt, she would do that too. There were those, especially those like Agent Paige, who thought every problem was a nail, and so they played the hammer. But Adele had learned from Robert that sometimes you caught more bees with honey.

"The thing is," she said, "if we wait half an hour, then more agents from the BKA may come by. It could become this whole thing. I really don't want to have to shut down your offices today. To be honest, it sounds unfair to me, but that's just the way policy works." She gave a helpless little shrug.

Director Mueller was frowning now.

Adele continued, "If you could just tell me what this compound is, we could be on our way in a minute. Please? I need your help." She kept her tone earnest, her arms still crossed.

Director Mueller rolled his eyes and met the gaze of the male assistant in the room, sharing a knowing look over Adele's shoulder. But finally, he waved his hand from behind his standing desk like a king imperiously summoning a subject. "Show me what compound," he said.

Adele turned and retrieved the folder from John—who flashed her a wink—before approaching Director Mueller.

He opened the folder and scanned it, his plastic features betraying no expression whatsoever. At last though, frowning, his eyes flicked up. "Where did you get this?"

Adele gnawed on her lip again. "I'm not really sure. But it's connected to something. It's not a big deal. But do you know where it's from?"

Everyone else in the room remained quiet, watching the strange exchange between the director and the FBI agent.

Director Mueller glanced at the file again and clicked his tongue.

He turned toward his standing desk and tapped at a laptop keyboard. A second later, his eyes scanned the screen, and he nodded. "I knew I recognized it. Yes. That was Project 132z. It was supposed to be a paralytic for the medical field, but we weren't granted the proper approvals from," he paused, and then very quickly recited, "the Bundesinstitut für Arzneimittel und Medizinprodukte." He smirked at Adele. "Do you know what that is?"

Inwardly, Adele translated the title as, *The Federal Institute for Drugs and Medical Devices.* But out loud, she said, "They sound important. So this drug of yours—it was forbidden?"

Director Mueller nodded. "We had to cancel Project 132z. It wasn't one of our bigger earners, anyway. What's this about? Did a competitor put you on this?"

Adele shook her head. "No, this has nothing to do with a competitor. So you're saying your lab did make the substance?"

Director Mueller paused, noticing a shift in Adele's tone. His eyes narrowed for a moment, "I think perhaps I have to speak with a lawyer."

137

But Adele leaned on his standing desk, looking Director Mueller in the eyes. "We're not interested in your company, sir. That I can promise you. We're here to find a murderer. I can't go into the details, but he's been using that substance of yours. And, as I said earlier, I have no interest in shutting down your operations, or having BKA agents swarming your company—who knows what they might find. I can't imagine that would do anything nice to your stock prices."

The sudden shift in Adele's posture and tone caught Mueller off guard. A flicker of annoyance crossed his features. A king rarely enjoyed being questioned by a subject, but Adele spoke quickly, not allowing his emotions to settle, hoping she would engage the part of him most concerned with his job rather than his ego. Robert had been a master at manipulating conversations, and some of his acumen had rubbed off on her.

"If you could just help us," she said, "we'll be on our way without interrupting anything. It is important to note that your drug is at the center of six separate murder investigations. Now, we could investigate your company…"

At this, the director's expression soured. "I have thousands of employees. I can't possibly know what all of them are up to."

On a lark, Adele asked, "Do any of those employees have red hair?"

Mueller frowned. "Employee information is private unless you have a judge's order…" He trailed off, glancing past her toward the other agents in the room with a questioning look. "No? Well, in that case—"

Here, Agent Marshall stepped forward from her position in the doorway, clearing her throat. "Actually, sir, the order is being written. But right now, we're under a joint task force. She's telling you the truth." Marshall lowered her voice conspiratorially. "Interpol is involved. But this doesn't have to become some sort of international investigation into your company—we wouldn't want what happened to Bedelwen Industries to happen here, now would we?" Marshall winced. "Bankruptcy, civil lawsuits… All because of a prolonged investigation…"

Mueller's face paled at this.

Marshall continued, "With your compliance, I'm sure we can limit the scope of our interference in your company."

Adele glanced back, flashing a look of gratitude toward the younger agent. Marshall kept her gaze on Mueller, her expression still polite.

The director glanced between the two women, still frowning. At last though, he sighed and said, "I can give you personnel files, but you can't stay here looking into them. It would be bad for business if it got out that private information was freely handed over to the government, understand? I'm expecting discretion here."

Adele nodded her thanks. "When can we have those files by?"

The director shrugged. "In a couple of days, I'm sure—"

"—Within the hour. Email them here." Adele grabbed an expensive-looking pen sticking from an ornamental desk set and scribbled on a notepad; she pushed the email address toward the director. "Please," she added. "We won't take any more of your time. The employee records need to be in that inbox within the hour, or I'm coming back with a crime scene team." Here, she leaned into the threat, fixing her gaze on the director.

Sometimes, even kings needed proper motivation. She didn't want to cause any trouble, but any delay could allow the killer to escape; that was something she simply couldn't afford. Adele turned and exited the office, leading Agents Renee and Marshall away from the office and through the circular, glass waiting room of the Lion Pharmaceutical company.

Somewhere in those records, they would find a red-haired man who'd been traveling in the last few weeks. Adele would stake everything on it. That would be their killer. They were closing in, and he didn't even know it.

CHAPTER TWENTY TWO

The smell of cheap takeout from a local Thai restaurant wafted on the still air of the borrowed office, hanging beneath the gray ceiling and pressing against the bare walls. Three uncomfortable metal chairs crowded around a circular wooden table. Adele wasn't sure where this warehouse ranked in the BKA's list of real estate assets, but she surmised it couldn't have been high on the list.

The limousine, coupled with this dingy office in the basement of an abandoned warehouse suggested that perhaps the BKA still wasn't thrilled about foreign agents operating on their soil. But Adele didn't care. All that mattered now: they had the files.

The three of them were on laptops, their devices set up on the circular table, emitting quiet tapping sounds as they pressed the keys and searched through the records provided to them by Director Mueller's office.

Adele cleared her throat, nearly choking on some dust that had fallen from the light fixture above. She coughed, then tried again. "Look for anyone who went on leave in the last couple of months," said Adele. "Especially if they travel frequently."

John grunted, making eyes toward Agent Marshall every few moments.

"Could we focus, please?" Adele said, her tone clipped.

Renee ignored her, but Agent Marshall went red and stared at her computer screen, dutifully searching the Lion Pharmaceutical employee records.

"No one," said John with a grunt, his accent heavy from continuing in English for Marshall's sake. "No red-haired employees. Surprising given how many of them there are, isn't it? Couple of them might've been, once upon a time. They're bald, now. Didn't realize how many chrome Germans there were." John snickered.

Adele passed a hand over her face, massaging her temples. The single naked bulb in the ceiling illuminated the cramped space with buzzing white light and further served to exacerbate her headache. The half empty cartons of Thai had tasted good on the way down, but Adele found they weren't playing nice with her intestines.

Still, exhaustion had settled, embracing her. She needed sleep and more food, and some time to think. But any time wasted was time gifted to the killer. By now, he could have discovered they were closing in. Director Mueller could have told his employees that agents were searching for them.

"Fine, ignore the red-haired part," said Adele. Briefly, she felt a jolt of regret. Robert had been so certain. Still, she would go where the evidence took her.

There's nothing," said John, rolling his eyes. "I don't speak German. What does *'der name'* mean?"

"I feel like even you can figure that one out," said Adele. "Just keep looking. Keep an eye out for the name of the drug and look for any mentions in the 'leave of absence' column I showed you. That'll be in numbers—you know those, right?"

"Funny," said John. "I'll have you know…" He trailed off, squinting at his laptop. It took him twice as long as the German-speaking women to cycle through one of the files, but this time, he took even longer, studying his screen. "Hang on…" he said, quietly. "I was looking through the technicians… What does *'leitender chemiker'* mean?"

Adele glanced over. "It means that person is the lead chemist. Why?"

John tapped a finger against his laptop.

"Please be gentle!" Agent Marshall interjected. "I need to return these in functional condition."

John, who'd already spilled spicy noodles on his keyboard, shrugged. "Look here," he said, butchering the pronunciation of *leitender chemiker* a second time. "He's in some supervisory role, right?"

He turned his laptop, facing it toward Adele.

She leaned in, peering at the screen and scanning the details. She frowned and reached out to push an arrow key to cycle through the contents.

"He requested leave five weeks ago," she said, quietly. She shook her head, her eyes widening.

"Look at the project he's in charge of," John said, inclining his head toward the computer. "I can read *that*."

Adele read the bio briefly and felt a jolt of electricity down her

141

spine. She exhaled, softly. "He was directly responsible for Project 132z. That's the drug." She looked up, staring at John. "He was responsible for the drug."

Agent Marshall glanced over from wiping fingerprints off the back of the laptop with a napkin. "The drug used by the killer?" For the first time, her nearly perfect English held a hint of her German accent. English was the only language the three of them had in common, but Adele knew neither John nor Marshall was completely comfortable with it.

Adele nodded. "Exactly. He was responsible for it. And he's been on a leave of absence for five weeks…" She glanced toward John. "I'm not sure if I want to slap you or kiss you."

Renee leaned back in his chair, crossing his hands behind his head. "Both, preferably. At the same time." He winked.

"But he doesn't have red hair," said the BKA agent.

Adele pushed away from the table, regaining her feet. "A wig, then. It's him. He's the supervising chemist on the project."

John frowned. "Look at him; he looks like a ghoul."

The photo of the employee in question didn't look that bad. In Adele's assessment, he resembled a man who didn't spend much time sleeping either. He had bags under his eyes, but he was probably in his forties, and despite depressed eye sockets, he had a cheerful smile and fading gray-brown hair.

"It's him," she said, pushing urgently away from the table and stepping over her seat. "Check his address. Agent Marshall, call some uniforms for backup—preferably without a limousine."

John was also getting to his feet and Marshall had already raised her phone, beginning to speak rapidly in German.

"Address?" Adele called over her shoulder as she strode hurriedly toward the door.

"Got it!" John called; then the sound of rapid, heavy footfalls gave pursuit.

"Hurry!" Adele said, over her shoulder, pushing out of the door into the stairwell up to the warehouse.

"He might not be there," John called after her. Glancing down at his phone. "What should I tell headquarters?"

Adele paused and looked back. "They should keep checking airports and train stations…" She hesitated, frowning. "He might not have come home—but if he did, he's ours. Now hurry?"

She strode rapidly out of the basement with her two companions following quickly behind.

CHAPTER TWENTY THREE

"You're sure that's the right address?" Adele asked for the third time in as many minutes.

"I'm sure," said John, growling. "Here." He shoved his phone in her face. "You read it."

Adele ignored the phone. "Can we go any faster?" she called through the glass partition.

But the vehicle kept a steady pace, following the flow of traffic.

Adele leaned back in her seat, trying not to let her impatience show. She counted slowly in her mind, breathing in, then exhaling and counting again. Finally, she said, "It's good his house is close by. I suppose that makes sense since he works at the company. What's his name again?"

"Peter Lehman," John supplied.

Adele wrinkled her nose. "He didn't come up in my investigation back stateside. Must've been using an alias. Dammit, can we go faster?"

Reluctantly, Agent Marshall raised a hand and rapped on the window. She called through the glass: "We're in a bit of a hurry!"

Adele heaved a breath. She wished the BKA had given them someone with a bit more experience. Still, working with any sort of interdepartmental task force sometimes came with unforeseen obstacles. Right now, the best way to smooth things over was to catch the killer and catch him fast. But would Peter Lehman even be home? He'd been on a leave of absence for five weeks and wasn't due back for another. He'd fled France, though—of that Adele was nearly certain. Where else could a German citizen go?

Adele clenched her fists. He had to be there.

The vehicle pulled up outside a house with two parked police cars already lining the street. In the distance, Adele heard more sirens as more vehicles responded to Agent Marshall's call for backup. Adele didn't have the patience to wait, though, and she burst out of the back of the car before they'd fully pulled to a stop.

"A2," John called after her.

Adele flashed a thumbs-up as she sprinted toward the townhouse and briefly scanned the structure; her eyes settled on the address. A2.

There was a light on inside, behind green drapes.

Her heart skipped a beat and Adele raced forward, surging toward Peter Lehman's residence. With the sound of boots to pavement, John raced after her, his gun leaving its holster with fluid ease. Adele also drew her weapon and squared her shoulders, feeling the reassuring weight of the Glock pressed against her palm.

John tried to sidestep Adele and took two lengthy strides as if he were preparing to kick down the door, but Adele quickly interjected an arm, tugging him back and giving the slightest shake of her head. She remained quiet as she reached out and tried the doorknob.

It turned.

She pulled the door open while John aimed through the gap, covering her. Then she lowered her weapon once more, brushing past the doorframe and entering a hall. Adele stepped over a pile of shoes by the door.

Peter had a family. There were children's and a woman's shoes next to a man's loafers.

John followed, his breathing heavy, his eyes fixed ahead, his cheeks taut, bearing the load of a solemn expression as he tracked the room over Adele's shoulder and kept his gun aimed safely off to the side. His posture allowed Adele full range of motion without crossing his line of fire.

She wasn't sure what the BKA policies were for breaching a home, but she would ask forgiveness later.

She stepped past a sink full of messy dishes and an old fridge humming and buzzing, emitting strange popping sounds, suggesting the appliance wasn't long for this kitchen.

Her feet padded against the ground as she made her way further into the townhouse. Through one of the walls, she heard loud music pulsing from the unit next door.

Adele felt prickles across the back of her neck. Hopefully the children would be in school. She wondered if they knew their father was a killer. And the mother? Adele passed a row of family pictures. Peter Lehman sat surrounded by his wife and three kids, all of them smiling out of the portrait, watching Adele. She noticed a certificate for a middle school science prize pinned on the refrigerator. One of Peter's children was following in their father's footsteps.

145

He had been the overseer for the entirety of Project 132z. He'd created the drug he'd used to torture six people to death.

"Don't split," John said quietly. "We check the bedrooms together."

"You coming on to me?" Adele quipped, barely cognizant of her words due to the adrenaline pulsing through her body.

Uncharacteristically, John didn't riposte. Whenever his sidearm appeared in his hands, his personality seemed to shift. He became quieter, more serious, more dangerous. His eyes were narrowed now, carrying a look that frightened Adele.

She was glad they were on the same side.

They moved to a door and John eased it open with his left hand, keeping his other gripping his weapon.

A bathroom, unoccupied.

They approached to the next door, and at that moment, through the thin wood, Adele heard movement. She held up a hand, teeth set, and pointed frantically at the frame; she tapped the side of her ear.

John glanced at her and nodded. In a barely discernible whisper, he said something in French, but Adele couldn't quite make it out. In English, he tried again "Should I go around the house? Check for a window?"

Adele thought for a moment, but then shook her head. Also keeping her voice low, quiet enough that she could barely hear it, she said, "On the count of three. Don't fire unless you see a weapon. No sense igniting an international powder keg."

Briefly, the thought caught her attention. She could only imagine what the papers would read if a French and American agent shot a German citizen on German soil. The repercussions would cost them far more than their jobs. Still, if the killer made any threatening moves, she would face the fanfare. It was up to her to make sure neither her life nor her partner's was put in jeopardy.

Adele counted down in her head, inhaling slowly through her nose, the weapon in her hand pointing toward the base of the door as she prepared to raise it the moment they entered.

Then John twisted the handle, pushed it open, and both of them started shouting at once.

"DGSI! Show your hands!"

"FBI! Don't move!"

Their voices blared into the room, and they stepped in, one after the other in perfect synchronicity, both of them immediately sliding past the door frame and putting their backs to the nearest portion of wall.

Adele found her shoulders scraping against the wooden knobs of a cabinet, but her eyes swept the bedroom.

A man crouched over a suitcase at the base of the bed, his silhouette framed by the light gleaming through the bedroom window.

At the shouting, the man whirled, startled, and reeled back, his face turning pale. The man didn't have red hair, but he matched the photo in the employee records of Peter Lehman.

"Show me your hands!" Adele shouted. "Now!"

Lehman didn't hesitate, and his hands shot to the sky, his fingertips illuminated by the fluorescent bulbs in the fixture above.

John quickly scanned the room and sidestepped to look into a closet, making sure all threats were contained. Then he reached for his cuffs, and in a couple of deft motions stepped over and handcuffed the chemist.

The German grunted as John handled him, and the breath left his body as he was knocked into a sitting position on the bed. Vaguely, Adele wondered if she was supposed to check with Agent Marshall when arresting someone—but it had all happened so fast.

"Don't move," John snapped, kicking at the man on the bed.

Adele walked over and noted the suitcase. "Returning from somewhere?" she said. "France, maybe?"

Peter Lehman was trembling now, his mouth quavering, his lips trying to form sentences, but failing. "Who are you?" he demanded at last.

"I said be quiet," John shouted in French.

But Peter glanced up with a look of confusion on his face.

John glared down at the man. "Don't pretend you don't speak French. That's how you lured that poor girl into the underpass, isn't it?"

Peter looked even more flabbergasted. He replied in German, "I don't understand. German. Do you speak German? Who are you?"

Adele flashed her FBI badge. At that moment, Agent Marshall also joined them, her own weapon raised in trembling hands. She surveyed the scene and released a small gasp of relief, quickly holstering her firearm as if she were discarding a hot coal. "BKA task force with Interpol," she announced, importantly through the room. "You, Peter Lehman, are under arrest for the murder of five US citizens and one French national."

At this, Peter's pale face turned downright ghostly. Sweat broke out

147

across his forehead beneath his fading gray and brown hair. "I didn't kill anyone!" he said, sputtering. "What is this about? A drug I worked on? I assure you, anything in my capacity for Lion Pharmaceutical is covered by the company's liability. If any patients are suffering side effects, we have a shield of immunity from prosecution as individuals. Which project is the issue?" He was shaking his head. "I know that hair regrowth cream isn't the best. But it wouldn't have caused anyone's death." Peter was talking rapidly now, the words spilling from his throat. He shook his head side to side, looking pleadingly from John to Adele and back to Agent Marshall.

Adele had to hand it to him. He was good. She could understand why Marion would've gone with him into the underpass. There was a sincerity in his words and his expression that would have put anyone off guard. Still, facts didn't lie.

"Check his suitcase," she said, pointing at John.

The large agent pushed Peter roughly in the chest, causing him to collapse backward, lying down against the bed. Then John dropped to a knee and unzipped the suitcase.

A pile of folded clothes and neatly arranged toiletries comprised most of the compartment. Adele frowned, wondering if they would find the knife. But as John tossed clothing from the suitcase, causing a couple of shirts to land on Peter's face, the tall agent froze.

"Sharp, look," he said, pointing.

Adele stepped further into the room and peered down into the case. She spotted a small white container with translucent glass. Sealed within the container, six small test tubes protruded from circular compartments, secured by rubber clasps.

"Project 132z," said John with a growl. He tapped the side of the glass with a long finger.

"Please, be careful with that!" Peter said, trying to sit back up.

John reached out an arm and pushed Peter back down on the bed.

"What do you know about the paralytic?" Lehman asked between hyperventilating gasps from where he lay, facing the ceiling, his hair sticking wildly out around him, jutting against the bed sheets.

"We know you used the drug to incapacitate your victims," snapped John. "We know you stole it from the lab, even though it was slated to be destroyed. And we know that the five weeks you've been absent from your company, you've been vacationing in the United States and France, killing citizens."

148

Agent Marshall pursed her lips, shaking her head side to side. "Mr. Lehman, I'm afraid you're under arrest."

Adele helped John back to his feet and patted him affectionately on the back.

As Agent Marshall muttered beneath her breath to Peter, advising him of his rights, Adele smiled at John. "Good job," she said.

Renee holstered his weapon, and his smirk returned like flowers in bloom. "Same to you."

Adele shifted her shoulders. "I have to say, I'm a little disappointed he didn't have red hair."

"You're a strange one, American Princess. Not bad in a day's work. Think we'll get a confession?"

Adele frowned, glancing over at the two Germans by the bed. "I'm—I'm not sure…"

"What is it?"

"Nothing… Just a thought, but… no, really, it's nothing." Robert had often told her to trust her hunches… but this time, she didn't want to. Peter Lehman seemed… so *normal.* He had to be the killer though, didn't he?

Adele frowned, scratching at the side of her chin.

Together, the three agents led their handcuffed suspect out of his home and over to the waiting police cars at the end of the street.

CHAPTER TWENTY FOUR

In Adele's opinion, all police stations, no matter what country they called home, shared a certain recognizable uniformity immediately apparent to anyone who'd spent much time around cops. There was a quiet order among the men and women of a police force. The arrangement of their offices would be different, the interrogation rooms might be in a basement or down a hall. But eventually, all police stations could be interpreted through the same grid.

Adele wasn't surprised they hadn't been taken back to a BKA headquarters. While Germany might've decided to play nice, allowing a DGSI agent and an FBI agent into their base of operations without preparation would have been a laughable proposition.

Still, the local police station would do well enough.

Adele stood in front of the vending machines, scanning the items.

She inserted a euro which she'd borrowed from Agent Marshall, clicked the button, waited for the tumbling sound, then retrieved an iced tea from the vending machine's slot. Clutching the cold beverage, she sidled past the desk clerk, and toward the long hall which led to the interrogation room.

She pushed open the door and stepped beneath the bright fluorescent light.

The naked room housed only two chairs, a long metal table bolted to the floor, and a glass mirror across the back half of the wall.

It wasn't a one-way mirror, but it served to convince the suspects, who'd seen enough TV, to assume that every police station had someone on the other side of that glass, watching them. In this case, though, it was just a mirror.

John was already seated in the metal chair opposite Peter. The suspected killer's hands were handcuffed in front of him and latched to the table through a metal hoop.

The man fidgeted uncomfortably, shaking his head. He could move his hands just enough to reach at his face to scratch an itch, but every time he moved one hand, the other one would lower, causing the chain to rattle as it slid through the metal hoop.

Adele placed the iced tea next to Lehman's left hand. She stepped back, leaning against the frigid mirror and watching the suspected killer.

"It's confirmed," said John. "Those test tubes contain the same substance that killed your victims. How about you tell me what you were doing in France last week?"

Peter shivered though, and shook his head. He glanced pleadingly at Adele. "I don't understand him. Is that French? Why am I being verbally abused by a Frenchman? What is this?"

Adele shrugged. "He says he can't understand you."

John threw his hands up. "He's lying!" He pointed a steady, thick finger toward Peter's chest. "You're lying—we know you are. You can speak French; that's how you tricked that poor girl to her death!"

Peter just looked back at Adele, his expression pleading. "I—I don't understand. I've told you, I didn't kill anyone! Please, you have to believe me. I'm not a violent man!"

"You've been gone from work for five weeks," said Adele, her tone even. "A strange coincidence that our murderer also travels a lot. What was the suitcase for?"

Lehman shifted again, shaking his head nervously. "I was just packing some things to store beneath the bed."

John growled, slamming his hands against the table. "What's he saying?" he demanded.

Adele found herself confused for a moment, switching from German to French, while trying to process her thoughts in English. "He says he was just going to stow the suitcase beneath his bed," she said, transitioning into French once more.

"Yeah?" John snorted. "Some things like illegal substances used to paralyze young women?"

Agent Marshall stood behind Peter, but she wasn't leaning against the wall. She seemed nervous, and was on the phone, quietly relaying the interrogation's entirety over the phone to her supervisors via video camera. Eyeballs in the sky, eyeballs on the ground. Adele glanced toward the security camera in the corner of the ceiling, then back at the blinking glass of Marshall's camera lens.

They would have to do this by the book. Then again, there wasn't much of a book for this sort of thing.

John continued to harangue the suspect, slamming a large hand against the top of the metal table with a resounding *thwack!* Peter

Lehman continued to shake his head and repeat, over and over, "I only speak German. I don't understand. Please. German."

Adele felt, surprisingly, the rumblings of pity burgeoning in her chest. She studied their suspected killer.

He had a pleasant face with a straight nose and high cheekbones. His hair was thinning, but not unduly so, and he wore an earnest expression as he stared across the table.

He hadn't even lawyered up. This unsettled Adele more than anything. Why hadn't he asked for a lawyer? Did he think he could fool them with spectacle?

She leaned forward, pushing off the mirror, and striding toward John. She stepped past his chair and faced Lehman. "Why were the test tubes in your bag?"

The man stared desperately up at her, his gaze flicking between John and Adele with rapid motions. He tried to twist, turning back to look at Agent Marshall, but his chained wrists hampered his range of motion. So instead, he glanced in the mirror and stared at Marshall's reflection.

"Please," he said, loudly. "This is a mistake. I haven't been to France. And I haven't been to the United States, ever. I don't know anything about killing. I-I did have the drug... yes... but for a good reason..."

He said this last part quickly, his cheeks turning red, and the slick sweat across his brow glistened beneath the fluorescent light. He muttered to himself beneath his breath, shaking his head wildly from side to side.

His voice was strained as he pressed on: "I can't—can't tell you why. Just please, I didn't kill anyone."

Adele was staring at him though, still frowning. "We're not interested in the theft of the drug. That's something for BKA to worry about. All I care about is the killer. You have the drug on you. There's no disputing that. The lab confirmed it. BKA has confirmed it, and local authorities have the evidence in custody." She didn't blink, and she kept her tone even, unaffected by emotion. "You can't escape that undeniable fact. Secondly, you had a suitcase at the foot of your bed. The man we're looking for has just returned from France to Germany. If you weren't traveling then why did you have a suitcase with the drugs in it? You have to understand; I'm asking the same question in different ways, but the facts remain undisputed. Unless you can explain away those two things, I'm afraid you're not going to like what comes next."

Peter Lehman's eyes bugged in his head, and he again muttered to himself in German, staring down at his shackled wrists. He did a double take at the chains, as if not quite believing what he was seeing.

At last, though, he muttered quietly, "Switzerland."

Adele leaned in, "What was that?"

"What's he saying?" John demanded in French.

But Adele held up a finger toward her partner. She turned back to Peter. "What about Switzerland? Did you kill someone in Switzerland, too?"

"I didn't kill anyone." Peter loosed a sigh, his chest puffing toward the light, and then descending as he crumpled in on himself, his shoulders trembling now. Tears sprang into the man's eyes.

He was better than Adele had given him credit for. No wonder his victims fell for him.

"Please," he said. "My family, my children. If I tell you—I didn't kill anyone. But you have to understand, I worked so hard on this project. The anesthesia was supposed to save lives. It would have been half the cost of normal anesthetic. There were some kinks; I admit that—some things that needed to be worked out, but we were rejected far too quickly. It was complete politics!"

Now his voice was rising, and the flush in his cheeks reddened further.

"What politics?" Adele demanded.

Peter was clenching his fists now, the tops of his hands turning white. "At our company. Lion is always gunning for contracts from the bigger fish. The competition wanted to put a stop to my project, to teach Director Mueller a lesson. I got caught in the crossfire. You have to understand, I've been working on this for three years. Me and my team have put in twenty hours days, sometimes staying over the weekends, just to make sure the thing was perfect. It *should* have been approved. We only had a couple more trials."

He released another puff of air and continued to wilt in his chair, sliding down so that the back of his head rested against the metal frame. "Dear God, I didn't kill anyone. This is a nightmare."

Adele circled to the edge of the table and lowered into a sitting position on the table next to Peter's clenched fist. She was only inches away from the man suspected of killing Marion, killing the three

153

Americans. The same man who had callously murdered his victims and left their bodies to rot. The same way Adele's mother had been left in that park.

She felt a flash of rage, which she quickly pushed deep down in her chest.

Somehow, though, she felt a burbling of pity, too. Perhaps Robert had been right. Perhaps even these sorts, the monsters of the world, were once destined to be masterpieces, but somehow vandalized.

Or perhaps her own instincts were trying to tell her something.

But what?

He couldn't be innocent, could he? It was far too damning of evidence for him to have stolen the drug, have a packed suitcase, match the employee records, request a leave of absence…

"Adele," said Agent Marshall, waving her phone.

But Adele held up another quieting finger and stared at Peter, studying the side of his face. "All right, let's say you took the drug. Where have you been for the last five weeks?"

"Here, in Germany! I swear it. I've been with my family; you can ask my wife, my kids! I was at my daughter's soccer practice last Wednesday. Everyone can tell you!"

"BKA is running your credit cards and passport right now," said Adele. "You're convincing, I'll give you that. But this charade is pointless. If they find that you've been spending money in France, or that your passport was spotted at any of the borders, you're going to spend the rest of your life behind bars. I hope you know that."

Peter Lehman's voice broke, shuddering with a sob. "I didn't kill anyone. I took the five weeks because of the politics. Like I said. Those bastards at Lion wouldn't stick up for us. I'm a chemist, not a killer. I was leading my team as best I could. I made promises, promises that they should've seen fulfilled. We all worked so hard…"

His voice strained, and he emitted another defeated sob. At last, he turned, meeting her gaze, his eyes laden with sadness. "I needed the time off to recover. I took the drug. I admit that. There's no sense pretending, you found it. But I took it to sell it."

He hesitated for a moment, his nostrils flaring as he realized what he'd said. But, shaking his head, he tried to steady himself. Then, soldiering on, with a grim look of determination like someone plunging into an icy river, he said, his voice strengthening with each word, "I was going to travel. I did pack a suitcase, but it wasn't because I've returned from France, but because I was going to leave for Switzerland. I told my wife there was a conference, but really, I was going there to meet a Swiss pharmaceutical company. I told them about the drug. I offered to sell it to them. You have to understand; I'm not a bad man. But I spent three years working on this project." He reached up as if to rub at his forehead, but his hand couldn't make it the full way. The chain rattled as his hand dropped limply back to the table. "To throw it away, so callously, with Director Mueller not even taking a second to try to salvage it…it's a crime. That's the real crime!"

Adele still sat on the edge of the metal table, her legs crossed, her hands folded in her lap, her shoulder brushing against Lehman's waving forearm as he gesticulated wildly, causing the chains to rattle back and forth and his hands to move up and down like a seesaw through the metal bracket holding him tight.

"Agent Sharp," Marshall repeated again, waving with her phone.

Adele sighed, and finally glanced over at the young BKA agent. "Yes?" she said.

Marshall winced apologetically. "He's telling the truth," she said, shaking her head. "BKA can't find any record of credit card purchases or travel outside the country. And the officer sent to speak with his wife has her swearing up and down that he's been home for the last five weeks, wallowing in it, in her words, but home."

Adele felt a pit forming in her stomach. She stared at Agent Marshall. "You have to be kidding."

The German agent winced again, shaking her head.

Adele glanced at Peter, who was hunched over now, crying, his forehead resting against his hands.

She turned to John, her expression grim. "There was no one else? No one in the employee records who worked on the project? Who requested absence? No one with red hair?"

John scowled. "Would you stop it with the red hair? *He* doesn't have red hair." He jabbed a finger toward Peter again. "He's the killer!"

But Adele shook her head and translated what Marshall had told her as well as what Peter had said. As she relayed the facts, John's expression morphed from one of anger to sheer contempt. He flung out a hand and grunted as if waving away everyone in the room. "He has to be the killer," John said, mulishly. "He had the drug on him, in the suitcase. You saw!"

"He does have a ticket for Switzerland," said Agent Marshall, once

155

again waving her phone like a child raising their hand to catch the attention of a supply teacher.

John growled again and opened his mouth to protest, but Adele interrupted, "No credit cards or passport out of Germany, John. He's been here."

"Can anyone else vouch for his whereabouts?" John demanded.

Adele turned to Peter. "Can anyone else corroborate that you've been in Germany?"

Peter hesitated, but then nodded wildly. "Yes, of course! My team. We met up for drinks only two weeks ago after the project was officially canceled. It was a wake, a sendoff, if you will. There were nearly twenty people there. They'll all be able to vouch for me. Please, just ask them!"

Adele felt her shoulders slump in defeat. "We're going to need names," she said softly. She reached out and patted Lehman on the shoulder, and then pushed off the table, turning toward the door to the interrogation room. "I need a breath," she said. "I'll be back."

As Adele pushed out of the cramped space, the smell of iced tea and sweat was replaced by cheap cologne and scented air freshener. She kept her eyes ahead as she walked down the hall, mulling over the possibilities. Either Peter was an Oscar winner, or else the real killer was still out there. For all she knew, he was preparing for his next victim.

Adele paused in the doorway of the police station, letting a couple of officers past, both who glanced at her with mildly confused expressions. She ignored them as she stared out into the street. The same ominous shudder she'd felt back at the DGSI headquarters crept up her spine—the same sense of foreboding, like a gust of chill breeze.

CHAPTER TWENTY FIVE

The man sat on the floor, leaning against the footrest of the grandfather chair, resting his head against the seat. He preferred the floor; chairs like this one were too comfortable. But he couldn't give it up. It had once belonged to his aunt, and she'd been kind to him once upon a time.

Still, comfort was for the weak.

The man stared at the TV screen, watching the events unfold.

A shakily held cell phone captured the moment when the chemist was escorted from his house in handcuffs.

A very tall agent with burn marks just below his chin was glaring at everyone within sight. A special glare was reserved for whoever was holding the camera.

The seated man returned the glare on the TV screen.

Next to the tall agent, he recognized the woman in the neat suit with the pretty, blonde hair.

"Agent Sharp," he murmured, tipping his head in mock greeting.

She was in Germany. The man kept his calm for a moment, counting in his head, but then his emotions bubbled over and he screamed, launching the remote at the glass cabinet across the room. He howled, cursing at the ceiling as the sound of shattered glass only further sparked his rage.

With heaving, huffing breaths, he managed to regain control of his temper, glaring toward the TV once more.

How had they followed him? He thought he'd been careful. Reaching the US had been easy enough. He'd traveled to Canada first, and then slipped through the border. It wasn't his first time.

Avoiding detection in France had been even easier; a matter of false papers. The government thought they were so clever. Yet in Germany, the US, and France, teenagers with fake IDs could fool even the most attentive of bartenders.

His tastes weren't so predictable as a teenager in search of a buzz, but fake papers on a train from France to Germany were far easier to procure with the right connections. The man rarely traveled by plane if he could help it.

The man leaned back again, resting his head against the cushioned footrest.

The US had been a delightful vacation, but future sojourns would be relegated to Europe. The man nodded, settling the matter in that moment with the simple bob of his head. The options were far better in Europe: bus, train, hitching a ride, driving...

The US border was too difficult to cross and getting more and more difficult with each passing month. No, his vacation had been cut short.

The man crossed his legs and pulled up the hem of his shirt, glancing down at his stomach and flexing his abdomen.

He couldn't quite make out the ridge of his muscles, and with a flare of annoyance, he quickly swiveled, placing his feet under the edge of the grandfather chair as he began to do sit-ups, grunting with each one and flexing his abdomen at the peak, holding the position until pain set in, and then releasing it and lowering down.

He listened as the news continued to announce the arrest of the chemist from Lion Pharmaceutical.

Of course, he knew all about the company.

They were closing in. This Agent Sharp was better than he'd thought. She couldn't have possibly tracked him by papers, so how had she found him in Germany?

"She hasn't," he said out loud, answering his own thought. He grunted again as he reached the pinnacle of his sit up, then lowered back once more. He shot off another twenty rapid sit-ups—then thirty—then forty.

He could feel a sweat breaking across his forehead and limbs, but he pushed himself, straining.

Youth required sacrifice. Longevity required commitment. Youth was wasted on the young. But it was a currency he would spend wisely.

He'd avoided vacationing in Germany; it was too close to home. But perhaps he could make an exception just this once. For a special person.

He reached his morning hundred, then stopped the exercise. Gasping, sweating, he pushed off his chair and went over to the kitchen table, retrieving his laptop from where he'd placed it on a counter. It took him a moment to boot up the thing, but then he stared at the blank screen displaying the search engine.

Everything was available on the internet nowadays.

That chemist's arrest had been captured by some neighbor's dinky camera. People fancied themselves reporters, though, really, they were in it for a buck.

The man sneered, wrinkling his nose in disgust. How many times had he seen videos of someone being beaten up, while fifty people surrounded them, instead of helping, videotaping the whole ordeal.

Humans were revolting.

This new one, this Agent Sharp... she was pretty. Not that it mattered. She was young, but not young enough.

Twenty-three was where he'd left off, and twenty-three was where he would need to start again.

He quivered in delight at the thought: how young could he go?

He'd never thought of exerting his routine over a teenager...Even a child? The possibilities were endless. But he could feel his strength rising. Every time one of them perished at his feet, bleeding out, he could feel part of them enter him. He didn't believe in immortality, but with the advances in science and medicine, he planned to make it to at least two hundred. And that required sacrifice.

Agent Sharp had to go. She was too close, too clever for her own good.

Anything could be found online.

He typed in her name, scanning articles. He paused for a moment, struggling to remember what his host family had mentioned back in the US.

He grunted in satisfaction as the memory clicked. "Adele," he said, quietly. He licked his lips and kissed the air. He typed "Adele Sharp" into the search engine and pressed enter. A split second later, he scanned the results and then stopped.

A German article, an interview, conducted with a Joseph Sharp. But what did that have to do with—

He froze as he scanned the article. Some bullshit thing honoring police veterans interviewed about their lives. Joseph Sharp worked for the police in Germany. The article was from more than a decade ago. His French daughter had won some sort of track and field meet in college, and there were rumors that she was planning on joining the German police. At least, that's what it sounded like Joseph Sharp expected.

He continued to scan the article. Joseph was still working in Germany. In fact, he wasn't far from here.

159

"Adele Sharp," the man said, quietly. "You wish to hunt me in my home?"

The old article still had a picture of Mr. Sharp, and had printed his address in the article. Ten years ago, people weren't so careful on the internet.

The article was nearly a decade old, but the information, would it still prove useful?

The man smiled, slowly lowering his hands from the computer. Perhaps it was time he paid Adele Sharp's father a visit.

CHAPTER TWENTY SIX

It had been a long walk from the bus stop, but Adele was sick of vehicles. Planes, limousines, cars, she was starting to feel like Robert.

Adele wasn't frustrated. No, she had passed frustration weeks ago. They were in a holding pattern once more. The BKA had reluctantly agreed to investigate the other members of Peter Lehman's team; double-checking their alibis and whereabouts. But Adele wasn't hopeful it would pay off.

She stared at the houses at the end of the cul-de-sac, her hands jammed in her pockets for warmth as she surveyed the yards. Her dad's house wasn't large, but it was just a bit larger than the other houses on the block. It wasn't particularly clean, but it was just a fraction cleaner than the other homes. He did have a white picket fence—the remnants of the American dream.

Her father had been born in the US, and had been deployed to Germany with the army. He'd stayed in Germany for Adele's mother at first. He didn't have any family back stateside. Part of Adele had often thought her father had fled something back home. He'd never returned to the US, not even on vacation after leaving the military and gaining his German citizenship. Now, very little of his American loyalty remained. Still, he couldn't resist showing up his German neighbors.

Even the grass, in the lawn, though it may have just been Adele's imagination, was a half inch taller after trimming than the other houses on the cul-de-sac. Her father did the yard work himself and painted the house himself. He didn't believe in hiring people to do something he could do. Of course, after eight hours on a job, coming home only to pick up more projects had left little room for time with the wife and kid once upon a time.

Adele twisted at her sleeves and stalked up the sidewalk, passing a fire hydrant and nodding toward someone peering at her through the window of a neighbor's home. She sighed in nervous little puffs of breath. She hadn't necessarily wanted to visit her father. It had been a few years since she'd actually seen him in person.

But if he found out from his law enforcement buddies that she'd been in Germany and hadn't visited him, she'd never hear the end of it.

"The ever doting father," Adele murmured to herself, jamming her hands back into her pockets as she strode toward the two-story, stone veneer house at the end of the block.

She could hear the neighbor's dogs yelping and barking, and vaguely thought of a childhood without pets. Her father hadn't wanted to clean up after them. Adele had gotten the turtle with Angus more out of spite than any actual desire to own the poor creature.

Already, bitter thoughts circled her head, and Adele felt like she was back to being twelve all over again.

She strode up the sidewalk, took the patio steps, and knocked politely on the front door.

The Sergeant hated it when people rang the bell. There were a lot of things that annoyed her father, and Adele had a memorized list. Walking on eggshells around Joseph Sharp wasn't only a necessity, it was a practiced skill. And of everyone Adele knew, she'd practiced best.

Still, though, she wasn't looking forward to the visit. She knocked again, politely, and heard a voice call from inside, in German, "I'm coming—hold on!"

Adele waited, and the door clicked as locks shifted and bolts rattled as chains were removed.

Her father was safety conscious. He didn't trust security cameras, but he had more locks on the windows and doors than most banks. And the collection of firearms permitted to him, thanks to his job, also served to provide him peace of mind.

The door swung open, revealing a bald man with an enormous mustache. He had a bit of a belly, but the arms of someone who spent a good amount of time in the weight room.

He had no tattoos, nor any sort of piercing. He was wearing a T-shirt with a stain down the front, and the smell of soup wafted in from the kitchen, gusting past him.

"Hey, Dad," said Adele, fidgeting and smiling nervously. She also spoke in German. Her father had been born in the States, but he'd lived in Germany now for most his life. She wasn't sure why, but he hated it when she tried to speak to him in English or French. Secretly, she suspected it reminded him of her mother.

Christ, she was thirty-two. Why was she acting like a ten-year-old all of a sudden? The Sergeant studied her, his bristling mustache twitching more than his lips. If she'd expected a smile in return, she'd been sorely mistaken.

It took her father all of two seconds to recover his wits, and then he nodded at her in turn. "Sharp," he said.

Her father had referred to her by their last name since she was five. At one point, she'd thought he'd done it to infuriate her mother, but after his ex-wife had died, Joseph had continued calling her by her last name. She supposed it was an old habit from police buddies; he'd always wanted a boy after all.

"It's good to see you," she said, still smiling. "I brought a gift." She reached into her jacket pocket and pulled out the can of condensed cream of broccoli she had picked up from the store on the way.

Her father's eyebrows shifted, and he reached out and took the soup from her, then turned and entered the house again. "Welcome," he called as an afterthought. "Come in if you want."

Her father liked soup. Especially if it came in a can. He'd been preparing for the Third World War for the last forty years, and he had turned the basement into a bunker.

"I just thought I'd stop by," said Adele calling into the house, still standing on the porch in front of the open door.

"Shut the door or you'll let the cold in!" he called back.

For a moment, the idea of turning and marching back down the patio steps and leaving her father was all too appealing, but Adele thought better of it, and with a quiet breath, she stepped into the house and closed the door behind her. She made sure to do it gently as her father had a pet peeve about slamming doors. She also followed her father into the kitchen, through the living room. Habitually, she flicked off the light near the entrance. A house rule: the last person to leave a room had to turn the lights off to conserve electricity.

Christ, she felt ten all over again.

Adele glanced back, half searching the ground for where she'd left her spine, but also checking to make sure she hadn't tracked any mud in the house.

She took her shoes off at the door to the kitchen and stepped onto the cold tiled floor with her socks.

"Hungry?" her father asked, leaning over a pot and stirring it with a wooden spoon. He peered into the metal container as tendrils of steam drifted up toward him, and his left hand finagled with the heat knob on the stove.

"Not really," said Adele.

Her father glanced back at her. "You should eat. You look horrible. Have you been sleeping?"

Adele sighed. "No, not much. I'm on a case."

"Can't solve the case if you can't sleep. You should know that."

Adele massaged the bridge of her nose and wearily collapsed in a seat at the kitchen table, leaning back, then quickly remembering how much her dad hated it when people rocked in his chairs; she leaned forward again, sitting upright, with her forearms on the table, but her elbows just off.

It was like a soldier rehearsing drills they'd learned when they first entered boot camp.

Her drill sergeant was still making soup.

"It's clam chowder," her father said, continuing in German. "Your favorite, right?"

Adele gave a half shrug. "I don't really like soup."

Her father made a clicking sound and poured a bowl, and then another.

"Soup is good for you. Comes in all sorts of flavors, and doesn't have many calories. Do you know what calories are? I was just reading about them the other day."

"I know what calories are, Dad," said Adele.

Joseph Sharp nodded at this and came over carrying the soup. He placed the bowl in front of Adele, and then placed another one on a tray on the table.

"Careful, it's hot. Don't eat it yet."

"I get it, Dad, why does everything you say have to sound like an order?"

He glanced at her, frowning slightly, and then reached up stroking at the edge of his mustache. "Just saying don't burn yourself."

Adele sighed once more and nodded again.

Coming here had been a mistake. Same old dad. Same old house.

He'd lived here for nearly thirty years.

She remembered growing up in this house. And, unsurprisingly, it was as clean and neat as she remembered. Her father took the tray with his soup and left the kitchen, strolling over to an old reclining chair facing a TV. He sat in the chair and set the tray on a coffee table.

Adele sat at the kitchen table, watching as her father ignored her and began sipping at his soup, staring at the TV, his profile outlined against a window at his side.

"I was hoping we could catch up," she said, trying to keep her tone even, calling out from the kitchen.

"Sharp, please don't shout. You know how it sets off the neighbor's dogs."

She got to her feet, leaving her soup, and went over to her father. "How have you been?"

He glanced over at her. "Working. Why? You don't need money, do you?"

"Dammit, no, I don't."

He frowned at the curse word and shook his head. "All right, what do you want?"

"I wanted to stop by and say hi."

"Do you need my help with a case?"

She tucked her tongue inside a cheek, counting quietly to ten in her head. Her father had never made it past desk sergeant with the German police force. He had always fancied himself a bit of an investigator, but his superiors hadn't seen it the same way.

"No, Dad. I mean, I could use all the help I can get on this one. But I'm not sure there's anything you can help me with."

"You going to eat your soup?"

"It's hot."

"Well, if you just leave it there, it can condense; the water will stain the table. Could you at least put a napkin or two down?"

Adele wanted to protest, but she just didn't have the energy. The exhaustion she'd felt over the last two days felt multiplied all of a sudden as she stood in the well-lit, cleanly kept house.

For the first time this week, she found herself missing John's company. Agent Renee was downright pleasant compared to this.

She stomped back into the kitchen, intentionally slamming her feet into the ground, knowing it would bother her father, and then took the bowl of soup and dumped it in the sink.

"What was that?" her dad called through the open door.

"Dad, do you want to watch TV, or do you want to catch up? Because honestly, I could use some sleep if you're not looking to talk."

"There's no room upstairs. Your old room is now my home office."

"I wasn't asking to stay here. We were given rooms at the motel across from the airport."

"The airport? How'd you get here?"

"Bus, then walked. But seriously, you're in good health?"

Joseph nodded, lifting his bowl of soup and drinking the rest of it, downing it in a couple of gulps. The bowl was still steaming, but the heat didn't seem to bother him.

He wagged his finger toward the TV, chuckling as a cop channel displayed a foot chase with a couple of dogs biting into the leg of a fleeing suspect.

"Been seeing anyone?" said Adele. The moment the question left her lips, she kicked herself. She had just been looking for something to say, but she knew her dad wouldn't take it well.

He turned at her, scowling. "How's that your business?"

Adele threw her hands up in surrender. "Sorry. You don't seem that interested in talking."

He sighed, heavily, and with much show of grave sacrifice, he reached for the TV remote and clicked the button. He turned, swiveling his large chair so he was facing her.

"What do you want to talk about?" he said.

"I just wanted to see how you're doing." Adele could feel herself easing back toward the front door. It had been a mistake coming here. She'd shown up, she'd said hi. That was all that could be expected. Her dad was the same as he'd ever been. She was amazed her mother had ever lasted to begin with.

"Do you want me to ask if you've been seeing someone? Is this one of those female things? You're not in poor health, are you?"

Adele just shook her head. "You know what, I can't really stay long. I just wanted to stop by and say hi. Anything you need? I can swing by the store and drop it off later."

Her dad waved away the offer and turned slowly back toward his TV, reaching for the remote. "Your German has gotten worse," he added as an afterthought.

Adele hesitated in the door to the kitchen, glancing at her father's profile. He was one of the few people who seemed happy in their discontent. And there was nothing she could do to change him. Stronger people than her had tried and failed.

"I'll see you later, Dad," she said.

The Sergeant nodded a couple of times. "See you, Sharp."

For some reason, Adele thought of Robert coming to pick her up at the airport. She thought of him tearing up at the thought of her moving into her room in his mansion. She thought of the way he smiled whenever he greeted her, of staying up late at night, talking by the fire.

But people couldn't choose their fathers. They couldn't choose their families.

Adele began striding back toward the front door, wishing she hadn't come to begin with.

"Sharp, make sure to clean your bowl. I'm tired of cleaning up other people's messes! Also don't splash the soup against the sink, the aluminum can rust."

Adele bit her lip, but backtracked to the sink, turned on the water, and rinsed out the bowl she hadn't asked for. She washed it with soap and water, listening to the hum and chatter from the TV room, and then turned to leave again.

A weight of sadness burdened her shoulders as she approached the front door. For some reason, unbidden, she thought perhaps she should go for a run in the morning. She didn't want to miss a day. She hadn't in years. Running always made her feel better.

As she contemplated the route she would jog, wondering if she could find a good trail nearby, she paused. A frown flitted across her features.

"Hang on," she said, softly. "What was that you said?"

But her dad ignored her, and she thought she heard him turn the TV up.

Tired of cleaning up other people's messes. Adele turned back toward the front door, heart hammering. The drug from Lion Pharmaceutical had been slated to be destroyed. But it was a highly controlled substance. There was no way they'd simply thrown it in the trash.

The samples that Peter Lehman had stolen were only part of the supplies destroyed.

So who had cleaned up the mess?

They would've had to hire a specialist. Adele's footsteps quickened as she hurried toward the door, and she put on her shoes.

"Don't run in the house! You'll leave scuff marks!"

She ignored her father and raced out the door, making sure to slam it as hard as possible as she jogged down the patio steps.

Her phone was already in her hand as she broke into a brisk walk, hurrying back toward the bus stop.

"John, meet me at Lion Pharmaceutical. I'm serious. I don't care who you're having drinks with. No, now. Please."

Adele closed her phone and jammed it back into her pocket.

Someone had to have cleaned up after the disposal of Project 132z. She needed to find out who was responsible for disposing of the samples. That, she was certain, had to be the key to everything. Whoever had disposed of the samples might have also known enough to steal some of them… And use them in America and France.

Adele quickened her pace until she was nearly jogging now, racing back toward the bus stop and away from her father's house.

CHAPTER TWENTY SEVEN

For the second time in the day, Adele burst through the door of Director Mueller's office without invitation. Again, he was on the phone.

Mueller scowled at Adele and threw his hands to the heavens. "What?" he demanded.

Agents Renee and Marshall followed closely behind as Adele came to a halt in front of the standing desk and peered across the smooth, varnished surface, meeting Director Mueller's glower. "Who disposes of your chemicals?" she asked.

"Excuse me?"

"I said, who handles the disposal of your chemicals? You can't just throw them in the trash, right?"

Director Mueller frowned. "If you must know," he said, testily, "we often incinerate, but sometimes we have contracts with agencies,"

Adele snapped her fingers, pointing one of them toward Mueller's face. "That second part. What agencies?"

"Excuse me?" Mueller glanced back past her toward Agent Marshall. "I thought I had the BKA's promise that I wouldn't be harassed over this. We complied by supplying the records. You arrested one of my employees. Right now," he wiggled the phone in his hand, "it's a PR disaster. So if you don't mind, I'd like to save this company before we lose contracts and go bankrupt."

Adele studied the man, weathering his frustration with a deferential nod, polite, but firm.

"Is he saying something annoying?" said John in French, with a growl. "I can tell he's saying something annoying."

Adele responded, "He's saying they do hire specialists to clean up their waste sometimes."

After a brief, muttered exchange with Agent Marshall, which seemed to calm him somewhat, Mueller finally threw his hands up and turned back to his computer.

He glanced at a couple of things, then clicked his phone, surveyed it, and pressed a number.

"Audrey?" he said. "Yes, right now. Keep them on hold. Yes, I need you to look who was responsible for hazardous disposals for the last two months."

Silence fell over the director's office.

Adele glanced out the floor-to-ceiling windows, scanning the fields surrounding the gated company, on the outskirts of the German suburbs.

A minute passed, then two.

Adele gnawed on the corner of her lip, hoping she'd been right. A lot was riding on this.

Not only could the killer escape if she was wrong. But Interpol's faith in her, faith in the collaboration between the DGSI, the BKA and the FBI, would be proven fruitless. Perhaps it would even cause difficulty arranging this sort of agency cooperation a second time.

After a few minutes, Director Mueller heaved an enormous sigh, his smooth forehead inching ever so slightly up, and he said, "Yes, two companies?" He lowered the phone. "Two companies were responsible for disposing of our chemicals these last two months."

Adele felt her heart quicken. "Who was responsible for disposing of Project 132z?"

"One moment." Director Mueller had the air of a man resigned to his fate. He lifted the phone again and parroted the question.

Another minute of pause, in which John tried to chat up Agent Marshall, but then Mueller returned with, "A local outfit," he said. "Medical Waste and Sanitation. Now, if you don't mind leaving my office... I don't have employee records for their company, and I really do have to take another call. Audrey, my assistant, will give you the number and address for the disposal team on the way out, all right? All right."

Then, ignoring them, he turned promptly, displaying his right shoulder toward Adele, and picked his phone up again, pressing it to his ear and ducking his head to make it abundantly clear that the conversation was over.

Adele turned toward John, her eyes glinting. "I was right; it's a company called Medical Waste and Sanitation. They're locals. They disposed of Lehman's project."

John stared at her. "You think a bunch of garbage men would've known what to do with those tubes?"

Adele shook her head. "I don't think they're regular sanitation

170

crews. They work for a place like this, so I'm not sure they're city-owned. I bet you one of them at the company was smart enough to know what they were looking at when they saw the disposed samples."

"You think it's a red-haired fellow?"

Adele shrugged. "We'll have to find out. They don't have employee records for the other company."

John nodded, turning away from Adele and starting to move back toward the exit to the office.

"Marshall," he said, "does the BKA have the ability to check records for us?"

Agent Marshall paused, chewed on her lip, then nodded. "Yes, just give me a moment."

Both John and Marshall took their phones out, and Adele hurried after them, leaving Director Mueller to his peace.

It felt like their last shot. Adele couldn't say why, but she knew that if this lead turned out to be a dead end, the killer would win. No other paths remained.

After this, Adele wouldn't have any other place to go. She *had* to be right. Someone on that sanitation team was a killer, and she was determined to find out who.

CHAPTER TWENTY EIGHT

Sergeant Joseph Sharp reclined in his armchair, his eyes flicking from the outdated TV to the clock on the wall. Three hours had passed since Sharp's visit.

Joseph watched a high-speed chase on the television with bland indifference, the red and blue lights on the screen pulsing and filling the room. A replay; he'd seen this one before—the no-good lawbreaker got his comeuppance. The Sergeant smiled at the thought, then, sighing to himself, he pulled the lever for the footrest and got to his feet.

"…for her own good…" he murmured quietly, continuing, out loud, a train of thought that had cycled through his mind the last three hours.

He glanced at the wall where his diploma from the police academy hung above newspaper clippings of the cases he'd been involved in. A hot flash of shame scoured his chest and he looked away in disgust, stomping into the kitchen.

Glowering, he turned on the hot water and began washing out his soup pot. On the counter, he spotted the canned soup Sharp had brought him. For a moment, as he eyed the can of soup, his movements became less agitated, and his internal monologue quieted.

"What?" he demanded of the soup can. He wagged a thick finger at the offending tin of creamed broccoli. He looked away and began washing the pot with large, agitated gestures, causing soapy water to splash against the inside of the metal sink.

Perhaps he was too hard on his daughter… But if he wasn't hard, she'd end up like everyone else in her generation: lazy good-for-nothings, mooching off the government and their parents.

Joseph hesitated… Still, it had been nice she'd visited. Maybe he should give her a call…

He glanced toward the old-fashioned phone dangling from its cradle on the wall, but then he shook his head and redoubled his cleaning efforts. No. Compassion was all well and good, but emotions got in the way of a good investigator. He wouldn't curse his daughter like that.

Once upon a time, he'd let his emotions get the best of him. He'd married a French girl—turned down a promotion to do it. Thirty years on the force and stuck as desk sergeant.

He rinsed off the pot and meticulously balanced it on the empty dry rack.

No; he wouldn't condemn his daughter to his same fate. She never admitted it, but he knew she was ambitious. He would push her, because she needed it. Because comfort bred complacency.

He nodded to himself, pursing his lips as he turned back toward the TV. Enough screen for the day; where had he placed that book? He glanced around the kitchen and patted at his back pocket.

Just then, the doorbell rang.

Joseph frowned and turned. Had his daughter returned?

"Sharp?" he called out through the house, the glow of the internal lights offset, now, by the darkness creeping in through the shuttered windows.

No answer.

The doorbell rang a second time.

"Darn it," he muttered with the same fervor a sailor might use to spew language that would have turned a priest's cheeks rosy. Joseph Sharp didn't believe in swearing, but the emotions behind the words? Outside his control.

And anything Sergeant Sharp couldn't control was best ignored or destroyed.

The doorbell rang a third time and he picked up his pace, hurrying to the front door, shouting through the house. "Keep your shirt on! I'm coming. Darn it, Sharp—you know how I hate it when—"

He pulled open the door.

No one was there.

"Sharp?" he murmured, frowning and peering out into the night. His only greeting was the flicker of streetlights in the night and the ashy smell of a neighbor's grill. He leaned forward, glancing to the side of the porch and down the patio steps. "Sharp—is that you?"

But he spotted no one. He glanced up the street, but the only car parked was the old green Nissan owned by the lady in 22C with that annoying, yip-yap mongrel.

The cool evening air gusted through the open door, sweeping toward Joseph Sharp and sending the hairs standing on the backs of his arms. Muttering darkly to himself, he began to close the door.

173

But just then, he heard a noise behind him. A creak of a floorboard. Sharp would have known not to ring the bell. She always knocked.

The Sergeant whirled around.

A man in a dark hood stood in his hallway, staring at him.

"Hello," the man said in German with a polite smile.

"Who in the double hells are—"

"Good evening," the man said.

Then his arm swung, there was a flash of metal, and something sharp jammed into Joseph's neck with an ominous *shnick*. He cried out in pain and tried to defend himself, reaching up with surprising speed and ripping the needle from his neck. Already, the plunger had been half pressed, though. Joseph cried out, smashing the needle against the wall, feeling glass bite into his hand.

The hooded man snarled. "That was my last one!"

Darkness pressed in. He felt light-headed, his movements sluggish. Joseph tried to reach up, grabbing at the hooded man, but his arm moved far, far too slowly.

The hooded man surveyed the Sergeant for a moment, clicking his tongue as the larger man slid down the wall. "Half a dose might not be enough, hmm? You're a big boy, aren't you?"

Vaguely, Joseph could hear the sound of his door closing, followed by the quiet click of a lock.

CHAPTER TWENTY NINE

Adele glanced into the passenger's seat at the printed page for the hundredth time in as many seconds. Her hands gripped the steering wheel, her heart pounding in tandem with the wild churning of her thoughts.

Porter Schmidt. The name at the top of the printed sheet. No photo—the waste department hadn't had any. The operator couldn't even describe what Schmidt looked like; apparently he worked remotely.

Adele growled in frustration. They would have to track down the suspects the hard way—door-to-door at night.

Porter Schmidt. Such a German name. One of *three* members of the waste disposal team who'd been tasked with destroying Project 132z. She had an address, a date of birth, and an identification number— nothing else. Records at Medical Waste and Sanitation were not up to the same standards of those of Lion Pharmaceutical. The operator hadn't even known if any of the men had vacationed recently.

Adele wracked her brain, recollecting the other two names. John was already hunting down Michael Xavi, and Agent Marshall had taken the third borrowed vehicle to find Artem Ozturk. The men lived on opposite sides of the township, and if any of Adele's teammates needed backup, it would take the others at least twenty minutes to arrive.

A lot could happen in twenty minutes.

Adele fidgeted uncomfortably in the seat of her loaner. At least she was no longer in the back of that ridiculous limousine. Adele had never worked with the BKA before, but—for the moment—they seemed accommodating enough. Though, she didn't doubt for a minute that the car was being tracked by GPS, and the dashcam blinked red, suggesting there was a live feed going directly back to German headquarters.

Adele worked best without pressure and too much oversight, but she could perform for an audience as well. Her father was not an affectionate man, but he had taught her how to succeed under pressure. For that, she was grateful.

Adele kept within ten kilometers of the speed limit, following the chirping GPS directions to the address on the printed file.

For a moment, as she turned off the highway and took the curling exit over a bridge, she glanced in the passenger's seat again and her eyes flicked to the rearview mirror, scanning the empty back seats. Strangely, she missed John.

Something about the tall, antagonizing agent had given her a sense of protection when shit hit the fan. Things were calm—almost too calm—as she sat in the car, studying the gentle flow of evening traffic. Most commuters had already returned home from work for the evening.

Still, despite it all, Adele felt like she was sitting on a powder keg, waiting for it to detonate. Agent Marshall had notified the appropriate units nearby to respond to calls for help, but still, if anything went wrong, the three agents were now on their own.

Michael, Artem, or Porter. Two innocent men who worked for a waste disposal crew were in for a rude interruption to their evenings. And, if Adele's guess was right, one murderer knew they were coming for him.

She felt a shiver down her spine and, inadvertently, her foot pushed on the gas pedal and her vehicle picked up speed as she took a right turn onto a long stretch of road.

"Right turn in two miles," chirped the GPS in German. "Then arrive at destination on left."

Adele felt her stomach twisting and, keeping one hand on the wheel, her other reached down to her side, checking that her weapon was still on her hip.

Porter Schmidt. A one in three chance she'd chosen the lucky number.

Two miles to go until she found out. Her thoughts continued to cycle, and Adele continued to push slowly on the gas pedal, now speeding through traffic and racing toward her destination.

***

Splitting up had seemed like the right call earlier in the evening. They would cover more ground that way.

But now, in the dark of looming night, as Adele exited her vehicle and stepped onto the sidewalk before the aloof, old house, she wished she'd reconsidered.

The darkness pressed in around her like hounds snuffling at prey. Adele doubled-checked her shoulder radio which Marshall had provided when they'd split up. She glanced back toward the dash cam of the now quiet car; the red light was still blinking even though the key was in her pocket.

Someone was still watching.

Funnily, this bolstered Adele's confidence. She hoped, if given a similar vehicle, John wouldn't take it personally and react in the way she assumed he might. Paying for a damaged dash cam likely wasn't high on Executive Foucault's agenda.

She pressed the outgoing button on the radio and said, "Hello, is this thing working? Renee? Marshall? Are you at your targets yet?"

There was a pause, a quiet crackling sound, then John replied, "Stopped for a coffee," he said. "And a donut. Will be there in five."

Adele bit her lip, cutting off the cuss that burbled to the tip of her tongue. Her father's influence stretched beyond the borders of his four neatly maintained walls. Still, she growled as she said, "We're on the clock here, John—maybe a bit of professionalism—"

"Sorry, coffee just arrived. They take Euros in this country, don't they?"

Adele stood on the sidewalk, feet at shoulder width, eyes narrowed now. Any sense of appreciation for John had faded to be replaced, once again, by annoyance at his lackluster approach to the job.

Before she could reply with a scathing remark, however, the radio buzzed again and Agent Marshall's voice blared out, far too loudly, "It isn't Mr. Ozturk," Marshall said. "He lives in an apartment and his landlord and three separate neighbors all claim they've seen him in the last week. Plus, well…" Here Marshall trailed off for a moment as if she were gathering her thoughts then, in a tactful tone, she continued, "I'm not sure he's in the physical capacity to subdue or harm anyone."

John snickered and said, "Is he a fatty? Are you talking normal chub or *American* fat?"

Adele pressed the button again. "John, please, could you just hurry up?"

A pause. Static, then, "What about you, American Princess; we're down to two, it sounds like. Is your man a red-haired devil?"

"Don't know yet," said Adele, glancing back up toward the old, well-maintained home. It was a busy street with cars zipping by every few moments, but otherwise, the house was normal looking enough.

The grass was cut, the leaves raked, two trash cans were set out on the curb for collection.

"Should I come meet one of you?" said Agent Marshall's voice.

Adele began to reply, but John beat her to it. "I'm closer. Come meet me. Afterwards, you can show me the best place to get drinks."

Adele resisted the urge to gag. "Could you stop flirting, finish your coffee, and go check your man?"

John snickered. "Don't forget the donut. It's almost ready."

Adele shook her head in defeat, but lowered her hand from the radio to her holster as she stalked toward the house. Her other hand went to her identification, preparing to lift it in introduction as she'd done many times before.

The investigative part was always easier. Adele had never been comfortable with a firearm, and even now she could feel old nerves coming back, threatening to derail her.

She inhaled deeply, then exhaled for a second longer, focusing on her breathing as she took the steps to the porch and raised a hand to knock on the door.

No answer.

She reached out and pushed the bell. A brief spurt of guilt caused her to cringe as she did. Her father's influence had extended to bell-pushing. *Christ,* she thought to herself. *How pathetic.*

She pushed the bell a second time with more confidence, holding it longer this time.

But again, there was no answer.

Adele slowly unbuttoned her holster and sidestepped to the nearest window. She frowned, pressing her forehead against the cool glass.

Through the window, she spotted a tidy room with an old grandfather chair facing a fireplace and a long kitchen table with a laptop.

Her eyes narrowed, staring at the laptop, trying to register what she was seeing.

A face on the laptop stared back at her.

A face she knew.

"Shit," she said, uttering the word in tandem with a huffing breath.

The laptop had a picture of her father's face displayed on the LED screen. Adele's gun ripped from its holster and she kicked at the door. Once, twice, leading with her heavy boot, but the door held firm. With an urgent huff of air, she sprinted around the side of the house and hopped a low, ridged wooden fence. Ignoring a bed of roses, she tore through the flowers and circled the backyard. A home gym was stationed beneath a tree, complete with a workout bench, weights and an old rowing machine beneath a tarp.

She ignored the strange set-up and surged toward the back door. This one was brittle, old—a wooden affair with chipped, flecked paint and a small glass semicircle which reminded her of the sections of an orange.

She kicked this door again, and again, desperately wishing she'd had John for backup.

Finally, with the third kick, on what felt like a sprained ankle, there was a splintering sound.

Adele felt a surge of exhilaration, coupled with dawning horror as she slammed her shoulder into the door and, with one final protesting crack, it gave way and swung inward.

She rushed into the room, sprinting over three neat sets of male shoes. She reached the kitchen table, her gun still raised, trained on the kitchen, then switching to the living room.

No one in sight.

She didn't announce herself, but spun around the rectangular kitchen table and, breathing heavy, her shoulder and ankle pulsing with aches, she stared at the computer screen.

It was open to the Berlin PD website. Her father's name and face filled the screen and her eyes flicked to the tabs of the browser: Google Maps was open. With a trembling hand, she lowered her gun, placing it on the table, and clicked the tab for the map.

A small red dot, like the laser on a sniper's scope pulsed over a house in the suburbs.

She stared, scanning the map and her eyes flicking to the search bar. It was her father's address.

"Dear God," she murmured, backing away from the table. Her hand fumbled in her pocket, but she finally managed to rip her phone from her pants and dial her father's number. The cold blue screen blinked back a single word: *Dad.*

Once upon a time, she'd stored his name only as *Joseph.* But things had improved since then. At least, so she hoped.

Five rings. Six. Seven.

No answer.

She dialed again. Sometimes her dad ignored the phone, fearing telemarketers.

Another five. Six. Seven. Dial tone.

No answer.

A third try—still no answer.

Adele rammed her phone back into her pocket and she darted forward, one arm extended as she grabbed her gun; rapidly, she gave the house a cursory scan, one last time, then broke into a sprint, back out the rear door, hopping the splintered frame and racing back through the rose garden.

"John!" she shouted into her radio, "John—it's Porter! Porter Schmidt is the killer. He's going after the Sergea—my dad! John!"

She reached her car, swung open the door, and spilled into the seat, tossing her gun onto the passenger side. It took her three tries with trembling fingers to jam the key into the ignition and another couple of tries, with the engine groaning, for her to realize she still had the vehicle in neutral.

Cursing, Adele put the car in gear and tried to focus on breathing, to calm herself.

But the trick didn't work this time.

Adrenaline met terror and did a number on her mind, sending her into a vortex of worry and fear. A physical clot of anxiety pulsed in her chest. Her dad. The killer was going after her dad.

She thought of her norther. Ribbons of red extending from the once beautiful woman, staining the clover leaves and blades of grass, spilling into the sodden ground in the park. A tapestry of swirling scars up and down her body.

"Fuck!" Adele shouted as she ripped from the curb and nearly hit a park bench. "Dammit!" She tore up the street, ignoring a vehicle half-pulled out of the driveway. The driver leaned on his horn in protest, but Adele ignored that too and floored the gas pedal, tearing through a stop sign and roaring up the street.

She'd just been at her father's place. Had she missed him? Would she be too late?

No. No, she couldn't think like that. She couldn't be too late. Not this time. *Please, God, not this time…*

"John!" she repeated, slapping at the radio. "Where are you?"

A buzz, some static. Then, "Sharp? What is it?" Some of the joviality had faded from John's voice. "Adele, are you okay?"

Tears were now streaming down her face. For a moment, Adele felt twenty again. Little more than a child, weeping at the news of her mother.

No. Not this time. Not her father too.

Still, she sobbed, trying to maintain professionalism, trying to suppress the emotions like she always did and always could. Emotions caused weakness. Emotions were distractions for an investigator.

But she couldn't push back the kaleidoscope of horrible images now playing themselves across her brain, suggesting all the *coulds* and *what-ifs* of the immediate future. Each thought brought a new wave of emotion and a new surge of speed as Adele ripped through traffic, receiving more than one blare from a horn. At last, she remembered to flip on her lights and siren—the BKA had been kind enough to at least supply that.

Siren wailing now, blue and red flashing across the glinting windshield and hood of her car, she zipped beneath a red light, surging back onto the highway, heading in the direction of her father's house.

"No," she said. "John—John he's going after my dad. It's Porter. He's going after my father!"

A pause. Then, a serious voice. "You're sure?"

Her voice cracked. " Yes, John, please—"

"Where does your father live?" he rattled off, his voice becoming colder, more calculated. The voice of a military man in the middle of a high-stakes operation.

Adele recited her father's address from memory, her eyes glued to the road as she wove in and out of traffic.

There was a staticky buzz, then John, sounding out of breath now as if he were running, said, "I'm on my way. Don't do anything stupid."

"John, it's my dad."

"Damn it, Adele, I know." The distant slamming sound of a car door interrupted through the static. "Just wait for me. Okay? Promise me you'll wait."

Adele didn't reply. She gripped the steering wheel, no longer attempting to suppress her emotions, but stewing in them as she sped through the city, racing toward her father's house and into the waiting arms of a killer.

CHAPTER THIRTY

She tore into the driveway, heralded by the yipping sound of the neighbor's dogs. She flung open the car door, not bothering to close it, only pausing for a second as she remembered to grab her gun from the passenger's seat.

She sprinted up the steps and reached the house, pausing only to glance through the windows, searching the interior of the house. But most the windows were shuttered.

Her dad was the type to shoot first and ask questions later, but Adele wasn't worried about being on the wrong end of a hair-trigger. Had she beat the killer here? She needed to enter the house.

Porter Schmidt. Such a German name. Nothing in that name suggested he'd killed six people, and yet, though she still had yet to meet him, Adele could practically smell the murderer, like a bloodhound with a sixth sense. She knew he was the killer as surely as she knew her father's life was in danger.

Her gun tapped gently against the window as she peered through a slat in one of the shutters—an old trick she'd adopted as a child when she'd returned home from school to make sure her parents weren't shouting at each other before entering the house.

Many afternoons had been spent sitting on the front porch for hours, reading schoolbooks or sketching in a journal, waiting for the shouting to stop.

Now, curling up her spine with tooth and claw, came a desperate, cloying, frigid sensation that set her teeth on edge more than the yelling ever had. Briefly, she thought fondly of the shouting, wishing that *some* noise would echo from the quiet, darkened house.

But no sound arose.

Adele abandoned her position by the slat in the window—all she'd managed to spot was darkness. She hurried to the door, reached out, and gripped the handle.

It twisted. The door remained locked.

For the faintest moment, she thought she heard a muffled groaning sound from within the house. Was someone in pain? She eyed the door up and down, her head movements frantic. She couldn't kick this door down, no matter how hard she tried. Her father had reinforced the front and the back door following a slew of robberies the town over.

With a snarl, Adele cast about, and her eyes settled on the porch furniture. Holstering her weapon, she hurried over, grabbed one of the hefty wooden chairs, and slammed it into the nearest slatted window. Glass shattered and spilled like fragments of starlight, twinkling as the pieces of glass scattered the porch and tumbled into the living room. She slammed the chair a second time, breaking the wooden shutters.

She would apologize later. Now, all she needed was to enter the house.

She used the chair to clear the worst of the jutting pieces of glass left in the sill. The silent alarm would have been tripped now—a call was already reaching the police station from the security system. Her father was nothing if not safety conscious. But they wouldn't reach her in time.

It was up to her. A foreign agent in a foreign country. At stake: the only family she had left.

She scraped the last of the glass away and shouted into the house, "Dad, it's me! Are you okay?"

This time, she was certain she heard a muffled groaning sound. She'd heard torture victims on a recording once that sounded like that.

She flung the chair aside and pushed through the window, ignoring the glass scraping at her side and against her forearm as she delicately tried to maneuver through the awkward opening.

With less grace than she would have liked, Adele tumbled into her father's living room, avoiding most the glass and splinters of wood. Still, she could feel a trickle of warmth down her arm and a sharp, pulsing throb in her right side along her ribs.

Injuries would have to wait.

Gun met sweaty palm; iron sights surveyed darkness.

Adele, foot over foot, in a shooter's crouch, stepped through the living room. Her feet made small crunching sounds against a few pieces of glass that had made it further along the carpet. For a moment, all she could think was where her father kept the vacuum. She needed to clean up before he saw it, or he'd let her have it for a week.

She gritted her teeth, staving off the thoughts brought on by the influence of the Sergeant's house. The crunching sound of her footsteps gave way to quiet padding as boots met carpet. The sharp pain in her

183

ribs still pulsed, but ignoring it, Adele stepped from the living room, swinging her gun into the kitchen.

Nothing.

Except.

The water was running.

Adele frowned at the faucet. She reached out with a trembling hand, turning the knob, shutting off the stream of hot water, which had now gone cold.

Her father would never have left a faucet running.

She struggled, desperately wondering if she should call out again. For all her father knew, someone had just broken into his house, and he was now crouched with a shotgun upstairs waiting to blow her head off the moment she popped into view.

Or, someone else was in the house.

Someone else waiting for her to make a noise, lying in wait, preparing to jab her with a needle.

If she called out in the first case, it might save her life, and save her father the trauma of blasting his only daughter in two. In the second case, though, any noise might alert the predator to her presence.

Adele maintained her quiet, moving along the cupboards, her body turned, presenting as small a target as possible toward the doorway, just as they'd been trained to do. This was her least favorite part of an investigation, but she'd drilled with weapons the same as everyone else.

She checked the safety, then slid through the door, crouched low, hoping to throw off the aim of anyone expecting someone of normal height. She kept her gun close to her chest, careful not to lead with her weapon too far in front, lest she give away her position before she had eyes on.

Again, she wished John had come with her. Some of her anxiety around weapons, around making an arrest, had been eased while with him. Back in the hotel in France, she hadn't felt the usual anxiety. Here in Germany, with the chemist, he'd known what to do.

Coffee and a donut. She shook her head in disbelief at the radio call, trying desperately to contain her emotions in the moment, to regain her composure.

She turned up the stairs.

No one.

The steps creaked as she stepped up the stairwell. Instead of facing forward, though, she backed up slowly, one at a time, gun raised toward the banisters above, keeping track toward the top of the stairs where someone might have been watching.

Again, nothing.

The carpeted hall was dark. Pictures framed the wall on either side in neat rows. Pictures of Adele and her mother. Pictures of a life long since lost. Yet pictures kept in positions of high esteem. The air smelled of detergent and lavender.

Adele stepped past her old room and glanced in.

Her father had lied.

He hadn't converted it into an office. Rather, her bed was exactly as she remembered it. Pink covers with pillows pressed against the headboards. Her stuffed animals were there; he'd also kept the old desk covered in the trophies she'd won at track meets. She frowned, distracted for the faintest of seconds.

There were other pictures too—pictures of the competitions in France. A shrine to his daughter's success. But also her stuffed animals.

Adele shook her head; her father was a hard man to read.

She heard a louder, muffled groan. Her attention shifted sharply back to the moment and she pointed her gun toward the large, closed chestnut door at the opposite end of the staircase. Her feet slipped along the thick, perfectly white carpet. It took a confident man to install white carpet. Yet, there had never been a stain in the near decade Adele had lived here.

Licking her dry lips, Adele shifted past the railing, moving past a bathroom and another guest room her mother had stayed in during the last couple years of their marriage.

She paused for a moment, standing in darkness in front of her parents' old room. Joseph's room. She'd never been allowed in the Sergeant's room; he'd hated the idea of a child messing around in his private space.

She felt an inexplicable surge of guilt as she reached down, slowly twisting the doorknob.

It turned.

More groaning, more desperate now.

Her heart skipped a beat, and she pushed the door, sharply, but instead of bursting in, she stepped back and dropped to a knee, allowing herself a good long look at the room before rushing into potential danger.

The door settled with a dull thump against the wall, spread over the white carpet.

In the room, in front of the neatly made bed, her father sat bound to a spindly wooden chair. His hands were tied behind his back; duct tape sealed his mouth. He was bleeding from cuts in his forehead and along his cheek.

Adele could just make out the edge of his fingers, from the way he was positioned facing the door, but turned slightly toward a window. Droplets of blood trickled from his fingertips and tumbled to the pristine carpet, staining the white beneath his chair and joining a larger stain caused by the blood seeping down his pant leg and soaking into the carpet beneath his foot.

"Dad!" Adele said, her hear in her throat.

She pushed off her knee and surged forward, rushing toward her father.

But he began shaking his head wildly, bucking and thrashing, a desperate look in his eyes she'd never seen before. He was staring at her, and kicking as wildly as he could, sending droplets off blood flying around the room, further staining his white carpet in complete disregard.

Adele hesitated for a moment in the doorway, entranced by her desperate desire to obey her father in all things, but also a sheer sense of duty to help those in danger.

Especially her parents. She only had one left.

Adele ignored his thrashing and bullishly entered the room, rushing to her dad's side and ripping the duct tape from his mouth as quickly as she could, like pulling a Band-Aid.

Her father's eyes narrowed as he winced, his cheeks bunched, but once the duct tape left his lips, his groaning and mumbling ceased and, in a loud voice, he shouted, "Sharp—no! Run!"

Adele heard the faintest of creaks behind her, from where the bookcase levied against the doorframe. She whirled around, gun raised. Something whistled as she ducked again, like she'd done before, and a heavy, metallic object swished over her head, rushing through her hair.

Her dad shouted incoherently.

There was a loud curse as a hooded shape swung a metal crowbar a second time, trying to crush Adele's upraised arm. Her gun went off, but she knew she'd missed before she lurched back, avoiding the attack.

At the same time, her father kicked out, trying to trip the assailant, but the man—though not particularly large—was clearly strong.

Adele raised her gun again and squeezed off a shot, blind, still reeling. She finally managed to reset, bracing her back against the window to her father's room, and she aimed now.

The hooded man cursed and kicked out, scoring a strike against Adele's wrist. She grunted in pain and her gun went flying. She tried to track it, but lost it as the killer surged at her, trying to overwhelm her. Still, she might not have enjoyed firearms, but she was a trained investigator; she knew how to find things.

And while she hadn't seen where the gun landed, she heard a quiet tick, suggesting the weapon had brushed the glass window, followed by a dull *thunk,* suggesting it had ricocheted off the jutting windowsill, followed by nothing further. Which meant, instead of landing on the carpet, it had likely landed on the soft pillow in the empty chair facing the window.

She didn't have time to check this theory, though, as the killer came at her like a bat out of a flooded cave. His hood obscured most his features, but now he had a scalpel in one hand and a crowbar in the other. Adele lurched beneath the swiping blade, but this time couldn't avoid the crowbar.

It struck her a glancing blow to the side of the head.

Immediately, she tasted iron in her mouth, and her head started spinning. Being struck in the side of the head was a lot harder to track than stories made out. It almost, inevitably, always came with a surge of shock and lost time.

Adele blinked and the killer seemed to have transported, the blow from the crowbar creating a gap in her memory. Still, she had the wherewithal to roll onto the bed as another swipe of the scalpel threatened to open her throat.

She couldn't move too far, though; if he reached the gun, it was over.

Adele didn't have time to look. She didn't have time to shout out a warning. If the gun was on the floor instead of the cushion, she was dead.

But while she struggled with firearms, she could follow clues to their inevitable conclusion. The soft tick, the dull *thunk,* the lack of any further sound.

The gun was on the cushion. It had to be.

The killer swiped at her again, this time with the crowbar. But instead of surging back, as he'd anticipated, she shoved forward, slamming her head into the hooded man's chest and sending him reeling into the window. Then, shooting up a desperate prayer to all listeners, she blindly groped toward the chair beneath the window, felt only cushion—horror flooded her—but then, at last, her fingers met metal.

She cried out in alarm and relief as her hand came back with her gun once more. She aimed it again, finger tightening on the trigger.

But the killer's eyes widened in the moonlight streaming through the window. This time, he didn't come for her again and instead, he flung himself backward, with impressive speed. Adele's finger stiffened on the trigger.

"Shoot him!" her father kept screaming. "Do it, Sharp! Kill the bastard!"

But Adele couldn't. The Sergeant was in the line of fire. She tried to shift, moving toward the door for a better angle, but the killer's eyes flicked from her, to her father, and then teeth flashed in the shadow of his hood as he grinned.

The scalpel fell, descending toward her father's neck.

The blade pressed against his throat and the Sergeant fell quiet, suddenly, swallowing.

"Hello, Agent Sharp," said the killer in perfect German, smiling at her.

He reached up and lowered his hood, revealing his face.

Porter Schmidt had the reddest hair Adele had ever seen. Robert had been right. He also had a nearly perfect nose and sculpted cheeks. He would have been alarmingly handsome, except something about his appearance seemed a little *too* intentional. Though Adele couldn't be certain, it seemed to her that Porter had booked appointments with the same sort of doctor who'd restored Robert's once fading hair.

"Mr. Schmidt?" Adele replied, also in German, breathing heavily, her chest rising and falling in rapid motions. The man frowned briefly, and Adele noted the reaction. "We know everything about you. There are ten officers closing in as we speak. They're downstairs. If you want to make it out alive at all—"

"Shh," the man said, quietly, drawing the scalpel across her father's neck and leaving a thin, red line.

The Sergeant winced and, for a brief five-second window, seemed to insert all the prohibited words he'd suppressed over the course of the year.

"Stop!" Adele said, desperate. "There are snipers just outside, and—"

"Shh," Schmidt repeated, smiling again. Another tracing of the scalpel, and her father hissed in pain, kicking his feet.

"Stop!" she screamed.

"Lower your gun," he said, quietly. "Please."

Adele hesitated.

"Don't, Sharp—shoot him. Do it now! Do it, or we're both dead." Her father's voice cracked. "Don't you—don't you dare. Please. Honey, please. Don't—I'll be fine. Don't—" This time he howled in pain as the scalpel bit deeper, dragging across his chin down to the collarbone, in the same position where John had his burn marks.

Adele dropped her gun like a hot coal. It hit the carpet with a muted *thud.*

"There are no snipers, no other officers," said the killer, studying Adele. "Are there? And, please, for daddy's sake, don't lie." He leaned down and kissed her father on top of his head, making a loud, smacking noise with his mouth as he did.

Her father tried to hit the killer with the top of his head, but the man was too quick. He chuckled and pressed the scalpel back to the Sergeant's neck.

"Well?" he said, quietly. "Tell me the truth."

Adele hesitated, then shook her head, staring at the knife. "No. I'm alone."

"Good. Please, darling, shut the door. I want to talk. How old are you, by the way?"

Adele frowned, but, with slow, morbid movements, she reached for the door and closed it. As she did, though, with her free hand, blocking it from view with her turned shoulders, she reached up and flicked the radio receiver on, while simultaneously muting the device.

When she turned back around, her hands were both back by her side.

Anyone listening would be able to hear, but she wouldn't be able to hear them.

The killer eyed her up and down, his gaze lingering on her radio for the faintest moment. Then, with a relieved sigh, he said, "Good. Now we're alone."

He collapsed into a sitting position on the bed, arm still out, scalpel still glinting in the moonlight in the dark room. The comforter flattened beneath his weight, puffing up around him and pressing against his hips.

He patted the bed next to him. "Come," he said, "sit next to me. You look so much like her, you know?"

Adele frowned. "Excuse me?" She didn't move, standing where she was in front of the closed door, still within view of the window.

"Elise Romei," said the killer, his tongue poking through his lips as if savoring her mother's name as it left his mouth. "You are the spitting image—believe me. Truly, truly," he began to giggle, shaking his head incredulously, "this is fate." He wagged a finger toward something on the bed.

Adele glanced over and felt her heart skip a beat. It was an old framed photo of Elise, the Sergeant, and Adele. Smiling. They hadn't smiled much together, and Adele couldn't even remember when the photo had been taken.

"We were meant to meet, Adele Sharp."

CHAPTER THIRTY ONE

"Romei," he clicked his tongue... "Elise changed her name, otherwise I would have realized sooner." He chuckled softly.

Adele glared at the man, a prickling horror giving way to a burning fury. This man, of all people, had no right to invoke her mother's name. "Romei was her maiden name. How do you know my mother?" she demanded.

The killer winked at her, reclining one elbow on her father's shoulder, using him like a table to prop up a weary arm. "Oh, she was a beautiful woman... I masturbated to pictures of her, you know..." Then he hesitated and frowned, as if realizing he might have said something offensive. "Not when she was alive, of course... I wouldn't do that to a married woman." He shook his head wildly from side to side. "Of course not. But afterwards? The pictures that were published in the papers, but repressed—they found their ways online... I have to tell you, I spent many nights—"

"Who the hell are you?" Adele demanded.

But the killer raised a hand, beckoning for her to come closer, smiling again.

With dread in her heart, but few options, she stepped over her gun, where it lay useless enmeshed in the thick carpet—stepping past her one defense—and approached the man with the knife to her father's throat.

"I don't understand, Mr. Schmidt," Adele said, slowly, wetting her lips with the tip of her tongue. "You knew my mother?"

Porter paused, reaching back with the hand not pressed to the Sergeant's throat and running a hand through his vibrant, red hair. "It's not what you think," he said, shaking his head, still smiling like a child discussing their favorite superhero. "I didn't kill your mother..."

"But you know who did?" Adele's voice rasped.

The killer frowned. "A gardener," he said. "They called him the Spade Killer. You should know that. He honored your mother—you owe him a debt of gratitude."

Adele rolled her fingers, clenching them into fists. She brushed her right foot back, seeking an anchor point with her gun, in case she needed to lunge for it.

The killer noticed this movement though and shook his head. He beckoned with a finger at her. "Come here. Give me your shirt and your radio."

Adele stared at him, and the Sergeant began thrashing again, indifferent to the blade against his neck.

The killer wiggled his pointer finger, gesturing at her. "I'm serious. Come on—give them, or I open a second smile in daddy dearest."

Adele stared over her father's shoulder, refusing to meet his eyes.

The killer rolled his eyes. "Puh-lease," he said, blowing air from out of a jutting lip and causing his red bangs to lift like dandelion fluff. "I'm not a perv—I just don't want you making any inappropriate calls, and I need to check you for a wire." His carefree tone morphed without notice and, with steel, he snapped, "Give me your shirt and your radio, *now!*"

He began to cut her father again, but Adele quickly ripped her shirt off, which took the shoulder radio and its wires with it. She flung both at Porter.

She glanced down, noticing the streak of blood along her ribs where she'd scraped against the glass window. She looked up and noticed the killer staring at her too, ogling the cut along her ribs. She'd worn a sports bra, modest enough—but Adele had never been embarrassed by her body, and if the killer was hoping to shame her, it wouldn't work.

His eyes weren't drawn to her chest, but rather remained fixed on her ribs, staring at the blood swirling down her abdomen. He let out a quiet sound of gurgling pleasure from the back of his throat.

As he stared, he was distracted. He extracted the radio from Adele's shirt and tossed it onto the bed, behind her father's bound form. But he didn't check it, nor did he flick the off-switch. If anyone was listening, they could still hear everything.

"I feel uncomfortable with my back to the window like this," Adele said, choosing her words carefully. "The moon is in your eyes; you have a pretty good look out the window, don't you? I bet that was intentional. And you kept the curtain open so you could see me coming. Clever," she said.

The killer frowned, listening to her, still mesmerized by the cut along her ribs.

Shirtless, Adele felt a chill now in the room. Her father's eyes were fixed on hers, wide, the whites stretched in the dark. She looked away, though. She needed her wits about her; long, meaningful looks of melancholy or unstated love wouldn't save them now.

"Second floor," she continued, speaking a bit louder than necessary, but refusing to look in the direction of the radio. "Smart to hole up here in the room facing the street. Gives you the perfect vantage point, and you've been one step ahead this entire time. No wire—can I have my shirt back? You're making my dad uncomfortable."

She stared, unblinking, unyielding at the killer.

At this, he tore his gaze away from the blood across her ribs and studied her for a moment. Then he began to giggle. He stood up, still keeping the knife to her father's throat, but now with his calf muscles against the frame of the bed. He watched her across the room. "You have a nice body," he said. "But I bet you don't have to work as hard as I do for it. See?"

He lifted the edge of his shirt, revealing his abdomen, and he flexed, grunting from exertion. Still flexing, in a strained voice, he repeated, "See? How old do you think I am—no, really, take your best guess." Now he was studying her eyes, staring out across the dark room and the bleeding sergeant.

She met his gaze, stepping, ever so slightly to the right.

"Hey!" he snapped. "None of that now; kick it away. Do it!"

Adele held up her hands in deference and reached back with a foot, kick-shoving her gun across the floor and sending it into the corner of the room beneath the chair. She used the motion, however, to take another, hesitant step to the right, out of the line of fire through the window.

Please be listening, John. If you stopped for another donut, I'll kill you myself!

"You never met my muse, did you?" said Porter, still studying her. "How old are you?"

"Does it matter?" she said.

He scowled, his smile disappearing. "What a stupid bloody question," he spat. "What a *stupid* question. Yes!" Spittle flew from his lips, speckling the back of her father's head. "Of course it matters. How old are you!"

"Thirty-two," Adele said, quietly.

The killer hesitated. His mood shifted again, just as rapidly as before. Instead of fury, his eyes now held awe. He glanced out the window, catching the reflection of the moon and glancing up as if looking to the stars. "Truly," he said. "It's fate. Elise faded away at forty-one, you know? The numbers equal five."

"A lot of numbers equal five."

The killer's eyes narrowed. "It's fate."

What is?" said Adele, still keeping calm, trying to stall, to give her backup as much time as they needed. What if they didn't come? What if they came too late? She suppressed these thoughts, forcing them, willing them from her mind.

The killer hadn't handed her shirt back, but still clutched it in one fist, bunched around his hand. He lifted it slowly, and sniffed at the fabric, especially lingering, his nostrils flaring, along the stretches streaked with blood.

"I like your perfume," he said, quietly. "It smells nice mixed with your sweat... Like flowers and sulfur..." He giggled and inhaled again, pressing her shirt against his mouth and nose now, his eyes rolling back in pleasure.

For a flash of a moment, there was an opening—he wasn't looking. But the moment passed as quickly as it came.

Adele couldn't risk her father. She didn't react, listening, allowing him to speak. The more he talked, the less he hurt the Sergeant. For now, that was a win. Eventually, though, he would lash out. She knew men like this. Killers always thought they were special. People romanticized serial killers—some people fantasized about being like them. TV shows, movies, books—serial killers were revered world 'round.

But really, deep down, killers were all the same.

Scared, vain, desperately alone, and looking to spread their own misery, like a contagion, to the rest of the world.

Adele was a surgeon. It was her job to remove the contagion— whatever the cost.

Her eyes narrowed as she slipped, once more, ever so slightly to the right. Now her shadow no longer played across the killer's chest. The moonlight struck him solid, illuminating his red hair and structured features.

"Forty-one," he said. "That was the Spade Killer's first, you know—Elise... your mother. His cuts are prettier than mine—I'll be the

194

first to admit it." He waved a hand, distractedly. "I'm a humble student—I don't desire to overtake the true savant of the trade." He shook his head. "But I did continue his work. He stopped at thirty, you know that? I picked up where he left off. Like Kepler finishing the work of Copernicus. Do you know who they are?"

Adele bobbed her head. "Astronomers. Both of them old. Both of them long dead." Her tone carried no undercurrent, but the killer still frowned at her words.

"Yes—yes, but immortal too, don't you see? You *know* them." His eyes had creased again and his brow furrowed in a summoned rage.

She needed to cut him off at the pass. Talking was fine, but eventually he'd hurt her father. Eventually, he'd kill her too—there was no way he didn't. The killer saw their meeting as fate. She needed to put him off guard, to give herself an opportunity, to turn the killer's violent attention from her father to herself.

Adele said, "Death scares you, doesn't it? Somehow, in that twisted brain of yours, you think by murdering these young, innocent people, that you're retaining your youth. Is that it? Whoever did the work on your nose, though, didn't do you any favors in that department."

The man's cheeks turned from red to white. He stared at her, his eyes bugging in his skull. The knife wavered for a moment as if his fingertips were trembling from sheer rage. "What did you say?" he said.

But Adele was tired of standing there, scared and shirtless in the dark, her father bleeding, her side aching, allowing the killer to toy with them. It was a gamble; but her father would die soon without medical attention. She couldn't keep stalling, or he'd bleed out.

"The gardener did your mother right," said the killer, seething now. "Honestly, it's *funny* you left Paris, you know that? Especially given where you worked. He who came before created a masterpiece. I may not be the artist he is, but there's a poetry to it, isn't there? It started at forty-one with Elise, and once you're out of the way I'll continue all the way down to… Well, until it ends."

Adele snorted in disdain. "Ends? You won't end shit. You're a murderer addicted to your own arrogance. You couldn't stop killing if you wanted to. A friend of mine, his name is Robert—he thinks that people like you can change. Maybe he's right; he taught me a lot, but you want to know what I think, Mr. Schmidt?"

The man's eyes narrowed across the room.

"I think you're too stupid, too *normal,* too *ordinary* and too old to change." She shrugged in a gesture of disdainful dismissal. "Can't teach an old dog new tricks. And hells, you're ancient."

The killer loosed a mewling snarl that started in the back of his throat as a whimper, but then exploded, shoved to the front of his lips with a surging vehemence that caught Adele off guard.

He screamed and lunged toward her, knife flashing, just as she turned, grabbing for her gun.

But he reached her first and kicked her in the chest, sending her stumbling away from her weapon and careening into the wall beneath the window. Her head clattered against the glass and her shoulders slumped as they scraped past the sill and she came to a stop against the plaster.

The killer continued to emit his shriek as he dropped on top of her, smothering her and holding her down. His one hand pressed against the exposed flesh of her abdomen, twisting against the blood and slipping along her ribs. The other raised the scalpel, trying to slash down.

Adele's hand was all that kept the knife from her throat. She had the killer gripped by the wrist, holding tight, keeping both their hands elevated.

She gritted her teeth, emitting a growl of her own to match the killer's snarl. Like a couple of huffing animals, they lay there, him on top of her, both of them struggling for control of the other's hand.

The Sergeant was shouting and thrashing now, but his movements had weakened as his wounds took their toll and blood loss had its say.

Adele screamed in pain as she felt a finger jam into the cut at her side, trying to twist the flesh open further. She howled and the killer screamed back at her, their noses almost touching. He managed to jerk his hand free from hers and shove his shoulder down, trapping her wrist against her chest and pinning it beneath his weight.

He was too strong, too agile.

She tried to kick out, but he was straddling her now, securing his grip before lifting the knife a second time, like an artist with a paint brush, holding their tool of choice aloft before setting to their next work.

Then there was a distant bang.

Followed, in near perfect succession by another.

The killer's hand was illuminated in moonlight—the only part of him still visible over the windowsill. The first bang saw the window

196

shatter as a bullet broke the glass and sent pieces tumbling onto both Adele and Porter.

The second bullet slammed into the killer's hand, demolishing a couple of knuckles and severing a finger at the joint. The killer howled as his finger fell from his injured hand and blood poured from his new wound.

The knife fell, landing next to Adele's cheek, along with more shards of glass, which nicked her face, but missed her eyes.

She grunted and shoved.

The killer was still staring at his disfigured hand, a look of horror across his features. Adele didn't hesitate. As some of his pressure lifted from the shock of being shot, she flung out her left hand, grabbed the scalpel, gripped it and brought it slashing forward. Once, twice, a third time, she used it like a knife, jamming the blade into the killer's neck.

Blood poured from the wounds and Adele felt his strength fading as he stared down at her, a quizzical look replacing his one of horror. His injured hand fell against his thigh and then, with a slight, questioning sigh, he toppled over, scalpel buried in his throat, falling from Adele.

Breathing heavily, covered in both her blood and the killer's, Adele slowly eased up, trying her best to avoid the falling glass.

"American Princess!" a voice shouted from the street outside. "Are you all right!"

An impossible shot. A perfect shot. One to clear the glass, a second to hit Schmidt's upraised hand. Adele shook her head in disbelief, shock running its course through her body.

Adele pushed doggedly to her feet, stumbling over to her father, shards of glass tumbling from her with each step and scattering on the ground. She reached her father, whose head was now lolled against his chest, his eyes half-closed.

"Stay with me!" she snapped, grabbing a nearby pillow and ripping off the case to press it against the cuts along her father's face and neck. Her father emitted a quiet moan, and his chest rose and fell, flooding Adele with relief. "John!" she shouted over her shoulder, toward the window. "John—call EMS! Now!"

She heard a muffled shout in response, but couldn't quite make out the words. Her own head was now spinning too. Slowly, she slid down the side of the bed, reaching out and snaring a piece of glass to start sawing at the duct tape around her father's wrists.

He moaned again. "Sorry about the carpet," she muttered.

Then, once her father's hands were free, she had him press another pillowcase to the wounds on his thigh.

Sitting on the edge of the bed, next to her father, they remained in silence, hands pressed to his wounds, staring at the open door, neither of them paying much mind to the body beneath the window. Adele had nearly forgotten he was there.

CHAPTER THIRTY TWO

Adele sat in the chair facing the opaque glass of Executive Foucault's door. Her feet were crossed, the fuzzy pink slippers Robert had given her poked toward the ceiling.

A voice cleared down the hall, and Adele glanced over at John striding toward her, a smirk on his face. "Nice slippers," he said.

She grunted in reply, shifting slightly, but wincing as her bandaged side moved against the armrest. "I'll give you one," she said. "I do owe you."

He nodded. "Yes. Definitely you're in my debt, hmm?"

She rolled her eyes. "Seriously though, that was a hell of a shot. I never did properly thank you."

John flashed a schoolboy smile. "I can think of some ways you could express your gratitude."

"You're a pig," she said, but her tone was devoid of any ill will.

John leaned against the executive's door, seemingly indifferent to the long, dark shadow he would cast through the glass into his boss's office. "Nice of you to advise me over the radio," he said, conversationally. "Gave me the information I needed to make the shot. To be honest, for a moment there, I thought I was too late."

Adele shrugged one shoulder, glancing back through the opaque glass.

John stared at her slippers again. "Not exactly *professional,*" he said, raising a dark eyebrow.

Adele smiled. "I'm on vacation."

"Yeah? Good for you."

"What?" Adele teased. "That's all I get? No jokes about how lazy American princesses are?"

But John didn't smile this time; he glanced off down the hall, his face darkening for a moment. "You deserve a break," he said, softly. "Don't let them drag you back too soon, hear?"

Adele sighed, feeling some tension leave her shoulders. "I've just got a last meeting with Foucault, then I'm off for the week."

"Going to spend it in Paris?"

Adele hesitated. "I think so, yes. An old friend offered me room and board for the week." She lowered her voice and winked conspiratorially. "He has a private swimming pool, so I think I might take him up on the offer." Adele didn't add the more important part. Her teeth pressed against each other and she felt her mood darken for a moment. The killer had said, *"Honestly, it's funny you left Paris, you know that?"* He'd been talking about her mother's killer. Why had it been funny, though? The way he'd said it kept repeating in Adele's mind... Almost... almost as if the killer she'd been looking for all along had been *in* Paris.

Adele had known he'd killed in the city, but she'd never known where he'd been from. *Funny you left Paris...* Maybe what she had been longing for was beneath her nose the whole time. A week of vacation wasn't a long time, but... enough time to turn up a new clue? Perhaps.

"How's the old man?" John asked, still leaning against the glass.

Adele paused for a moment. Only three days had passed since closing the case of the German vacationing killer. Her father had emailed her earlier; he'd returned from the hospital to more than one can of condensed soup waiting for him on his front porch: gifts from his work buddies. She shrugged toward John. "Tougher than me," she said. "But he agreed to video call me later today—so that's progress." She chuckled and shook her head in incredulity. "By the sound of things, though, he's heading back to work tomorrow."

John nodded, no longer smiling. "I doubt it," he said, softly.

She frowned. "For all the things he is, my dad isn't a liar."

"No—not the work part. I doubt he's tougher than you."

Adele hesitated, studying her French partner. "John, am I hallucinating, or did you just compliment me?"

He studied her, his eyes laden with something she couldn't quite place... A sorrow, but also a relief. Just as quickly, he covered with a chuckle and a wink. "The way to a princess's heart; lavish with compliments. This could be the start to an illicit French romance, hmm?"

Adele didn't react at first. She looked at the tall agent leaning like a tomcat against the door, his eyes hooded as if he didn't have a care in the world. He really was quite handsome, even with that burn mark. "Maybe we can test that theory," she said with a smirk of her own. "Indoor pools are always more fun with two people."

John blinked, taken aback for a moment, and Adele hid her smile of satisfaction.

After a bit too long of a pause, John finally retorted, "I'm a really good swimmer."

"We'll see," Adele said, sweetly. Then she got to her feet, stretching her long legs as she did and rolling her shoulders.

John, still staring at her, hadn't noticed the shadow approaching from the other side. He jolted like a scalded cat as the door to the executive's office opened.

Foucault glanced out in the hall. He looked up at the tall agent, frowning, then turned his attention to Adele. "Agent Sharp," he said, "join me, if you please."

Adele brushed past John, looking up and winking at him before following Foucault into the office. The door shut with a quiet rattle of glass.

Adele suppressed her smile at John's startled reaction. It took her a moment to quell the satisfaction, but she finally turned to face Foucault's desk. To her surprise, he wasn't the only one in the room.

The TV screen was on behind him, depicting the face of Agent Lee from back in San Francisco. Additionally, the same woman from before—the one from Interpol, was standing by Foucault's desk with a phone in one hand and a paper file in the other. The large woman eyed Adele from behind thin glasses, her intelligent eyes twinkling.

Foucault was now sitting in his chair, peering across the desk at Adele. Both the chair and the desk seemed perfectly proportioned to suit the DGSI executive's frame.

Adele felt a sudden flash of embarrassment at her choice in footwear.

For a moment, Foucault frowned, glancing down at Adele's slippers, but before he could say anything, Agent Lee spoke from the TV screen.

"Hey, Sharp," she said. "I hear you're doing good things across the pond!"

Adele smiled at her friend and gave a little wave. "Can't complain," she replied. "How are things stateside?"

Agent Lee nodded and flashed a thumbs-up. "Same ol'. I've been hearing some interesting thoughts from Ms. Jayne, here, though…"

Adele glanced at the Interpol correspondent, who had lowered the paper file and was studying Adele with a look of quiet contemplation.

For a moment, Adele felt a flash of nerves. Had she done something wrong? She cycled back through the events in Germany. The killer had died before EMS had arrived—perhaps that's what this was about. Surely they weren't questioning the self-defense nature of the killer's wounds. She opened her mouth, preparing to defend herself, but before she could speak, the correspondent identified simply as Ms. Jayne, spoke first, "I'd like to offer you a job," she said.

Adele closed her mouth, her eyebrows inching slightly up. She cleared her throat. "Excuse me?"

Ms. Jayne spoke in crisp, precise tones, and, without a hint of impatience, she repeated, "I would like to offer you a job."

Adele stammered, "I-I'm afraid I don't understand."

Foucault cleared his throat. "Look, Agent Sharp, I'm sorry for calling you in on your vacation, but as I promised on the phone, this won't take long. Ms. Jayne here works, as I'm sure you've gathered—"

"For Interpol." Adele nodded.

"Yes," said Ms. Jayne. Her clear, crisp tones were devoid of any accent whatsoever. The occupants in the room spoke English, likely for Agent Lee's benefit, but Ms. Jayne had the sort of voice that suggested while she wasn't a native English speaker, she had perfected the craft. She continued, "Well, you'll need to come with me to our headquarters in Lyon, once you return for work, and we'll iron out the details there. For now, I'm simply looking for a verbal commitment to take back to my supervisors. They're, of course, fully apprised of the idea."

Adele glanced from the DGSI executive, to the FBI supervisor and back to the Interpol correspondent. "I'm still not sure I understand. *What* job?" she said.

"Ah, yes," said Ms. Jayne. She rubbed her thumbs in small circles on the back of the paper file, in a sort of soothing motion. "You are uniquely positioned, Adele. Interpol has realized this. As a citizen of three countries, coupled with your involvement with multiple agencies, you're a prime candidate for a program we've been working on."

Adele stared, stunned. Agent Lee and Foucault were both watching her, motionless, as if waiting for her reaction.

"What program?" Adele said, her throat suddenly dry. She really wished she hadn't worn the slippers now.

"A special license," said Ms. Jayne, her head bobbing. "An experimental license to operate as a domestic agent in all three countries." Her expression remained the same, her tone held only polite, matter-of-fact delivery.

And yet, Adele felt her heart skip a beat. "You mean like the CIA?" she asked.

But Ms. Jayne shook her head. "No. Rather, you'd be working as a shared resource between the United States, France, *and* Germany. You would be consulted whenever it is suspected that a relevant case has an international component. Do you understand?"

Adele paused. She glanced again between the three supervisors, not quite believing her ears. She frowned, studying the carpet beneath her feet for a moment, but then glanced back up.

They seemed to be waiting for something, though, and the silence stretched, occupying the space for a moment.

"Well?" Ms. Jayne said, at last, tilting her head ever so slightly.

"Well, what?" Adele said.

"Are you interested in the position? You are still welcome to your vacation—seven days, correct? And well deserved, of course. But your verbal agreement will allow me to start setting things in motion on our end; understand?"

Adele hesitated again. She glanced toward the screen with Agent Lee and met her friend's quiet, encouraging smile. She glanced at Foucault; his lips were pursed and he carried an air of solemnity, watching her, waiting for *her* decision.

"I..." she began, thinking. "I think I'd like to," she said, slowly. More time overseas meant more time around Robert. Around, even, John... And, perhaps, a chance to track down her mother's killer. She said none of this though. Instead, she said, "But on one condition."

Foucault was smiling as if washed in a wave of relief, but the expression became rather fixed at this last part. Ms. Jayne folded her hands. "If it is a matter of compensation, I assure you—"

"Not that," said Adele, quickly shaking her head. As she spoke, her words came quicker, and she nodded at each one, uttering them with conviction. "I'll do it, but only if Robert Henry is hired as a consultant. I'll need people I can trust; he was my mentor at the DGSI, and he's traveled his fair share too."

Ms. Jayne frowned and Executive Foucault began to shake his head. He glanced up at the Interpol correspondent. "Agent Henry is of an older generation," Foucault said, clearing his throat. "He's been instrumental in the *early* days of the agency. But now, the direction we've been taking it, perhaps it might be better to—"

Adele frowned. "Exactly. If you don't need him anymore, then I do." She turned back to Ms. Jayne, nodding once. "I'll do it—I'll come to Lyon tomorrow, if that's what you want. But first, you have to give me assurance that Robert will be involved. If it's an issue of salary, you can take it out of mine."

Executive Foucault looked ready to protest again, but Ms. Jayne spoke over him at the mention of salary. "Done," she said, simply. "I can't promise what capacity, but we'll find a place for Agent Henry, you have my word."

Adele felt a small jolt of satisfaction which she hid behind a cough and a swallow. "Well," she said, slowly. "I—"

But before she could continue, her phone started to buzz. Adele frowned for a moment, but then her eyes widened.

"I'm so, so sorry," she said. "So sorry." She held up a finger and fished her phone from her pocket.

The blue screen carried a single word: *Dad.*

"It's—it's important," she said, backing slowly toward the opaque glass door. "I'm sorry," she kept repeating. "But I have to take this."

Without waiting for a reply, Adele backed out of the room full of supervisors—all of whom held her career in their hands—and stepped into the hall, lifting the phone and staring at the answer button.

She swallowed, brushed a few loose strands of hair from her face.

Perhaps it wasn't the wisest course, stepping foot into the DGSI headquarters wearing pink slippers, then leaving a meeting with powerful members of the intelligence community to take a personal call. But then again, perhaps Angus had been right. Perhaps the job couldn't come first *every* time.

Adele answered the phone, hurrying toward the elevator and stepping into the empty compartment. She held the phone up, staring into the camera. Her father's face blinked into view and, for a brief moment, he almost seemed to smile. He had bandages on his face, but otherwise, he looked healthy enough.

"Hey, Dad," Adele said. "You look good."

Her father studied her for a moment. And this time, he actually did flash a smile. The elevator doors closed with a quiet *ding.* "Hello, Adele," he said, his voice rasping. "How are you?"

Adele tried to respond, but found a lump in her throat. Her dad never called her by her name. The elevator whirred to life, carrying Adele back down to the lobby, the walls and floor vibrating softly around her. "I'm—I'm doing fine," she said, quietly. "I've got some good news. It sounds like I might be visiting Germany quite a bit now…"

The Sergeant's eyes widened at this. "Good," he said. The word seemed to take an effort to utter, but after he did, his gaze almost seemed to soften. "Tell me about it," he said.

The elevator dinged, but Adele didn't get off. She stood in the empty compartment, facing the lobby, holding up her phone and chatting with her father. She'd once upon a time lost a parent in France. But there, standing in the elevator, hunched over her phone with a smile on her face, Adele felt perhaps she wasn't so alone as all that. A father from the US, living in Germany, married to a French woman… Adele could only shake her head softly at the thought.

But, for a moment, she thought of Robert's comments to her. *"Perhaps it isn't you don't have a home. But that you have more than one."*

NOW AVAILABLE!

LEFT TO RUN
(An Adele Sharp Mystery—Book 2)

"When you think that life cannot get better, Blake Pierce comes up with another masterpiece of thriller and mystery! This book is full of twists and the end brings a surprising revelation. I strongly recommend this book to the permanent library of any reader that enjoys a very well written thriller."
--Books and Movie Reviews, Roberto Mattos (re Almost Gone)

LEFT TO RUN is book #2 in a new FBI thriller series by USA Today bestselling author Blake Pierce, whose #1 bestseller Once Gone (Book #1) (a free download) has received over 1,000 five star reviews.

A serial killer is ravaging the American expat community in Paris, his kills reminiscent of Jack the Ripper. For FBI special agent Adele Sharp, it's a mad race against time to enter his mind and save the next victim—until she uncovers a secret darker than anyone could have imagined.

Haunted by her own mother's murder, Adele throws herself into the case, delving into the grisly underbelly of a city she once called home.

Can Adele stop the killer before it's too late?

An action-packed mystery series of international intrigue and riveting suspense, LEFT TO RUN will have you turning pages late into the night.

Book #3—LEFT TO HIDE—is also now available!

LEFT TO RUN
(An Adele Sharp Mystery—Book 2)

Blake Pierce

Blake Pierce is the USA Today bestselling author of the RILEY PAGE mystery series, which includes sixteen books (and counting). Blake Pierce is also the author of the MACKENZIE WHITE mystery series, comprising thirteen books (and counting); of the AVERY BLACK mystery series, comprising six books; of the KERI LOCKE mystery series, comprising five books; of the MAKING OF RILEY PAIGE mystery series, comprising five books (and counting); of the KATE WISE mystery series, comprising six books (and counting); of the CHLOE FINE psychological suspense mystery, comprising five books (and counting); of the JESSE HUNT psychological suspense thriller series, comprising five books (and counting); of the AU PAIR psychological suspense thriller series, comprising two books (and counting); of the ZOE PRIME mystery series, comprising two books (and counting); and of the new ADELE SHARP mystery series.

An avid reader and lifelong fan of the mystery and thriller genres, Blake loves to hear from you, so please feel free to visit www.blakepierceauthor.com to learn more and stay in touch.

BOOKS BY BLAKE PIERCE

ADELE SHARP MYSTERY SERIES
LEFT TO DIE (Book #1)
LEFT TO RUN (Book #2)
LEFT TO HIDE (Book #3)
LEFT TO KILL (Book #4)
LEFT TO MURDER (Book #5)

THE AU PAIR SERIES
ALMOST GONE (Book#1)
ALMOST LOST (Book #2)
ALMOST DEAD (Book #3)

ZOE PRIME MYSTERY SERIES
FACE OF DEATH (Book#1)
FACE OF MURDER (Book #2)
FACE OF FEAR (Book #3)
FACE OF MADNESS (Book #4)
FACE OF FURY (Book #5)
FACE OF DARKNESS (Book #6)

A JESSIE HUNT PSYCHOLOGICAL SUSPENSE SERIES
THE PERFECT WIFE (Book #1)
THE PERFECT BLOCK (Book #2)
THE PERFECT HOUSE (Book #3)
THE PERFECT SMILE (Book #4)
THE PERFECT LIE (Book #5)
THE PERFECT LOOK (Book #6)

CHLOE FINE PSYCHOLOGICAL SUSPENSE SERIES
NEXT DOOR (Book #1)
A NEIGHBOR'S LIE (Book #2)
CUL DE SAC (Book #3)
SILENT NEIGHBOR (Book #4)
HOMECOMING (Book #5)
TINTED WINDOWS (Book #6)

KATE WISE MYSTERY SERIES

IF SHE KNEW (Book #1)
IF SHE SAW (Book #2)
IF SHE RAN (Book #3)
IF SHE HID (Book #4)
IF SHE FLED (Book #5)
IF SHE FEARED (Book #6)
IF SHE HEARD (Book #7)

THE MAKING OF RILEY PAIGE SERIES
WATCHING (Book #1)
WAITING (Book #2)
LURING (Book #3)
TAKING (Book #4)
STALKING (Book #5)

RILEY PAIGE MYSTERY SERIES
ONCE GONE (Book #1)
ONCE TAKEN (Book #2)
ONCE CRAVED (Book #3)
ONCE LURED (Book #4)
ONCE HUNTED (Book #5)
ONCE PINED (Book #6)
ONCE FORSAKEN (Book #7)
ONCE COLD (Book #8)
ONCE STALKED (Book #9)
ONCE LOST (Book #10)
ONCE BURIED (Book #11)
ONCE BOUND (Book #12)
ONCE TRAPPED (Book #13)
ONCE DORMANT (Book #14)
ONCE SHUNNED (Book #15)
ONCE MISSED (Book #16)
ONCE CHOSEN (Book #17)

MACKENZIE WHITE MYSTERY SERIES
BEFORE HE KILLS (Book #1)
BEFORE HE SEES (Book #2)
BEFORE HE COVETS (Book #3)
BEFORE HE TAKES (Book #4)
BEFORE HE NEEDS (Book #5)

BEFORE HE FEELS (Book #6)
BEFORE HE SINS (Book #7)
BEFORE HE HUNTS (Book #8)
BEFORE HE PREYS (Book #9)
BEFORE HE LONGS (Book #10)
BEFORE HE LAPSES (Book #11)
BEFORE HE ENVIES (Book #12)
BEFORE HE STALKS (Book #13)
BEFORE HE HARMS (Book #14)

AVERY BLACK MYSTERY SERIES
CAUSE TO KILL (Book #1)
CAUSE TO RUN (Book #2)
CAUSE TO HIDE (Book #3)
CAUSE TO FEAR (Book #4)
CAUSE TO SAVE (Book #5)
CAUSE TO DREAD (Book #6)

KERI LOCKE MYSTERY SERIES
A TRACE OF DEATH (Book #1)
A TRACE OF MUDER (Book #2)
A TRACE OF VICE (Book #3)
A TRACE OF CRIME (Book #4)
A TRACE OF HOPE (Book #5)

Made in the USA
Monee, IL
14 July 2023

39297989R00132